OXHERDING TALE

Charles Johnson

GROVE PRESS, INC.
New York

First Evergreen Edition 1984
First Printing 1984
ISBN: 0-394-62123-9
Library of Congress Catalog Card Number: 83-49379

Library of Congress Cataloging in Publication Data

Johnson, Charles Richard, 1948-
  Oxherding tale.

  I. Title
[PS3560.03735096 1984]   813'.54   84-4490
ISBN 0-394-62123-9 (pbk.)

Printed in the United States of America

GROVE PRESS, INC., 196 West Houston Street,
New York, N.Y., 10014

5 4 3 2 1

To the memory
of
Ruby Elizabeth Johnson

Portions of this novel, in slightly different form, have appeared in Antaeus *and* Nimrod. *Acknowledgment is made, gratefully, to the National Endowment for the Arts for a grant to finish the work, and I must also thank my novel-writing students (spring 1980) for their merciless criticism, especially G. W. Hawkes for one of his jokes, and Cheryl Mathisen for her hours spent typing the manuscript.*

Noli foras ire, in te redi, in interiore homine habitat veritas.

Saint Augustine

I do not know what I am like here, I do not know in relation to what I can say, "This I am." Bewildered and lost in thought, I wander.

Rig Veda

Desolate through forests and fearful in jungles, he is seeking an Ox he does not find.

Ten Oxherding Pictures

There exists in the same human being varying perceptions of one and the same object which differ so completely from each other that one can only deduce the existence of different subjects in the same human being.

Franz Kafka, *The Great Wall of China*

OXHERDING
TALE

PART ONE

House and Field

I

MY ORIGINS.
PRÉCIS OF MY EDUCATION.
MY LIFE AT CRIPPLEGATE.
THE AGREEMENT

Long ago my father and I were servants at Cripplegate, a cotton plantation in South Carolina. That distant place, the world of my childhood, is ruin now, mere parable, but what history I have begins there in an unrecorded accident before the Civil War, late one evening when my father, George Hawkins, still worked in the Big House, watched over his owner's interests, and often drank with his Master—this was Jonathan Polkinghorne—on the front porch after a heavy meal. It was a warm night. An autumn night of fine-spun moonlight blurred first by Madeira, then home-brewed beer as they played Rummy, their feet propped on the knife-whittled porch rail, the dark two-story house behind them, creaking sometimes in the wind. My father had finished his chores early, for he was (he says) the best butler in the country, and took great pride in his position, but he wasn't eager to go home. He stayed clear of his cabin when my stepmother played host for the Ladies Prayer Circle. They were strange, George thought. Those women were harmless enough by themselves, when sewing or cleaning, but together their collective prayers had a mysterious power that filled his whitewashed cabin with presences—Shades, he called them, because they moved furniture in the cabin, destroyed the laws of physics, which George swore by, and drove him outside to sleep in the shed. (Not that my father knew a whole lot about physics, being a slave, but George knew sorcery when he saw it, and kept his distance.) He was, as all Hodges knew, a practical, God-fearing man who liked to keep things simple so he could enjoy them. He was overly cautious and unnerved by little things. So he avoided his cabin and talked about commonsense things like poli-

3

tics and the price of potatoes on his Master's porch long after the last pine-knot candles winked out in the quarters. Whiskey burned, then exploded like gas in his belly. He felt his face expand. His eyes slid slowly out of focus. Hard old leaves on magnolias overhanging the porch clacked, like shells, in a September wind sprinkled with rain.

Twelve o'clock. A typical Saturday night.

"George," said Jonathan, his voice harsh after consuming forty-eight ounces of Madeira in what my father figured to be half an hour, "if I go up to bed at this advanced hour, smelling of spirits, my Anna will brain me with a milkstool." Low and deep, George laughed, then hiccoughed. He rubbed his legs to start blood circulating again. "And your wife, Mattie," Jonathan added, passing his bottle to my father, "she'll chew your fat good, won't she, George?"

Because he had not thought of this, my father stopped laughing, then breathing for a second. My stepmother frowned on drinking—she frowned, in fact, on most things about George. She was no famous beauty, fat as she was, with brown freckles, a rich spangled voice, and more chins (lately) than a Chinese social register, but my stepmother had—or so George believed when Jonathan arranged their wedding—beautiful ways. Her previous owners, friends of the Polkinghornes, were an old New England family that landed with the Pilgrims at Cape Cod Bay. Mattie, their servant, was sure some days that she had married below herself. She was spiritual, high-strung, respected books, and above all else was dedicated to developing George into a real gentleman, even if it killed him—she selected his clothes for him, corrected his speech, and watched him narrowly for the slightest lapse into Negroness, as she called it. Added to which, and most of all, George liked his women big and smart (you could have cut two good-sized maids out of Mattie and still had leftovers). As he uncorked a bottle of gin, poured a glass for Jonathan, then toasted his Master's health, he could not bear the thought of disappointing her by stumbling into their cabin reeking of liquor—it would destroy her faith that he was not, after all, a common nigger with no appreciation for the finer things; she would be waiting, he knew, turning the tissue-thin pages of her Bible, holding her finger on some flight of poetry in Psalms, which she planned to read to George for his "general im-

4

provement." She made him bend his knees beside her each night, their heads tipped and thighs brushing, praying that neither jealousy nor evil temper, boredom nor temptation, poverty nor padderolls, would destroy their devotion to each other. "You have me, I have you," Mattie whispered, "and we both have Jesus." It made George shudder. Why were black women so mystical? Religion was fine, but if you carried on too much about it, people were liable to think something was wrong with you. "No," he said, shaking his head, glancing left at Jonathan, "I'd best not go home tonight."

"Nor I." Jonathan sat back heavily on his cane-seat chair, crossing his knees, and lit a cigar. "But there must be *some* alternative."

My father raised his shoulders in a shrug.

They drank on in the darkness, grinning more and more now under the influence of gin-and-water. The porch fogged with smoke. At length, Jonathan lifted his head and touched my father's knee.

"George, I have it."

"Yessir?"

"*I* can't go upstairs to face my Anna. And *you* can't return to the quarters." Thoughtful, he picked at his lip. "Are these premises correct so far?"

"Yessir," George rocked his head. "I think so."

"But there's no harm in switching places for one night, is there, with me sleeping in the quarters, and you upstairs?"

George gave him a look. He was sure it was the gin, not Jonathan, talking.

"George, when*ever* I advance an idea you have a most annoying way of looking at me as if I'd just suggested that we strangle a child and sell its body to science. No good will come of this. Goodnight," Jonathan said, steadying himself with one hand on the porch rail as he stood. He rocked off for George's cabin. "I'll see you at breakfast."

How long George waited on the front porch, sweating from the soles of his feet upward, is impossible to tell—my father seldom speaks of this night, but the great Swiss clock in Jonathan's parlor chimed twice and, in perfect submission to his Master's will, he turned inside and walked like a man waistdeep in weeds down a hallway where every surface, every shape was warped by frail lamplight from Jonathan's study. His Master's house was solid and rich; it was established, quiet, and so different from the squalid quarters, with vases, a vast library, and great rooms of imported furniture that had cost the Polkinghorne's dearly—a house of such heavily upholstered luxuriance and antiques that George now took small, mincing steps for fear of breaking something. In the kitchen, he uncovered a pot of beef on the table, prepared a plate for Mattie (he always brought my stepmother something when he worked in the house), wrapped it in paper, drained his bottle of gin, then lit a candle. Now he was ready.

My father negotiated the wide, straight staircase to Anna's bedchamber, but stopped in the doorway. In candlelight like this, on her high bed with its pewterized nickel headboard, Anna Polkinghorne was a whole landscape of flesh, white as the moon, with rolling hills, mounds, and bottomless gorges. He sat down on a chair by her bed. He stood up. He sat down again—George had never seen the old woman so beautiful. Blurred by the violence of his feelings, or the gin, his eyes clamped shut and he swallowed. Wouldn't a man rise new-made and cured of all his troubles after a night in this immense bed? And the Prayer Circle? Didn't his wife say whatever happened was, in the end, the Lord's will? George put his plate on the chair. He stared—and stared—as Anna turned in her sleep. He yanked off his shirt—wooden buttons flew everywhere, then his coarse Lowell breeches and, like a man listening to the voice of a mesmerist, slipped himself under the bedsheets. What happened next, he had not expected. Sleepily, Anna turned and soldered herself to George. She crushed him in a clinch so strong his spine cracked. Now he had fallen too far to stop. She talked to George, a wild stream of gibberish, which scared him plenty, but he was not a man to leave his chores half-finished, and plowed on. Springs in the mattress snapped, and Anna, gripping the headboard, groaned, "Oh *gawd*, Jonathan!"

"No, ma'am. It ain't Jonathan."

"Geo-o-o-orge?" Her voice pulled at the vowel like taffy. She yanked her sheet to her chin. "Is this *George*?"

"Yo husband's in the quarters." George was on his feet. "He's, uh, with my wife." None of it made sense now. How in God's name had he gotten himself into this? He went down on all fours, holding the plate for Mattie over his head, groping around the furniture

6

for his trousers. "Mrs. Polkinghorne, I kin explain, I think. You know how a li'l corn kin confuse yo thinkin'? Well, we was downstairs on the porch, you know, drinkin', Master Polkinghorne and me. . . ."

Anna let fly a scream.

She was still howling, so he says, when George, hauling hips outside, fell, splattering himself from head to foot with mud deltaed in the yard, whooping too when he arrived flushed, naked, and fighting for breath at his own place, the plate of beef still miraculously covered. He heard from inside yet another scream, higher, and then Jonathan came flying like a chicken fleeing a hawk through the cabin door, carrying his boots, his shirt, his suspenders. For an instant, both men paused as they churned past each other in the night and shouted (stretto):

"George, whose fat idea was this?"

"Suh, it was *you* who told *me*. . . ."

This, I have been told, was my origin.

It is, at least, my father's version of the story; I would tell you Anna Polkinghorne's, but I was never privileged to hear it. While Jonathan survived this incident, his reputation unblemished, George Hawkins was to be changed forever. Anna, of course, was never quite herself again. All this may seem comic to some, but from it we may date the end of tranquility at Cripplegate. Predictably, my birth played hob with George's marriage (it didn't help Master Polkinghorne's much either) and, just as predictably, for twenty years whenever George or Jonathan entered the same room as Mattie, my stepmother found something to do elsewhere. She never forgave George, who never forgave Jonathan, who blamed Anna for letting things go too far, and *she* demanded a divorce but settled, finally, on living in a separate wing of the house. George, who looked astonished for the rest of his life, even when sleeping, was sent to work in the fields. This Fall, he decided, was the wage of false pride—he had long hours to ponder such things as Providence and Destiny now that he was a shepherd of oxen and sheep. It was God's will, for hitherto he and Mattie—especially Mattie— had been sadditty and felt superior to the fieldhands who, George decided, had a world-historical mission. He had been a traitor. A tool. He refused Jonathan's apologies and joked bleakly of shooting him or, late at night when he had me clean his eyes with cloth after a day of sacking wool, even more bleakly of spiritual and physical bondage, arguing his beliefs loudly, if ineffectively, on the ridiculously tangled subject Race. My father had a talent for ridiculing slaveholders in general and the Polkinghornes in particular—who knew them better than their butler?—that ultimately went over big in Cripplegate's quarters. When I look back on my life, it seems that I belonged by error or accident—call it what you will— to both house and field, but I was popular in neither, because the war between these two families focused, as it were, on me, and I found myself caught from my fifth year forward in their crossfire.

It started in 1843 when Jonathan realized he would have no children, what with Anna holed up with his flintlock and twenty-five rounds of ammunition in one half of the house. What had been a comfortable, cushiony marriage with only minor flare-ups, easily fixed by flowers or Anna's favorite chocolates, was now a truce with his wife denying him access to the common room, top floors, and dining area (he slept in his study); what was once a beautiful woman whose voice sang as lovely as any in this world when she sat at the black, boatlike piano in the parlor, one foot gently vibrating on the sostenuto pedal, was now an irascible old woman who haunted the place like a dead man demanding justice, who left terrible notes on the kitchen table, under Jonathan's cup, who, locked in her bedchamber like a prisoner, finished the plates the housemaid left outside her door, but would not throw the latch: a rotten business, in Jonathan's opinion. He came half-asleep to her door night after night, night after night, night after night, and asked helplessly, "Can we talk about it?"

She sat up and shouted, "No!"

"We *all* make mistakes, Anna. For God's sake, George and I meant no harm. . . ." He paused. The inevitable question still nagged him. "Anna, you *wanted* George, not me, to be there, didn't you?"

Silence. After a second: "Is that boy still here?"

"In the quarters," he said. "He's living with George, and he's beautiful, Anna. He has your hair, your—"

"You send him away!"

The old man gulped. "He's your son as much as George's, isn't

8

he?" He rubbed the floor with the toe of his slipper. "We should do for him, you know, like he was ours. . . ."

"I know no such thing!" Her voice became flat and tired. "Go away."

"This is *my* house!" he barked, trembling with fury. "I live here, too!"

"Go *away!*"

Exactly five years to the day George sprang from Anna's bedsheets, Jonathan sat in his study until dawn, writing advertisements for a tutor, which he sent to the best schools. So September, October, and November passed; and on a cold morning in December a gloomy but gifted teacher—a graduate of William and Mary—arrived unannounced on foot from Hodges. By a riverboat, by a stagecoach, by a wagon, by a horse, by a rail—by traveling for five weeks he came with a stupendous headcold to Cripplegate, bearing letters of reference from Amos Bronson Alcott, Caleb Sprague Henry, and Noah Porter, who wrote, "This candidate knows as much about metaphysics as any man alive, and has traveled in India, but you must never leave him alone for long in a room with a little girl."

Porter wrote:

"He is, let us say, born to Transcendentalism by virtue of a peculiar quirk of cognition that, like the Tibetan mystic, lets him perceive the interior of objects, why no one knows; whatever his faults, he is perhaps the only man in North America who truly understands the *Mahàbhárata,* and has a splendid future as an Orientalist ordained for him, provided he isn't hanged, say, for high treason, or heresy. He is well suited for the tutorial position you advertise if, and only if, you do not set him off. Never," wrote Porter, "mention his mother."

That winter, the worst in South Carolina's history, five men froze to their horses. Up in the hills, they weren't found until March thaw, their bodies white pap and bloated fingers inside the horses' bellies for the bloodwarmth. In this bitter season, snow sat on the rooftops, where its weight cracked wooden beams like kindling; snow brought a silence like sleep to the quarters, where it frosted the great family house and, like a glacial spell, sealed off the hills, the forests, and the fields in blue ice. This drowse of winter released a figure who evolved in pieces from the snowdrifts, first a patch of bloodless fingers and a prayerbook, then a black coat, a hatbrim dusted with ice crystals. Snow lay like a cloak on his shoulders and like spats on the tops of his boots. He sloshed, coughing, up a path made by the wagons to the paddocks—it was eight-thirty—and there he stamped his feet. Jonathan bounded outside in his housecoat, he picked up the stranger's portmanteau, then pushed a tumbler of claret at him. My tutor brushed it aside. "I never drink before noon."

"Nor I," chuckled Jonathan. "But it must be noon *some*where." He threw down the tumbler, then took the stranger's arm:

"How are you called?"

Dropping his gloves into his hat, he pulled back, did a heelclick in the hallway, and bowed. "My Christian name is Ezekiel William Sykes-Withers."

"Of course," Jonathan said, blinking—he couldn't stand people with two last names. "I wouldn't have it any other way."

They sat, these two, on straw chairs by the windows in the study. As Jonathan served hot cups of milk tea with honey, dickered over Ezekiel's wages, and spelled out his chores, Anna must have whiffed trouble, because the slumbrous feel of the morning was broken by a crash from her bedchamber upstairs, then a groan; the plank-ribbed ceiling buckled, Jonathan spilled boiling tea on his lap, and yelped, "Pay no attention—we're having some work done upstairs." In the doorway, I listened; the interview did not seem to be edited for my benefit.

"You're welcome to the guestroom," said Jonathan. "It's right below my wife's bedroom, so you can look in when she rings her bell."

"By your leave," sniffed Ezekiel—he blew his nose into his handkerchief, looked inside to see what he'd got, and said, "I will sleep closer to the boy."

"My thought exactly." Jonathan finished his tea, then placed his cup and saucer on a candlestand. Unconsciously, he swung his left foot. What he thought we shall never know, but this was clear: my tutor, he learned, was, as Porter hinted, an Anarchist and member of George Ripley's Transcendental Club—a brilliant man, a mystic whose pockets bulged with letters, scraps of paper, news clippings, notes scribbled on his handkerchiefs, his shirtcuffs, and stuffed inside his hat. He looked in the study's weak light like engravings I'd seen of Thomas Paine, or a Medieval scholar peering up from his scrolls, and at other times reminded me of a story-book preacher (Calvinist), and was, we learned, one of the two or three authorities on the Rhineland sermons of Meister Eckhart. He was thin as a line in Zeno, with a craglike face, wild goatish eyes, and blood pressure so staggeringly high that twice during the interview he ran outside to rub his wrists with snow. His tight, pale lips were the whole Jeffersonian idea of Insurrection. Whenever he pronounced the words "perceiver" and "perceived," which he referred to often that morning, he smothered them in his long nose into "per-r-rceiver" and "per-r-rceived" with a kind of solemn quiver as he rolled them out. He smelled of laudanum. He smoked while he was eating, disdained comfort, and died, ten years later, under circumstances that left the exact cause of death a mystery. "You don't drink heavily, do you, Ezekiel?" asked Jonathan. "No," he said. "Or take opium?" "No." "And you have no wife, no relations?" Ezekiel's brow wrinkled and he shook his head violently. "I've stayed to myself since the death of my parents, Mr. Polkinghorne."

"I'm sorry." Jonathan tapped the end of his broad, bell-shaped nose. "I lost my father not long ago, too—I know how you must feel."

"*My* father," said Ezekiel, "deeply loved the things of this world, he held his family and work in the highest esteem. He was piously religious to his Creator, loyal to his country, faithful to his wife, a kind relation, a lasting friend, and charitable to the poor." He sat stiffly on his chair, fists clenched tight. "He shot my mother and sister, and would have blown me to Kingdom Come, too, I assure you, had I not been away that evening. When I arrived home, they were all dead, over their *apéritif*, at the dinner table. Have you," Ezekiel asked, "ever considered suicide?"

"Why no!" Jonathan rubbed his nose. "Never!"

Ezekiel said, "You should."

"And what is *that* supposed to mean?"

"I only mean," said Ezekiel, "that we do not think of death until we are well within her jaws." What he meant by this, he did

11

not say. From his pocket he withdrew a tobacco pouch and a big Nuremberg pipe, thumbed down a pinch of Latakia, and said, "This boy, you say, is a mulatto?"

Jonathan nodded yes.

"In his horoscope Mars confronts Mercury at three angles, and this is promising," said Ezekiel. "It signifies the birth of a philosopher. Is he yours?"

Witheringly, Jonathan glanced toward the door, wagged his head, and said, "No." The reply and gesture nihilated each other. "What I mean to say is that Andrew is my property and that his value will increase with proper training." He looked away, quickly, from the door, then sighed. And what was I thinking? What did I feel? Try as I might, I could not have told you what my body rested on, or what was under my feet—the hallway had the feel of pasteboard and papier-mâché. A new train of thoughts were made to live in my mind. Jonathan hung his head a little. He said to Ezekiel, without looking up from the floor, "Five dollars monthly, and board, are all I can offer. Are you still interested?"

Ezekiel's face wrinkled into an infernal, Faustian leer. "He *isn't* your son?"

"Are you," Jonathan asked, crossly, "interested?"

"I will teach the boy, yes, using a program modeled on that of James Mill for his son John Stuart, but I am never to be disturbed on Sundays, or during the evening. I never eat meat. Or eggs. I would like one wall of my room covered with mirrors. Don't ask why—I live a bit to one side of things. Do you," he asked, stretching out a hand soft and white as raw dough toward Jonathan, "agree to these conditions?"

"Yes." My Master blinked and pushed back his chair. "Agreed."

By the age of eight I began, with Ezekiel, learning Greek; by the time I was twelve I had read Xenophon and Plato. Next came Voice, Elocution, and Piano lessons. He gave George and Mattie orders that I was not to touch silver, gold, or paper currency; nor was I allowed to listen to the Mixed Lydian and Hyperlydian Modes in music, lest these melancholy strains foul Ezekiel's plans for what was—in his view—a perfect moral education. By the age of fifteen I began to fare badly. I could ask to use the silver chamber pot in George's cabin, where I slept curled up on a pallet, in Latin more perfect than my native tongue; I received lectures on monadology, classical philology, and Oriental thought—the better to fathom Schopenhauer, a favorite of Ezekiel, who often spent days in his cabin, reading Hegel and Thoreau, with whom he'd corresponded earlier, and Marx, who paid him a visit at Cripplegate in 1850. (Of Karl Marx's social call more will be said later.) He taught me the 165 Considerations, Four Noble Truths, the Eight-Fold Path, the 3,000 Good Manners, and 80,000 Graceful Conducts; but I must confess that reading Chinese thought was a little like eating Chinese food: the more one read Lao tzu and Chaung tzu, or ate subgum chop suey, the emptier one's head and stomach felt hours later. Too, I could never remember if it was ▽ before ⊥ except after 🁢 , or 𝕏 before 𝕐 except after 🀆 , and always got the meanings confused. And there is also this to say:

Soon all life left my studies—why I couldn't say, but I had, at least, this theory: these vain studies of things moral, things transcendental, things metaphysical were, all in all, rich food for the soul, but in Cripplegate's quarters all that was considered as making life worth living was utterly wanting. And so I became restless and unquiet. So restless, in fact, that on the eve of my twentieth birthday, a rainy Sunday evening, I rose from my pallet in George's dreary, two-room cabin, and carried all my confusions to Master Polkinghorne.

May 6 of the year of grace 1858.

My clothes were soaking, my frock bunched up like a woman's bustle in the back as I scaled a hillslope between the quarters and house. The yard, as wide as a playing field, was wet and slippery to my feet. Farther on, around the lee side and behind long chintz draperies, a chandelier glowed faintly with fumes of golden light like luminous gas in one ground-floor window. For an instant, I paused beside the broad bay window, watching an old woman, all wrinkled, nothing but pleats and folds, almost bedridden now, burnt down to eighty pounds, dying faster than Dr. Horace Crimshaw in Hodges could feed her pills for migraines, pills for stomach cramps, and potions (Veronal and chloral hydrate) for rest. Jonathan loved his old woman, I knew, and me as well, but could not live with us both. He would slip away some evenings, yes, riding his one-horse chaise off on the remains of old plank roads to tumble, it was rumored, the wives of farmers gone to market in Greenwood. He became, in fact, a hunter of women—a broken-down old man, perfumed, who wore powdered wigs and ribbons in his hair like a Creole dandy. The sort of man who told women, "My wife and I live like brother and sister," or, "Older men make, of course, the best lovers." So it was for years with my Master before sickness brought his wife back downstairs. His chest shrank, his stomach filled, and duty replaced his desire for Anna. But he never thought— he was too loyal to think—of abandoning her, although now she could only stare back at him through burnt-out eyes, coughing blood into her brass thunderpot, crepitations like the dry induviae of brittle leaves in the folds of her nightgown: a fragile mass of living jelly, and no more wife to Jonathan now than a stump of firewood.

A thousand drubbing fingers of rain flew against my face as I leaned forward from my hips and climbed the six wooden steps of the dry-rotted porch. The nerves of my teeth reacted to the cold. Shivering, I lifted, then let fall once—twice—the long brass knocker on the door, waited, then stepped back quickly. For now the latch was thrown, and the huge door opened with a splinter of milkblue candlelight and a dragging sound. It opened, old hinges grating for want of oil. And in the doorway stood my Master, his back hooped like a horseshoe, breathing as if he'd been running for hours. His eyelids were puffy. He scuffed in his stiff, sliding walk onto the porch, lifted his candle higher, oblivious to hot wax trickling down his forearm into his sleeve, and winced when he saw me. A tic twitched in one of his eyes. He saddled his nose with wide spectacles, and asked, full of affection (for the old quop did, indeed, love me like a son), "Is this Andrew?"

"It is, Master Polkinghorne." He pressed his cold lips in a moist kiss against my forehead, and I, in return, affectionately squeezed his arm. "May I come in, sir?"

"You can't stay," he said. "My wife is up and about, you see."

"This won't take long." I coughed into my right hand to clear my throat. "You'll not be troubled by me again."

"You're not in any trouble, are you? You haven't murdered someone, have you?" Jonathan signed. "If so, I hope it wasn't anybody white, Andrew."

"No, sir. Nothing like that." At that moment I decided to tell him nothing, and confide only in you of my brief but unsettling encounter earlier that afternoon. Near the southern hills, close to the backroad, just where the plantation approaches a dark stretch of woods, I had been herding my father's Brown Swiss calves, his Leicester sheep, when the girl—this was Minty—appeared in an osnaburg skirt and white blouse, beneath an old Leghorn hat, with a blue satin ribbon, toting a washtub of clothes. I had known her since childhood—whenever she saw me, her lips made a kissing-sound and she called me away. To Master Polkinghorne's big twelve-stanchion barn. There, beside bins of old oats going bad, in a loft of straw and musty hay, I think I saw her—*really* saw her for the first time. Not, I say, as the wild daughter of Jonathan's maid, who teased me when I traipsed off for my sessions with Ezekiel, hid my books, and mocked my speech, but as all the highbreasted women in calico and taffeta, in lace-trimmed gingham poke bonnets and black net hose, that I had ever wanted and secretly, hopelessly loved. What seemed physical shortcomings, defects in her child-hood—eyes too heavy for a child's small head, a shower of sienna hair always entangling itself in farm machinery—seemed (to me) that afternoon to be purified features in a Whole, where no partic-ular facet was striking because all fused together to offer a flawed, haunting beauty the likes of which you have never seen. Do not laugh, sir: I was stung sorely, riveted to the spot, relieved, Lord knows, of my reason. How much of her beauty lay in Minty, and how much in my head, was a mystery to me. Was beauty truly *in* things? Was touch in me or in the things I touched? These things so ensorceled me and baffled my wits that I prayed mightily, *Give me Minty*. And, God's own truth, I promised in that evanescent instant that she and I, George and Mattie—all the bondsmen in Cripplegate's quarters and abroad—would grow old in the skins of free man. (Perhaps I was not too clear in the head at that moment.) But how long would this take? Forty years? Fifty years? My heart knocked violently for manumission. Especially when, as we straightened our garments, I saw her eyes—eyes green as icy mountain meltwater, with a hint of blue shadow and a drowse of sensuality that made her seem voluptuously sleepy, distant, as though she had been lifted long ago from a melancholy African landscape overrich with the colors and warm smells of autumn—a sad, out-of-season beauty suddenly precious to me because it was imperfect and perhaps illusory like moonlight on pond water, sensuously alive, but delivering itself over, as if in sacrifice, to inevitable slow death in the fields. Her name, now that I think on it, might have been Zeudi—Ethiopian, ancient, as remote and strange, now that something in me had awoken, as Inca ruins or shards of pottery from the long-buried cities of Mu. But this is not what I said to Master Polkinghorne. I said:

"She has never liked me, has she?"

"Perhaps you will find forgiveness in your heart for her, Andrew." Now we entered his study. "Our relations are somewhat on the stiff side." There was a bureau with swinging brass handles, a diamond-paned bookcase, and a soft calf-bound set of Hawthorne. On an elbow-chair near the fireplace my Master lowered his weight, then looked up. "Would you rub me along the shoulders, Andrew—the pain is there again." As I did so, Jonathan talked on, as if to himself. "My Anna is mad, gloriously mad, and it's all my doing." He forced a laugh, full of gloom. "And I'll tell you true, I hate her sometimes. Many a night I stand by her door, listening to Anna breathe—it's horrible. Just *horrible!*" His voice began to shake. "I pray that her lungs will fail, and when they *do* stop, faltering sometimes in a hideous rattle, I pray just as desperately for her to breathe again, and when this happens . . . ah, Andrew, I'm sorry once again." He rubbed his face with both hands as I crossed to the fireplace and stood with my back to the flames, facing him, opening my palms to catch the heat, closing them. The next time he looked up there were tears in his eyes. "What business brings you here tonight?"

"With your permission," I said, "I have come to tell you that Minty, your seamstress, and I plan to be married. That, however, is not all, sir."

"Oh?" He squinted suspiciously.

"Meaning no disrespect to you, sir, I want you to draw up my deed of manumission."

My Master was silent so long I could hear rain patter, lightly, against the windowpanes. Make no mistake. That night I trembled. A pulse began to throb in my temple. Beneath the sausage-tight skin of slavery I could be, depending on the roll of the dice, the swerve of the indifferent atom, forever poised between two worlds, or —with a little luck—a wealthy man who had made his way in the world and married the woman he loved. All right—be realistic, I thought. Consider the facts: Like a man who had fallen or been rudely flung into the world, I owned nothing. My knowledge, my clothes, my language, even, were shamefully second-hand, made by, and perhaps for, other men. I was a living lie, that was the heart of it. My argument was: Whatever my origin, I would be wholly responsible for the shape I gave myself in the future, for shirting myself handsomely with a new life that called me like a siren to possibilities that were real but forever out of reach. My Master sat, blinking into the fire, then up at me, the corners of his mouth tucked in, his expression exactly that of a man who has come suddenly across cat fur in a bowl of soup. I walked to the study window. Air outside still smelled of rain. Breezes flew over the grass like shadows or grandfather spirits—so I imagined—in search of their graves. Clearly, I remember the night sky as applegreen, the chirring of grasshoppers in a crazy sort of chorus. Abruptly, Jonathan Polkinghorne brought out:

"You haven't been smoking rabbit tobacco again, have you, Andrew?"

"No, sir."

His eyebrows drew inward.

"Touch your thumb to your nose."

I did so.

"Now say, 'The rain in Spain falls mainly on the plain.' "

I assured him I was sober.

"Then, Andrew," he said, "you will understand that you are too young for these freedom papers. All our bondsmen will be released after Anna and I close our eyes. This is in our will. You haven't long, I suppose, to wait." His face was pale and strained and vague—Jonathan rather hated all discussions of death, especially his own. Moving toward the door, his shoe knocked a chair, and he swore irritably. Massaging his toe, he turned to ask, "Is there anything else?"

"Sir," I said, struggling, the reflections of the balls of my eyes so utterly without depth in the window that even I could not tell what I was thinking. "Long ago, you would not have me, and you turned me out to the quarters, then over to a teacher. . . ."

"Ezekiel Sykes-Withers." He drew his mouth down. "That was a mistake. The man was crazy as a mouse in a milkcan. Should've been a monk. He was hired to teach you useful *skills*, Andrew— things like book-keeping, and market research, and furniture repair, and what have we to show for his time here?"

"He taught me to read," I said.

"Well, that's some consolation."

"He taught me to control my heart and, when I walk, leave no footprints."

"Are these what they call *metaphors*, Andrew?" As always when facing figurative language, my Master was a little flummoxed. "I think I'm a pretty clear-witted man," he said, "but this outdoes me, Andrew." It's only about once in a lifetime that you stumble upon a first-rate philosophical metaphor, and when you do, people are bound to say, "Huh?" and take all the starch out of it. "You got out of bed to tell me all this?" He scratched his head. "Manumission and marriage?"

"Yes, sir."

"And what shall you do if I sign these papers?"

"Work for myself," I said, too loudly. "Within a year I'll be back to buy Minty, then George and Mattie from you." Our eyes met— mine squinted, small as sewing needles, like a murderer's; my Master's cold and critical, the eyes of an eagle, infinitely wise.

Softly, the clock in the corner chimed twice.

"I see."

He did not, I knew, see it at all.

"Then I tell you what, you *will* have an opportunity to work for yourself—or at least work this foolishness out of your system." He went to his bureau, taking out paper, ink, and a quill, but his jaw was set—that meant something. "However, as I say, I will sign no freedom papers until you return, as promised, with the money for the others."

"You will have it," I said. "Every penny."

Glasses clamped on his nose, he wrote quietly while I paced, and in a cramped, arthritic script that made his letter resemble a cross between cuneiform, Arabic, and Morse code. When he finished this tortured message, he folded the paper, and pressed it into my hand.

"This letter will see that you get work with one of my old acquaintances in Abbeville. We have not corresponded in years, but I believe she will put you to work." He said this woman—Flo Hatfield—would see to all my needs (he didn't say what needs), and would keep me busy (he didn't say how). Standing, he rumpled my hair, which I hated, and said, "Now go and tell George and Mattie where you're off to."

I started to hug him, then thought better of it, and ran down the hallway, though I had no reason, and leaped from the porch. The beauty of the night made me shout a cry that set sleeping dogs to barking and hummed for minutes afterwards in my ears. A fine rain fell. I sang out, now to trees that nodded respectfully in return, now to invisible blackbirds that called back from the bushes. Then I hurried on through foamy mud to the quarters, the letter tucked inside my shirt, sank slowly to sleep, and, dreaming, saw myself counting coins at the end of the week.

But first I had to work for Flo Hatfield.

II

———◆———

HOMELEAVING

Traveling with me to Abbeville, George told a story, very strange, of Flo Hatfield's appetites. A widow, and forty if a day, she lived on a five-hundred-acre farm—she called it Leviathan—and often picked a slave, preferably male, from her fields. Him she bathed, rested, then washed in cassia and tamarind, massaged with castor oil, which relaxes the muscles, tied his hair in bright ribbons, added cologne, then placed him in her late husband Henry's clothes before a platform of banquet proportions—all the good things of the earth baked, basted, broiled. He'd died and gone to Heaven, you might say. No other servants were permitted near the house. She kept her door barricaded. The shutters were closed. For days, whole weeks, Flo Hatfield entertained him—how George couldn't figure, but eventually a black Maria eased in from town, and a veterinarian examined the body. Then a mortician dragged a pine casket down her front steps, hauled it away, and her bondsman was listed among slaves who'd fled to Canada.

"Hawk," George said, grim, "I don't 'spect to see you again 'til Judgment Day."

"Stop joking," I studied his face. "You *are* joking, aren't you?"

"I just know what I hear."

We rode on, the sunlight ripening from blonde to brick-red at our backs, sweat trickling down my belly, George very quiet now, thinking his own thoughts, tired, and weakly cracking his short-handled whip over the horses across backcountry that smelled mucilaginous and faintly sweet. He was old now, with pyorrhea of the gums, big waxy hands, and a broken hip. Talking wearied him, so he said nothing as we rumbled through dreary villages and tobacco

20

fields, the wagon listing like a great ship on its broken springs. And then, without warning, he reached over and gently pressed my hand. "Mattie and me gonna miss you, Hawk." A stronger pressure. " 'Specially me. I know we ain't been the best parents to you, fightin' and all," he frowned, "but you know one thing, son?"

"What?"

Another squeeze.

"No matter what *any*body tells you, 'specially Master Polkinghorne, you Mattie's son, and mine. We had some rough spots, you know, Mattie and me. But you blood. You belong with us." Chewing his lower lip, he glanced at me quickly, then away. "You wouldn't never pass for white, would you?"

"No, I don't think so."

"You know ain't nothin' as beautiful as yo own people?"

"Yessir."

"You know Africa *will* rise again someday, Hawk, with her own queens and kings and a court bigger'n anythin' in Europe?"

"Yessir." I'd heard this so often before; my father spoke of it the way the Prayer Circle sang Christ's resurrection. "I hope it will."

"And that you belong there?"

"Yessir."

"You *could* pass," he said, "if you wanted to. But if you did, it'd be like turnin' your back on me and everythin' I believes in."

"I'd never do that."

"Don't" he said. "Whatever you do, Hawk—it pushes the Race forward, or pulls us back. You know what I've always told you: If you fail, everything we been fightin' for fails with you. Be y'self."

"I will," I said. "I promise."

No sooner than I said this I felt wrong. More than anything else, I wanted my father's approval—I did, in fact, clomp along in his boots when I was a child, but he was so bitter. And his obsession with the world-historical mission of Africa? I didn't *want* this obligation! How strange that my father, the skillful, shrewd, funny, and wisest butler at Cripplegate—so faithful, on the surface, that he was even permitted to keep a shotgun before the Fall, and still had it—was beneath his mask of good humor and harmlessness a flinty old Race Man who wouldn't cook, wouldn't clean, who left his bedpans unemptied, who loosened his belt after my stepmother's meals, broke wind loudly, and, as often as not, fell asleep in the middle of her conversations. He nearly killed Mattie. The skin on his face was as thick as the callouses on his palm. But Mattie was, according to her lights, soft and deeply religious. A tall, thick-waisted woman, she attacked dirt in his cabin with a vengeance, singing "My God Is a Rock in a Weary Land" as she scrubbed tobacco stains off his porch, her crisp hair in a bright headscarf, shampooed his filthy rugs, which threw up biscuit crumbs, dust bunnies, and pips of calcified bone when George, tramping in each evening, stomped from room to room in his stockingfeet and nightshirts (Mattie kept the fireplace smoking, even in summer, and George, tight as an owl some nights, rocked around the cabin in nothing but his boots and Beardbox—he was absolutely the last man at Cripplegate to sleep in a Beardbox), but my stepmother stayed cold, very cold, after the incident with Jonathan. She bundled up in George's big workshirts and woolen scarves, grabbed the seat of her dress, threw it out behind her, then rested, a kitten on her lap, in George's favorite chair—she did not so much sit as bend the space around her. God only knew where she got her voice. It resonated, I remember, deep and clear like a belljar, but a bit of Cambridge clung to her vowels: when she said "dear" it always came out "dare." They argued. They fought. They paced circles round each other like cats. Mattie made him fix broken floorboards, then the front steps—this was no work, George argued, for one of the avant-garde of the African Revolution. It was (he said) a sin to Moses the way she made him finish his vegetables and, later, live *only* on herbs and roots. Or wipe his feet. Or smoke outdoors. (He pinched out his handmade, black-tobacco cigarettes when she caught him, dropping them still smoldering into his shirt pocket.) Or say grace above his usual mumbles: "*Gawd*," groaned George, hands squeezed together under the table, "forwhatweare-abouttoreceivethankyouAmen!" Crying shame too (said George) to be put out like this in your own place. (They fought, for example, over soup each Sunday, what with George drinking twice as fast as my stepmother and, ready for more, shoving his cup at her for a refill before she finished. Mattie took to bolting down her soup to beat him to the last cup—they looked rather like two huge, boiled lobsters by the end of the meal.) She made him comb his hair, which George never did, because once unkinked, he could not wear his hat, but it was not until a December evening in 1846, a bone-chilling Christmas eve, that their differences exploded in violence.

We were eating in his cabin, the table enhaloed by soft yellow lamplight, when I bit into my huge sandwich of split cornpone, with a thick slice of fat bacon inserted between the halves, and the Lord made it fall apart (so Mattie claimed), then a dollop of meat dropped to the floor, and George's hunting dog Daisy, a hound my father swore was the best friend he ever had ("You kin make a damn fool of yoself with a good huntin' dog and she won't rag you," he'd say, "she'll even make a fool of herself, too")—well, Daisy snapped up that scrap. She took one gulp, gagged, showed her blue-black gums, spat the meat straight across the cabin, then fainted with her legs in the air like an upended chair. "She's just playin'," said George, but Daisy fainting dead away like that was, for my stepmother, an *actus Dei*.

She went on a liquid fast for a week. She borrowed cookbooks, then biology texts from Ezekiel, and, each evening, made me read them to untangle for her whether animals or plants had souls and if eating them was evil. (True enough, I discovered, theologians of our time had weighed the soul in at eight-tenths of an ounce, and even one-celled chlamydosauria have (I read) a refined taste and a respect for beauty, but I found no proof that, say, a mushroom's got a scientific mind like you or me.) Mattie suffered, so to speak, from bad conscience. She claimed, contrary to reason, that men were so god-awful cruel, unchristian, and lowbrow (maybe she was trying to tell my father something) because meat eating—the essence of it, you might say—violated every civilized value since Saint Paul; and all that suffering could be overcome, if my stepmother was right, by doing away with corned Willie. "Well, Hawk," George told me, "yo Mama's gone off her pegs for sho this time. Next thing you know, she'll be talkin' with spirits and studyin' phrenology." The more George thought about this, the less he liked it. Too much imagination, he decided, was unwholesome. And white. If you were George Hawkins, you were coldly courteous to a Master who banished you to the bleakest life possible, a life spent among animals, away from the center of culture at Cripplegate; but wasn't this exile a blessing? Didn't it prove that whites were not, morally, Nature's last word on Man? They were, George swore after three fingers worth of stump liquor—his eyes like torches—Devils or, worse, derived in some way he couldn't explain from Africans, who were a practical, down-to-earth people. He hated, really hated, Ezekiel. Logic was not, I'm afraid, my father's strong point. "If they say *hup*, Hawk, it's gotta be *down*." He stood Jonathan's world on its head, to speak plainly, inverting Big House values at every turn. As for Mattie, well, this: She made her discovery, she was ready to expand on and explore this thing, to experiment with recipes, fried milk, to talk ethics all day with Ezekiel—I think all they did was talk—and revolutionize George's meals.

"Woman!" he barked. "You *got* to kill *some*thin' if you gonna eat! That's *Nature!* Don't take four years of college to see somethin' as simple as *that!*" Two weeks after she took George off his feed, they squared off in the cabin. It was quiet, rather like New Year's dinner in a work camp. George held his spoon in his whole fist. Mattie, her hair divided into eight partings, kept her back to the woodstove. She sent me out to wash my hands and, returning, I saw her bite into a cathead biscuit sharply, as if it might be the end of George's nose. She asked:

"George, is something wrong? You're eating your shirt collar again."

"That's 'cause I'm *hongry!* I stay hongry enough to chew the ass out of a dead goat!" When he looked up, his forehead was tortuously wrinkled, then suddenly smooth when he sighed, "Sorry."

"Then be so good, George," she sniffed—my stepmother hated it when he swore—"as to eat your dinner."

"You want me to *eat* these funnylookin' roots and raw tubers, eh?"

"Vegetables are good for you, George."

"Eat this paste, rice, and wood fibre without salt or syrup or anythin', like I was a bird or an English poet, or," his eyes shifted like a crab's, "one of them big wotchermercallits—what's the word, Mattie?"

She pulled her blouse away from her body.

"I couldn't say."

"Bronchitis? Naw, it ain't bronchitis. It's on the tip of my tongue."

He scratched his neck. "Begins with *b* and has a neck two miles long."

"Brontosaurus?" I asked.

"There you go, Hawk!" George looked at Mattie, his fingertips on the edge of the table. "Like that, huh? Honey, you know I ain't askin' for quail on toast. If I was to have Hawk run over to the henhouse, and if you was to fry an egg sunnyside-up for me, it wouldn't be the end of Western Civilization, would it?"

"Isn't a fool a wonderful thing, Andrew?" Mattie glanced from George to me. "It would end the *egg*, dear." (Was he about to choke her? I couldn't tell.) "Science *proves* that if you thump one brown egg in a basket, *all* the other eggs panic. Life," she said to turn him off, "is *process*, dear. We know that now."

"Which we you talkin' about?" asked George. "Whitefolks-*we* or blackfolks-*we*?"

She ignored him. Daisy was under the table, covering both eyes with her paws. The house was, just then, as quiet as a church on Monday. So quiet, I could hear Daisy—she had a touch of asthma—draw her little thimbleful of air. "You like soybean spread, don't you?" said my stepmother. "I can fix that. It does no *harm* to eat soybeans."

"Soybeans ain't hardly *food!*"

It was then my father decided, I think, that these sophisticated shenanigans had gone about far enough. Night pressed against the cabin window. He stood up, chewing his cheek, then hauled his shotgun and a fifth of topshelf whiskey from the pantry. "Beans or vegetables are okay for extras, but *I* need somethin' that'll fill hup this emptiness and stick with me!"

"George," said my stepmother, "what Ezekiel thinks—and what I think, too, is that meat eating is evil."

"And that's what *wrong* with him, Mattie!" Now his stomach grumbled. He broke off a toothpick from a broom in the pantry, then gnawed it. "He's the biggest fool in Hodges, and he's *ruinin'* this boy! If he don't wanna eat meat, okay, but *I* works hard for a livin'!" I could smell, as he stomped back to the table, the soap and starch in his collar. Now he'd begun to sweat. "He'd bring back the wolves! Naw," said George, "eatin' vegetables and walkin' round the woods nekkid like I seen Ezekiel do—oh yeah, I seen him—is for

white people. Colored folks got enough sense to stay in their clothes."
He stopped, pulling deeply for wind, then said, all righteousness,
"Some things you *got* to kill for survival!"

Mattie said, piously, "Our Lord Jesus Christ never ate meat."

"Right," grumped George, "and His life wasn't exactly one
long hallelujah from start to finish either!" He examined two shotgun shells, snapped both triggers, checked the firing pins before
loading both barrels, then closed the breech. Maybe you could
outargue George Hawkins, but you couldn't starve him. Daisy padded over. She put her black paws on my lap. After cocking both
triggers, George placed the gunstock under his arm, against his
side, the butt in his armpit, said, "Woman, I'm tired of talkin',"
then whipped open the back door. "And you best learn how to
cook like a black woman before I gets back!"

My stepmother shrank back. Guns terrified her. Her voice shot
up two octaves. "George, where are you going with that?"

"Get me some food," he said. "*Real* food, y'hear?"

It was the darkest night I could remember, seeing now my
father, hopping mad, and I tramped for hours through crusty
heaps of frozen snow, his finger rusted to the trigger, iced through
as he railed against the helplessness of black men before masters
and Modern Women. "They just a mouthful of grousin' and a
handful of Gimme." He uncorked a bottle with his teeth. Veins
stood out in his temples as he drank. When he finished the bottle,
he blew a few sour notes off the top, and raged on: "Hawk, I've
got to kill *some*thin' tonight or I'll go crazy!" For all the snow, and
for all his drunkenness, Death in the form of George Hawkins
tracked down a deer and dropped it—both barrels, which he steadied on my shoulders as I stooped, brought him crashing from a
dead run into the bushes, but he kept on kicking, looking back at
me, his voice leaping and pitching so loud I thought it was my own.
The explosion of gunpowder echoed in my throat. I turned away,
sick deep in my stomach (I'd seen George kill a hog once by leaping
on its back, burying the knife between its shoulder blades, riding it
round the yard until it dropped, then he hung it in the smoke-
house, its belly slit like an envelope, so I knew—or thought I knew—
what was coming next). Squatting on his hams, breathing heavily,

my father said, "You skin him, Hawk. I ain't got the wind left to do a decent job."

The knife he handed me sliced clean into its windpipe. I slid it sideways, severing the biggest arteries, then tied the buck's legs to a tree to keep its belly up. It was hot work, I can tell you. The effort left me panting. Then it was as if someone ran a finger across my mind. What if all Ezekiel's talk about how poleaxing preceded porkchops was saying that violence of the shotgun blast, the instant before the final explosion of dust, stayed sealed inside like a particle, trapped in the dying tissues, and wound up on the dinner table—as if everything was mysteriously blended into everything else, and somehow all the violence wars slavery crime and suffering in the world had, as Ezekiel suggested, its beginning in what went into our bellies? I screwed shut my eyes. An uneasy feeling came to me through my legs. Despite the cold, I was gulping air, my heart fluttering and unstable in my chest when I cut along the soft belly, pulling the blade from pelvic bone to chest, through tissue tough as rubber. My fist inside then, holding down the hot coils of intestines, I slid my sleeve in deep as I could, cutting loose the diaphragm, the windpipe—it felt like an old hose with wires on it—and then, against my will, I began crying softly into one hand as the other pulled free a handful of smoking heart, lungs, and intestines onto the snow-covered ground.

"Ah now, look at you, Hawk," George chuckled. "What's all that rain in yo face for?"

"You dress him," I said meekly.

"Go on." Now he sounded cross. "You doin' fine."

"It's wrong," I said. "It's all *wrong!*"

My father stared at me as if I had slapped him. In my refusal he saw everyone who had ever hurt him. Furious, he rode down on me, snatched away the knife, and finished skinning the deer himself. On the way home, with ice forming in his hair, he was touchy. He would not speak to me, nor for days thereafter. But sometimes in the middle of supper he would look up and hiss, "Y'all *against* me," banging his big fist on the table. "You even turned this boy against me!" Then, sure as day, came paranoia. From his porch, George held mad conversations with someone. Nights, he

Charles Johnson

whispered that he was being followed by a man, perhaps a padder-oll—a slave catcher, who rode an Andalusian with rags tied to its hooves, and who was assigned to murder him if he went too far, nurtured the flimsiest hopes, or forgot his place. "Hawk," he said, shaking, "someday you'll see him, too. No matter how edjoocated you git, he'll *be* there." He cracked his knuckles. His brow wrinkled, then went smooth, as if in astonishment. "Just when things git to goin' good, you know, when you finally think you kin lift hup yo head a li'l, he'll lay his hand on yo shoulder." My father believed, rightly or wrongly, in this specter, he slept with his shotgun, never sat with his back to the cabin door, and started at every strange sound.

George Hawkins and Jonathan Polkinghorne differed in ways doubtlessly important to them, but in my father's cabin, in the family house I saw the same ancient war—or, more precisely, the same crisis in the male spirit. This frightened me, I confess, for in philosophy's long history the heart was a mystery. Men had glimpsed, as my stepmother claimed, the algebra and alphabet of Nature, but knew nothing of feeling; men had charted Being and knew its mutations like the Periodic Table, but men were as children when it came to the heart. The emotions were not at issue here—each had its essence, but feeling was something else again: a process, plainly metaphysical, with its own grammar. What grammar was this? All the more urgent, then, was it for me to know, in this age of sexual warfare, my heart, make it my meditation, and be forever creating some meaning for what it meant to be male, though with what real satisfaction, and with how much resemblance to the promise of my gender, I did not know. During my third year with Ezekiel I began this exercise with etymology, tracing the heart's genesis to the Sanskrit *hrd*, or *kerd*, which led to the Greek *Kardia* (καρδία), and finally *thumos*, meaning soul or spirit, a sort of clearing, or aporia, or hollow carved primordially in the midst of things—it was planted (so we say) in the chest's deep cavity, *buried* in Being like a stake, centered in popular terms ("To get to the heart of") at precisely the point where Matter and Mind, spirit and flesh, heaven and earth, subject and object, Self and Other, locked like fingers. This theory was fine, as far as it went, but it hardly went far enough. Perhaps the narratives of Gustavus Vassa and Venture Smith are,

28

as confessions, clearer about slavery and sexual politics, but I (alas)
was lost in the ideas at Cripplegate, lost in the emotions, lost in
others, and, as always, when I exhausted my wit, I turned to Ezekiel.

There was no one like Ezekiel.

What he did about women was anybody's guess, but he never
brought them to his cabin. His two, tiny eight-by-ten–foot rooms,
with their three-decked stove, its sheet-iron stovepipe turned at a
right angle, warped piano shipped from St. Louis, and large pine
cupboard, were an extension of my tutor's mind—namely, a catas-
trophe of books, periodicals, copies of *Neue Rheinische Zeitung*, the
only issue of *Deutsche-Französische Jahrbücher*, Indian sculpture (The
Dance of Shiva), and papers Ezekiel was writing—articles on Patan-
jali, the poet Shankara, and the anonymous *Cloud of Unknowing*
that would someday be called "brilliant" by people who still cared
about the life of the spirit, and "pretentious" by those who did not.
Vulgarity he hated; and, after that, Vanity. There was something
feminine in his tastes. Yet, he was the only man in Hodges who
needed gin to lower his nervous system, gear down his ganglions
to the level of general torpidity we called "normal." Women frightened him. He was afraid also of cripples. He slept in his clothes—
the one-button sack coat so ragged he could, when pacing, reach
right into the lining and lock his hands behind his back, or rather
he collapsed in his clothes at his writing desk after feverishly writing letters to confound his enemies, or pouring over the Pali texts,
his shirt collar open, throat bare, and great Adam's apple bobbing;
but he never touched newspapers because the Press, Ezekiel said,
trafficked in trivial froth about politicians, features about stage
personalities with less wit than a toadstool, gossip, lies, and facts
lumped together, page upon page, without analysis, without truth,
without system or order, or even once asking, as any right-thinking
man would, how the heart might find peace in a world where the
spirit seemed exiled. He was awesome to me. He could not, it was
clear, live without certainty. And then there were his looking glasses,
dozens of them on his study door and wall. His room was all iri-
descence, a blinding shimmer to me when I tipped in with my black
lesson book, for his lamplight was magnified a thousandfold, re-
peated across the room in every nook and cranny—as were Ezekiel
and I—like a sound ricocheting into infinity. Everything inside looked

like a vision. When he saw me squinting, he would stand, coughing—he seemed to keep a cold—and say, "Let us step into the next room, Andrew." His eyes, redwebbed, puckered when he looked down at me. "In Missouri, before the accident, my family was very poor." He took paper spill from a sheaf on the mantelpiece and began lighting an oil lamp in the front room. "I discovered that looking glasses open up a room, so I never feel confined—they are openings, I think, or doorways." Ezekiel placed the cloudy lampglass over the flame, paused a moment, then turned up the wick.

"Was it really an accident?" I was sitting now on a milkbench. "Your father?"

"It was," he said, "and it wasn't." Lamplight threw his shadow and mine high against the wall. His nose was lit by the glow of his pipe. "My father was no fool. He never wanted pity. He didn't *want* to die, Andrew. When I found my parents dead, I wept, of course, but only briefly, because my grief, it struck me, was a ghastly pose— mere histrionics, clichéd outrage when the situation called for something else. Do you see?"

"Yes," I said, quietly, but I wasn't sure.

"My father's need for consolation did not dawn on me, or anyone, until it was too late to console. This is the way with all suicides. Because we didn't listen well, or Lord knows what, he shambled home after work and shot himself." Ezekiel blew his nose. After a moment of silence, he said, "My father spent twelve, maybe fifteen hours a day in a brass foundry, where I was employed for a time when I was fifteen, and for a pitiful wage. If all he could expect was poverty—if, I say, Andrew, all he could see ahead was sixty years of bad news, the breakdown of his family, debts and disappointments, without hope of change, without consolation, wasn't it better to be done once and for all with the person feeling, eh? It is not easy to be a full-grown man, Andrew. We are not like women." He swung his eyes toward me. "We are weaker."

"Weaker?" It made no sense. "How are we *weaker?*"

"Spiritually, I think. Perhaps all philosophy boils down to the simple fear that the universe has no need for us—men, I mean, because women are, in a strange sense, more essential to Being than we are. Have you never felt that? Don't you feel oftentimes that we have been banished from the earth? That we approach the universe as an adversary because she turns her back upon us? In the East," he said, "men believe themselves to be off-springs of the sun, creatures of light, made of the same stuff that powers stars. They worship Being as a female, the Mother. But we in Europe and the Americas have settled for something else. Something less, I daresay. We build machines, Andrew, create tribal languages in philosophy—like little boys with secret codes in their clubhouse—to get back at the universe because she has failed to give us a function. All our works, *male* works, will perish in history—history, a male concept of time, will vanish, too, but the culture of women goes on, the rhythms of birth and destruction, the Way of absorption, passivity, cycle and epicycle." Ezekiel smiled, remote. "I haven't put any of this very well, but this is the heart of my meditation, the reason for all these papers stacked around us. In India, near the town of Gaya, there is an illiterate man I know, a sannyasin named Trishanku, who believes that good is good, Andrew, and that evil is good, too. Not far from him, in a city, a couple is completing a love affair that began twenty-five centuries ago in Sparta. . . ." His voice trailed off. His lips went white. Now he had forgotten me altogether. "Sometimes I feel so close to how he must have felt that day, and at other times . . . when I think of him with half his head blown away like that, sometimes I think. . . ."

Ezekiel didn't explain what he thought.

But my tutor and I often crossed the border of Jonathan Polkinghorne's plantation to take solitary walks on springtide evenings along the shelfy beach of the river. Oddly like a sacrament, the sand was penciled with patterns by porridgy waters that came crashing in, carrying catfish to shore, eternally collapsing and re-forming like—what?—vorticed, breaking in a fine spray of foam and ammonites on clusters of stone covered with weeds and great patches of slime. The blue haze of the salt-scented air, as I listened to Ezekiel, soaked into my white linen frock and lemon-colored breeches like a stain. He thought obliquely, in language reshaped like soft wax, the power of his arguments vivid, their precise meaning veiled. He made me feel, strangely, that each smell, each sound was sheer magic—that he and I, these frothy waves, this dust-seamed wind were somehow essential for the world to be, as if the twisted straw, clumps of driftwood gnarled and knobby like old

31

human bones, upon which our boots fell, the heart-shaped stones and scree, very smooth, thought themselves in me and were full of some queer godstuff I could sense these nights in my blood, but could never, never grasp. Nor could I decide, before we returned to the quarters, if what I felt was, finally, an intimation of my freedom—my *real* freedom—ordering these objects now into love, now into beauty, or merely the fantasies a crackpot Anarchist had flowered in my thoughts. Unable to penetrate these things, seeking at that time only to be penetrated, I traipsed along with him at night, wondering over the objects thinging on the banks, studying the bright orb that mooned brilliantly above in a dark sky tinctured with vermeil. In the clutch of this calm intoxication I heard Ezekiel speak of his teacher in India, the strange, naked, nut-brown man named Trishanku, who (said Ezekiel) had worn out seventeen meditation cushions and, at age fifty, mastered the eight occult powers. If his tale can be believed, this Trishanku, living by the Ganges in a detoxified body, conversed often with Brahma, and on one such occasion Trishanku asked, "I have often heard holy men speak of something called *Samsara*. Can you tell me what this means?"

"Ask something else." The question made Brahma uncomfortable. "Anything else. How to win a woman's heart, or gain wealth— these things I can easily tell you."

"I asked about *Samsara*. That, and only that, is what I do not fully understand after a lifetime of meditation."

Though reluctant, the Most High said, "All right, but this knowledge of *Samsara* will take some time. It is the highest knowledge, Trishanku. First, we must prepare ourselves—the ground beneath us is very hard. Have you a pillow I can sit upon?"

"I will find one," said Trishanku, and, after bowing deeply and pulling on a loincloth, he took off for Magadha, the nearest village. It was a long walk, and you must remember that Trishanku, after thirty years of fasting, standing on one foot, and yoga postures was not a very physical man. Soon he was breathing heavily and his legs buckled, yet the village seemed no closer than before. Like a mirage, it seemed, moving backwards as the old sannyasin planted one blistered, brown foot before the other. When at last he reached the first hut at the fringe of the village, Trishanku was too tired to knock. He tripped through the doorway, and would have shouted

32

Water! but he was too parched, and besides, what Trishanku saw inside the hut took away his breath, and that was no small thing (said Ezekiel), for the sannyasin was a master of breath, *chi, prana,* and a number of other cardiovascular tricks. What he saw, lifting his eyes, was a woman so beautiful his heart whispered *Oh!* and his old knees smacked together, and for a time the sage, the rsi, the swami Trishanku only stared. "Do you need help?" asked the woman, whose name was Lila. Trishanku pointed at his lips and croaked, "Water," which she brought, then food for him—a little fruit on banana leaves—and then Lila, who was unwed and hungry for companionship, looked at him. Trishanku looked at her. Their bodies moved closer, then twinned together like those of two eels. By morning, they had not moved from their spot near her door. But Trishanku had, from guilt and love, asked Lila to be his wife, and to this she agreed.

Their first few days of marriage were a delight to Trishanku. Before retiring to the forest he had apprenticed as a carpenter, and to this trade he returned, taking only a few assignments at first—he wanted to spend all his time with Lila—then more when a daughter, then a son came into their lives. He worked harder then, traveling sometimes to other villages and towns—Kurukshetra and Brahmapura—building homes and for himself the reputation of being the best carpenter in all India. But always his joy was in returning home to his family, the root and fruit of his happiness, his great elephants groaning with garments from Persia for his wife, and toys for the boy and girl. There, at home, his house buzzed with activities. Babies to feed. Younger boys to teach, as his family grew, and the affairs of his servants, the kitchen maids and mahouts, to see after (for Trishanku was a good employer). To her credit, Lila loved Trishanku and was as prudent as she was shrewd about money—she balanced her husband's books, for he could not read, and with her help he made many wise investments. His holdings tripled, as did his household, and after eight years there was no wealthier estate in twenty provinces than that of Trishanku of Magadha.

And then their eldest son was of an age for work, and his daughter ripe for marrying. The boy, who was a blessing to Trishanku, took the hardest part of his father's business, which gave

Trishanku time to be with his grandchildren, or to gamble (lightly) with other rich men of the village; his girl married well, snaring the son of a local Brahman and, with him, political connections for her father. Once or twice, though, it came to Trishanku that his duties were too much. He felt, now and then, as if he might one day drop in the street and die in harness like a horse. But he tried not to complain—one look at Lila's smile of pleasure at their prosperity was enough to dispel his doubts. Late some nights, they lay in each other's arms, kissed, and when he could manage it they made love as passionately perhaps as when he first stepped through her door. "How dear you are to me," Trishanku whispered as he rolled off his wife. Lila, knowing how men are—he would be complaining again in the morning—simply nuzzled closer, her head on his chest.

But as often happens in India, there came a flooding of the Ganges, an overflowing that swept away the houses Trishanku had built. The roar awoke him and Lila in the night. From his doorway he watched the waters rise above the temple roofs, carrying away the families of his friends; then his bins of grain; his house, which splintered as if slapped by the great toe of a god; and then it carried away as well his wife and children, his grandchildren—they were torn from him, each of their deaths like a dagger in his mind; the entire village washed away, and only Trishanku, broken and bleeding, remained, clinging to driftwood, crying aloud, *Lord!* for he now drifted toward a cliff with a hundred-foot drop, *Lord!* but he was not even sure now that he wanted to live.

Instantly, the flood was gone. Where the remains of Magadha had stood there was Brahma in a sea, a miracle, of light. He was a little impatient now, tapping his foot. "Trishanku," asked the Most High, "where is my pillow?"

"Wake hup, Hawk." George elbowed me. "We heah, son."

Covered with dust, and just an hour before twilight, we arrived at an old Hanoverian hip-roofed house that, large, dark, and imposing, hunched high up in the hills. The sky was fast losing light. My father looked, or so I thought, uneasy—but was he? And afraid—but was George afraid? Swinging his feet down from his seat, he said, "All this heah, up to the mines north-northwest, belongs to Flo Hatfield."

"You've been here before?" I pulled my bag from beneath tarpaulin in the rear of the wagon. And then, suddenly, the answer trumpeted through my thoughts: "You've been here before with Master Polkinghorne, haven't you?"

"Gimme a hug, Hawk."

"Why?"

"I'm saying goodbye, son." He opened his arms. "From here on, you go by yoself." I hesitated for a moment—I saw him chewing my meat for me when I was a child, softening it before spooning it toward me; he would wiggle, I remember, his big ears for me, and let me look through his pockets for coins, and keep them. I squeezed George round his neck until he grunted. Then my father took out his handkerchief, dusted me off, and wiped his eyes. He clapped me on the back, climbed back on the wagon, then turned it around. "Be y'self." His voice began to creak. "That's all I'm askin', Hawk."

Therewith, I bunched my shoulders, marching up a footpath along the hill, stiff from sitting so long in the wagon, but the path ended abruptly, leaving me standing near sawmills fallen into perdition, leaf-heavy trees, hot houses near Augean quarters—they once had been quarters, I decided, but were now rotting sheds that smelled worse than Hell on housecleaning day. Slouching women too old for the fields—Wolof and Fulah by their crimped faces—stirred clothing in their boiling pots with willow wands. I labored on through weeds, gulping air. The wind rolled through my hair. Griffinlike wolfhounds wuffed at my ashey ankles. Worksounds—sawing, hammering, the lilt of a spiritual struck up like a lay—whorled round my head in great humping arcs. Was I to work here? In this dreary factory? Each sound, blunted by the heat, stuck to me like a burr. Thereaway were trees that shot out branches favoring the writhing feelers at the front of a squid. Closer were summered-over yards full of soapwort and boneless snakes. Children waved. Whistled. Yoohooed. Away to the left were different strains of sunblackened slaves (Marabous and Griffe) tinkering with rickety plows, repairing mule harnesses, and one looked up with curiosity from the casket he was building as I stumbled along.

"My name," I told him, "is Andrew Hawkins. I'm here to see Flo Hatfield. Can you help me reach the house?"

"You *folks?*" he asked, and I swallowed. This man or boy—he

35

might have been either—had a hoarse, carrying voice, like a slab of granite grunting, that went through you, that burst inside your head like thought, or intelligence felt telepathically. He was obscenely bald like an egg, but his ears bristled with hair. His body, which ranged in color from coal black (arms) to brown (palms), was large, but not tall, with the look of a wrestler who'd let himself go. On his cheeks was scarification. In his left nostril, a dull ring. This was Reb, I learned later. Leviathan's Coffinmaker. He squeezed shut one eye asking again, "You *folks*, I say, or white people?"

"Oh, folks," I assured him. "Definitely folks."

"You ain't folks or white," he snorted. His eyes studied me. "You fresh meat, boy." Two dirty children came up to stare at me, but the Coffinmaker waved them away. He lay his long saw down inside his casket, dusted his hands, then stood up. "Oh, she gonna like you awright—all that curly hair and them brown eyes. And that ain't good."

"No?" My breath went out of me. "Why?"

"C'mon." Gently, Reb shoved me toward the house. I said no more, but stayed as close as I could to him, lugging my bag. Moving along like a wind-up doll, locomotively, both arms flat at his sides, he looked back at me and laughed. It was the laugh, you'd have thought, of a hangman. Had you entered with us that day, you'd have passed through outside odors arranged in a strata so that we moved, slowly like a funeral procession, from room to room through curtains of smells that included cabbage, hominy made from Indian corn, and fresh fish. You'd have seen a white-pillared doorway leaded with sidelights, then, as Reb stepped aside, an oak-paneled, high-ceilinged boudoir of whorehouse luxury.

"She's in there?" My voice was shaky. I offered him my hand. "Thank you."

"Boy," he said, turning away. "You don't wanna thank me."

He left me outside the door. Thinking I might charm this woman Flo Hatfield and thereby earn my quick return to Cripplegate, I breathed deeply to steady myself. *Be steady,* I thought, then, straightening my cravat with two fingers, I stepped slowly inside.

III

IN THE SERVICE OF THE SENSES

After looking over Jonathan Polkinghorne's letter, Flo Hatfield peered at me for perhaps a minute through a black lorgnette, first my dusty boots, then my lap, and, finally, my face before she intoned:

"Well, you are *here* now, Andrew Hawkins. And I will not send you home. You shall work. However, it is vital that you know a few things about Leviathan. And me."

She settled herself more comfortably on a long horsehair sofa with round, tasseled pillows, both her knees drawn up, then made a pause, which I dared not break. So here was Flo Hatfield, wearing clothes of a period I could not place, but the material was embroidered to look like a landscape—forests and fauna—and cut tightly over an extraordinary bosom. She was a beautiful woman. A sumptuous woman with a little red mouth, and an uptilted nose. I placed her age at forty. Forty-five. In the darkening room her face looked at first sharp and highly stylized, then old and spidered with wrinkles. Arranged in broad basket plaits, ornamented with pearls, her brown hair made her appear, in twilight silting through windows of storied glass, much older than her hands, which had a vegetable sensuality that, at first, frightened me. You would have thought Flo Hatfield had found a way of speaking that perfectly twisted the English tongue to fit her voice, which was deep and steamy: a kind of soft, deer language. And what of her boudoir? It was, in the truest sense, Decadent. Lush curtains near her door resembled paired Ionic columns. Closed in comfortably by chairs with cabriole legs, her paintings, and a bust of Dionysius, Flo Hatfield lounged, feeding herself an egg from a demitasse cup, swinging her left

37

foot, her head thrown back against the cushions of her sofa. I did not so much listen to her words as I listened to Flo. She made me feel larval and lazy. She had a way of stroking her breasts up, letting them fall back, then looking—all innocence—at me for my reaction. A nerve trembled in the center of my belly. I kept my eyes on the plates and bric-a-brac behind her, to the left, and she said:

"Leviathan belonged to my late husband Henry. It is a profitable affair for me, Andrew, but I sometimes find it necessary to hire our people out to the mines during off-season." A grin, elastic, tightened around her mouth. "We work well together here," she said. "I am Leviathan's sovereign, its soul. All others are, in a manner of speaking, the joints, tendons, nerves, and tissues that sustain the soul. You have read Jeremy Bentham? No? Well, no matter. Leviathan supports, oh, fifty slaves and that human sloth Earl, my second husband. I have been," she watched me narrowly, "married eleven times—I'm sure I hold some kind of record. Does that surprise you, Andrew?"

"No," I said. "I mean, I think it generous, very Christian of you to support your last husband."

Laughing, her teeth flashed white. "Each year I send Earl five hundred thrips inside a mule, Andrew."

"In a mule, I heard you say, ma'am?"

"Yes, we mix the money in with their feed." Flo Hatfield's cackle went through me like a shock. "You see, I *never* just let a man walk out of my life. This doesn't," she asked, "seem *cruel* to you, does it, Andrew?"

"Oh no." I could feel my smile freezing. Hereupon, I plaited the right leg of my trousers with my right hand. "Whatever you think is fair."

"I'm so glad you see it that way." She clapped her hands twice, why I didn't know, but lifting her arms—her armpits were stippled black from shaving—also lifted her breasts, which fell again. She caught me staring and smiled. Head cocked to the left, sly, she leaned back, turning a brilliant ring on her finger, watching me watch her cleavage, and said, "I am selfish, Andrew—I know my faults and virtues—and I stay dissatisfied. Often, I believe I was born on another planet, perhaps Venus, which is a world of spoiled, pampered women, who are all geniuses of love, ravishing and forever young, but somehow, by some terrible cosmic accident, I was brought here by slavers, millions of miles from my true home and sisters. I *knew* a monstrous error had been made when, as a girl in Georgia, I took a hard look at the great soft toads who called themselves my parents. I felt a bit like a changeling. Does that make any sense to you?"

"Yes." I wiped sweat from my brow with the back of my hand. "You're an artist, Mrs. Hatfield."

She brightened. "You can *tell?*"

"The thrips inside the mule gave you away." She saw me perspiring and pulled from under her pillows a lace handkerchief scented with patchouli. "Creative types," I offered, "often feel so . . . misplaced."

"You *are* charming," smiled Flo Hatfield. "And I like your breeding. Jonathan has done handsomely by you."

"It was my tutor Ezekiel," I said, "And you are too kind."

Into this steamy room came some species of butler—a young man close to my age, but well-heeled, and with a voice like a tuba. He had an easy, loose-hinged walk. His face was clean-shaven, with an explosion of dreadlocks like the cowboy Nat Love. He saw me sitting by Flo and stopped. He took two steps back, then, looking from Flo to me, holding a tray with a glass and a decanter of Bordeaux, he asked—a whisper—"You wanted refreshments?"

"For both of us, Patrick, yes," she said. "Will you get Andrew a glass?"

"Get him a glass, too?"

Flo dipped into her egg cup, finished it, then licked the back of her spoon as Patrick watched. "That's what I said." Angling upward, her gaze crossed his, and for a second I thought her look was to reassure him. His shoulders relaxed. "And before you go," added Flo, "please measure Andrew for a new wardrobe, something like what you're wearing—he looks as if he lifted his clothes off a scarecrow." She wound hair close to her ear around one finger, watching Patrick's reaction to me. She seemed, I thought, to swell, growing larger on her sofa as he glared back at me, feeding on his anxiety. And after a second: "What kind of wage did you have in mind, Andrew?"

"Mrs. Hatfield." I sat up with a jerk. "Maybe I should tell you

my purpose for coming here. In a year's time I hope to earn enough
to buy my parents and the girl I wish to marry"—I felt her stiffen
at the word "marry," and, as I said it aloud, I felt silly—"from
Master Polkinghorne."

"Well!" Flo Hatfield said violently. "Do you mean to say that
you love this girl?"

"Yes," I said. "Yes, I do."

"And does she love *you?*"

For a moment I struggled. Time and again, I'd told myself that
it only mattered if I loved Minty. Now the thought bothered me. I
buried it. I said, "She does—she does love me."

"Does she *really?*" Flo put back her head. "And is she pretty?"

I bobbed my head: *yes, yes, yes.*

"We shall see, then, about this—what is the girl's name? Does
she have a name, Andrew?"

"Minty. . . ."

"Yes, Minty." Flo made the name sound like root medicine.
Her high bosom heaved. "We will see how you feel about all this in
a year. Now, if you will please disrobe, Patrick can take your
measurements."

That threw me off stroke. I asked in a tight voice that had no
tie to my mind, "Ma'am?"

"Your trousers." The stones of her eyes, very blue with shades
of brown as if spring water rushed over bright riverbottom pebbles,
ranged over me. "We do not stand on ceremony here, Andrew, but
if you wish, I will leave the room."

To this hour, sir, I wonder how in Heaven's name I had brought
this upon myself. Flo glided to the door, passing Patrick, shutting
it behind her, and left me with her butler, who gave me the kind of
look I had seen Conjure Doctors use to paralyze birds. Irritably, he
waited beside my chair, pins in his mouth, holding a bolt of brown
cloth. The air around me, tight. Despite my schoolboy shyness, and
despite the weakness in my knees, I pulled the cord around my
waist and my trousers sprang open. At this point, Flo Hatfield
bounded back into the room. "I have forgotten something." As this
was said, she walked to the sofa, found her lorgnette, and, turning
toward me, drew breath suddenly. Her mouth snapped shut. Then
it slipped sideways. She stretched her neck toward me, blinking

through her glasses, then hurried back out the door with the tray of Bordeaux. In the hallway, she said, "*Do* hurry, Patrick"—her voice quavered—"We haven't all day." I heard her pour herself a goodly measure of wine, knocking glass and bottle—*clink!*—nervously as the butler, finishing, called, "We's finished now, Flo."

"You call her Flo?" I asked.

"Just me." His lips curled back, he said, like a thug, with his mouth wrenched to one side, "Think you *some*thin', don't you, comin' in heah with all them books."

"Huh?"

"Why doan you go back to Hodges," he said. "Doan nobody want you heah."

"Has Andrew," asked Flo, "covered himself?"

"Yeah."

Exhaling deeply, Flo Hatfield eased back into the room and onto her sofa, slowly, like someone on stage. Her mouth fell back into place, relaxed. There was, just then, a half-wistful, half-perverse look in her eyes as she glanced from Patrick to me, like a woman comparing chunks of pork at Public Market.

"Well," she said, "you are *most* welcome, as Jonathan Polkinghorne's servant, in my house. But," her nose wrinkled, "don't you dare get fat, Andrew."

I assured her I would not.

She told Patrick to take me to a tiny, topfloor room down the hall from her bedchamber—the room was a kind of catchall space, full of luggage, round-topped leather trunks, but it looked lived in. Showing me inside, he tossed my portmanteau and books like so much trash onto the bed, then slammed shut the door. He cuffed me hard behind my ear and pushed me into a chair. His knuckles, five black knots of wood, slammed into my chest.

"You and me best get one thing straight from the get-go, Chief." He was panting a little now, spitting in anger. "There ain't *room* enough for two splibs in this house. You understand?" He began gathering up clothes and shoes in the room, talking to me over his shoulder. "I've put up with a *whole* lot since I left my Papa's shed— I worked like hell to make somethin' of myself. Is that clear, Chief?"

"Is this *your* room, Patrick?"

"Nigguh, nobody told you to talk! This ain't *no*body's room.

Look at them walls. *Hundreds* of nigguhs been in heah. You know where they all went?"

"Can I talk now?"

"No!"

Clothes crushed under his right arm, he stamped to the door, threw it open, and said, "They went to the mines, Chief, and that's where you're goin'—I'll see to it—if you mess hup this thing for me."

"By my heart, Patrick," I said, "I'm only here to work with you." I lifted my hand toward him. "We can work together, can't we?"

And then, incredibly, Patrick's lips released a rippling volley of laughter so sudden that his head tilted back, tears hopped from his eyes, and, doubled over, he strangled. I slapped his back; he struck down my hand, and said, "Don't you *ever* touch me, Chief." Slowly, he wiped his eyes. "How people gonna work *together* heah? You tell me that!" He hoisted his bundle higher, turned in the doorway, said, "You ain't gonna last a week," then closed it behind him with a click.

Needless to say, I did not entirely trust Flo Hatfield's butler, or even Flo for that matter—they seemed, now that it's out in the open, more than half-crazy, and I thank God, sir, that you ain't a lunatic, too. Nor was I happy sleeping in Patrick's former room. (Flo sent him to sleep in the quarters.) The house was huge, with sliding panels, I discovered, and rooms into which Flo and Patrick often disappeared, and which, strange to relate, I was forbidden to enter. My bedroom had thin walls. The door did not close properly, the piece of looking-glass on its back was held there by three rusty nails, but slowly I slipped into the rhythms of life at Leviathan. Lavish meals were served twice a day. There were so many courses I could not finish what was on my plate. Since the catfight between George and Mattie over eating flesh, I took no meat. Flo, who ate no more than a child, and mainly candy at that, was ill pleased with my vegetarianism. "There is something *lowbred* in self-denial, Andrew," she announced over breakfast. And this saying, too: "Eating a good piece of meat is like making love," swinging her eyes toward Patrick, as if he might be a six-foot chicken quiche. This observation, I daresay, was narrowly true, but the phrase bothered me because her words laundered a much larger problem, concealed something in me I could not unkey. Let me explain.

I don't want to wrong this woman, who treated Patrick and me like family, so I won't go so far as to say her appetites were well known to the county sheriff, although this was possible. Self-denial was, however, the only sin for our mistress. She put tremendous pressure on my masculinity. Don't get me wrong—I am not, nor have I ever been, a prude; I love making love. But if you scratch a man deeply enough, particularly one with Pico's *Oration*, or my father's vision of the black future in his bloodstream, you'll find him suspicious of pleasure as a Final Cause. For the men of my period the dream of contributing to the Race, of Great Sacrifice and glory, drew us back from desire. We wanted to do something difficult—see?—like tame the West, spearhead a Revolution, or pin the universe down like a butterfly on the pages of a book. We wanted trials. Tests of faith. We could not live, the men of my age, without a cause. A principle. Something greater than merely *living* from day to day, and to which we could devote ourselves entirely. And pleasure? It was hard to square pleasure with having a world-historical mission. Sex was subhistoric. Plutarch's *Lives of Great Men* didn't portray—if memory serves—anyone who simply had a good time. I knew, as Flo knew, my weakness for heroic visions; it was dangerous, I knew that, too. But it was me. These, as I say, were things that troubled me about Flo Hatfield's philosophy.

And one other thing:

Despite her plain talk about pleasure, she was not sensual. My mistress was too obsessive to be sensual. The erotic difference between my Minty and Flo, it seemed to me—though I could have been wrong, fooled by first impressions—was the difference between growth and decay, the spirit flowering in efflorescence and the spirit so paralyzed by past pleasures, impoverished by desire, that now it needed the most violent stimulants to register sensation. Long ago she had ruptured the capillaries inside her nose, but with what chemicals I cannot tell you. If you looked carefully, light passed *through* her nostrils. Her awareness of sounds, of colors, even her paintings, seemed anchored less in passion than—how shall I put this?—in mechanical response. And what more? She was trigger-happy with snap judgments, vengeful, so cunning the act of crossing her knees was equivalent to a frontal attack in a military operation, and, like Aristotle, couldn't stomach children. And yet how lovely she was, and gentle with everyone generally, except her ex-husbands, whom she considered subhuman.

But I would do wrong, and I would lie, if I left you with the impression that she was, in any sense, anything but fair my first few months at Leviathan. Flo Hatfield bought me gifts. Two months after my arrival, she gave me a silver bracelet, a beautiful dog collar (Patrick had one identical to it). From the start, Flo took it upon herself to make me more worldly. I did not resist. One must, I reasoned, make allowances for a woman who lives on candy and at any hour of the day only had a few ounces of chocolate in her. So I followed Flo everywhere. To horse races. Cockfights. (She'd gamble on anything—the weather, which way a cockroach would turn next on the wall.) After finishing my chores—helping Patrick clean the dishes, scrubbing her cabinets, made in Flanders and Germany, or tidying up her huge bedchamber (once I saw Flo, wearing one of Patrick's shirts, stumble out to bathe, with wheezing, whistlelike breath, and insomnia, her skin mottled from sleeplessness; but mostly our mistress stepped from her bedroom at ten each morning, incredibly put-together after her toilet, yet if you tipped in behind her, as I had to do, peering round her dark bedroom, you saw a disaster, as if, magically, her bedroom's disorder—an order I reestablished daily—passed through osmosis into Flo, who blithely left behind a disheveled chrysalis of broken jars, her paintings atilt, clothes, stockings, haircombs, and pillows tossed everywhere)—after these chores she called me into her boudoir to play Rummy or Coon-can.

Yet, despite Flo Hatfield's noisy eroticism, or because of it, she was lonely. At her easel, where she mixed paint on the palm of her hand, or in her fields beneath a straw bonnet, Flo Hatfield looked lonely. Waxing her eyelashes, or pulling a comb through her hair before her immense mirror, her right leg crossed over her left, and Patrick standing nearby to fetch, his back straight, holding a tray as he gazed at her reflection, she looked lonely. There was something wrong, something she'd done to herself, but I couldn't put my finger on it. At any rate, I pitied my new mistress being so successfully independent, so liberated from convention, that no one in Abbeville would touch her with a barge pole, except—it seemed—Patrick, who was no Don Juan. Little wonder then that as the days became months I began, I think, to love her thereness, the beauty and spiritual brilliance that was Flo Hatfield.

She would have me read Sir Walter Scott while she painted, then suddenly place her hand over my book—this, during afternoons on her lawn in late summer, when she wore a paint-splattered tunic, and said, "Tell me about philosophy, Andrew."

"Whose philosophy did you want to hear, ma'am?"

"It doesn't matter." That afternoon her eyes were strained and pointed as though she'd been chewing some controlled substance. "You have a way," Flo fanned herself with a scrap of sketching paper, "of pitching your voice just so that it runs in my head and gives me gooseflesh." She lowered her eyelids a little. "I wonder what you'd taste like."

Patrick bit down on the side of his finger.

I told her all I knew of Gnosticism, taking each question of Theodotus singly. Her eyes became quiet; she blurred the sense of my lecture, listening only to the stream of my speech. She seemed, I thought, unnecessarily harsh that afternoon on Patrick. "Men," Flo said, more to him than to me, "don't enjoy sex at *all*. They're afraid to experiment. Things are so one-sided. Men don't know how to relax. They make love as a *task*. They don't know how to imaginatively use pain."

I closed a finger on my book to keep my place. Patrick looked away, sadly, toward the mines, and with such melancholy I could hear, faintly, a whimper rise, then die in his right ventricle. I turned to Flo, and asked, "Pain?"

"The artful use of pain, Andrew." She talked on like this. "Men orgasm too quickly. You must learn to indefinitely prolong tension, longing, thirst, discomfort, desire, the burning sensation of the genitalia just before they sneeze. I came of age in Venice, Andrew," said Flo, as if this explained everything. "I was educated there, and I discovered techniques of maximizing pleasure seldom permitted in a country as backward as this one, except maybe in New Orleans. Pain," she said, "is the precondition for pleasure. Have you ever been licked unconscious by four naked women?"

"No." My voice broke. "I don't think so."

"Well, if you had, you'd remember it, Andrew. I mean you'd hardly forget a thing as delicious as that, would you?"

"You've done this?" I asked.

Flo Hatfield only smiled and pushed my nose.

Whoever is wise, and will observe these things, will see that this woman had no equal on earth, that only a fool would not open himself to her, though, yes, the races at Leviathan, as elsewhere, only lived *alongside* each other in an uneasy truce. Example: Reb the Coffinmaker avoided Flo Hatfield at all costs. My mistress bothered him a whole lot. Everything about Flo raised his Ebenezer: her laughter, her clothes, every order she gave, orders she didn't give. Was Reb, I wondered, as scarred by slavery as my father? As unfirm in his gender as Ezekiel? Clearly, it was Flo Hatfield's air we breathed, her clothes dispensed to the quarters once a year (hard leather clogs, one blanket, Lowell pants, one mackinaw hat, five yards of coarse homespun cotton), but Reb's feelings of discomfort sprang, I discovered, from a different source, a deeper outrage. Permit me, then, in a plain way, to backpedal a bit and speak of the Coffinmaker's life in Africa.

There were days, whole weeks, when my duties kept me close to the house (Flo managed, however, to dodge all discussion of my wages), but on the day when my struggle with Patrick for male preeminence in the house ended in murder—I will speak of it in a minute—I descended on a gray medley, leisurely, at a handgallop to the quarters and found the Coffinmaker grimly sealing cracks and seams in a casket with wood putty, painting the top and interior with tar, his trousers and the front of his shirt covered with pinewood powder. It was a hot afternoon, and the sky was clear and deep and the road to Reb's shack was dusty. For a long time he ignored me. He was, as everyone knew, the most disagreeable man in South Carolina. His face naturally relaxed into a frown. You would know him in a crowd of thousands. He was the man, at country market, who looked at the stands and rejoiced at what he *didn't* need; the man who, when most vigorously at work, seemed resting. Reb did not believe in getting sick or tired and, therefore, never was. It was said that when he first arrived at Leviathan he found himself confronted by two white hunters on a backroad. They'd caught no game that day. They leveled their shotguns at

Reb. When he failed to run, one hunter said, "Nigguh, you lookin'
at somebody who kin blow off yo head without battin' an eye." It is
said the Coffinmaker blinked, pushed aside both shotguns like
treelimbs in his path, and, passing on, replied, "You lookin' at
somebody who can *be* shot without blinkin' an eyelash." I did not,
therefore, wish to upset him. He was building—so it seemed to
me—his most elaborate coffin, but no one had died at Leviathan
since my arrival. I said, to start him talking:

"It's a beautiful casket. You do fine work."

"*I* didn't *do* anythin'," said Reb. He looked up for an instant,
straight ahead, scowling at something I couldn't see in his mind.
"Things are done, that's all."

Often he had this way of talking, which baffled me.

"Each casket you do is different, though," I said. "There must
be some technique. . . ."

"Technique?" Reb laughed. "You wanna know what I do? I
don't do nothin', Freshmeat, leastways, nothing you'd understand.
Before I even open my toolbox I go off by myself into them woods
yonder for a week. I try to forget about every casket I've made.
After a day I can't remember none of 'em. After two days, I forget
whatever instructions the family of the dead person give me, and
whether they gonna like it or not. After five days, I forget the fact
that I makes coffins. Seven days go by, and I forget all about myself, and that's when I start looking round for a tree that wants to
be a coffin."

"Is it," I asked, "for someone in town?"

"You *know* who it's for, Freshmeat."

His hacksaw cut harshly against woodgrain, and he swore. "My
boy Patrick was down heah this mawnin'. He ain't been right since
you got heah." Dusting his hands, he came slowly to his feet. "This
heah box is for you. Or Flo Hatfield."

Reb had said nothing before about Patrick being his son.
Knowing Flo's butler, it was, I supposed, the sort of thing you tried
to keep quiet. "But," I said, "I haven't *done* anything! And if he
does anything to Flo. . . ."

"You still don't git it, do you?" Reb's voice was rusty. He spoke
softly, picking his words as if placing his feet on the swaying logs
of a suspension bridge. "There can't be *two* of you at the top, boy.

47

Is that hard to see? Before my boy moved into the house there was a li'l nigguh go by the name of Moon who stayed as close to that woman as a pimple. Then she saw Patrick was growed-hup. You see what I'm sayin'? He's gonna close somebody's account—yo's," said Reb, "or that woman's."

"What," I asked, "happened to Moon?"

"You really want to know?"

I did not.

After fastening up my horse for me, Reb waved me inside. "You might as well stay for supper." His place was unpainted, a two-room shed with a lean-to kitchen. For light and air he pushed open one of the boards. Sacks of feed and mash were stacked in the corners beside a tub and washing stick, and carvings—when not shaping caskets he made figures of wood for Leviathan's children. "It ain't right," he said, "to eat 'less you feed at least one other person." From the peck of cornmeal, brackish messpork, and quart of molasses Flo rationed, Reb prepared a meal—sucamagrowl and sowbelly—which he placed in front of me. "She's dead," he said, without warning. "That's what you came down heah to ask, ain't it?"

I'd come to ask Reb how best to approach Flo Hatfield about my wages, but I did feel—and felt still—at Flo's center something unhealthy, like hysteria.

"Flo Hatfield been dead, oh, for goin' on fifteen years now, Freshmeat." Reb gave his lopsided smile. "I was buildin' caskets before you was born, so can't nobody tell me I doan know a dead person when I sees one. She had heart failure. She *died* in her sleep. We worked on her—her husband Earl and me—and when she woke up she never knowed she'd been dead. But you kin tell. You kin feel it. That's why you heah."

He ate in a way I thought quite telling for his age—chewing, like a cow, on one side of his face, feeding himself with black fingers gnarled like gingerroots. Reb shucked off his boots, brought out whiskey, then talked as he struggled to capture a likeness of me with a knife and a piece of balsa wood. The Coffinmaker was, not Wazimba, as I first thought, but from the ancient clan-state of the Allmuseri, concealed for centuries in the bush between Cape Lopez and the Congo River. "I was from a good line of people." He thumped his chest, "Me!" I tumbled down his voice into a clearing of circular houses built of clay, date groves dotting the countryside, and markets of watoto and viazi. The history of the Allmuseri, I learned, was intimately bound to the life of Reb's great-grand-father, Rakhal, a powerful *osuo,* who was cheated out of half his land by Akbar, the village king who late in life became a Moslem and hated Rakhal because he held fast to the old religion. Seeking revenge, Rakhal told the king that within a week he would bring a rain that would produce madness. Naturally, Akbar collected and hived away all the jugs of fresh water he could find. When the storm of insanity came upon the Allmuseri, everyone went mad, including Rakhal, who, standing below the king's window, laughing in the doorway, drank the waters of madness, too. But the king was untouched. He had saved himself from the shaman's curse, though he could not understand why Rakhal chose madness with the oth-ers. Soon Akbar knew. His subjects, in their lunacy, were all the same—they took the fantastic world of their madness to be real, understood each other, and he, their king, could not speak a word to them that made sense. For weeks he wandered among them, lugging his jug of fresh water, shouting, "I'm *sane,* you're *not,*" and everyone laughed, especially Rakhal, and pointed significantly at their temples as he passed, for the Real, if it was anything at all to the Allmuseri, was a matter of consent, a shared hallucination. So it was, said Reb, that King Akbar finally threw aside his stash of fresh water, drank the waters of insanity, and Rakhal's revenge was complete. All was as it had been before, except that Akbar couldn't have told you, at gunpoint, what a Moslem was.

The Coffinmaker, being Rakhal's great-grandson, was selected to follow him as the master of Yaka powders and Yohimby roots, rituals for rainmaking, rhymes for killing rats, and charms from the Ndembos tribe and Ekpe cults of the Cameroons. By dumb-show, he learned from Rakhal biting satires to blight an enemy's crops and, more importantly, how to send his *kra* forth to dwell in oxen in the cattle kraals. It took up ten thousand hosts, this I, slipped into men, women, giraffes, gibbering monkeys, perished, pilgrimaged in the animal and spirit worlds, dwelled peacefully in baobab trees. He learned intimately the life of these objects and others, died their unrecorded deaths, and ever returned to himself richer, ready to assume a sorcerer's role. Which did not come to pass. The hours passed quickly. Despite my duties the next day, I drank and listened. The Coffinmaker went on, softer now. Reb spoke of the slave clippers. Of the voyage of a hundred days into history. Washing with buckets of cold salt water. Squatting to sing still vivid Allmuseri melodies. Then he was called Agamemnon by the ship's captain, he thumped tom-toms on the deck of *The Fortunata*. On the forecastle sailors drank and danced a double-shuffle to his music, because now he was not rainmaker and magician but the shaper of gentle songs. He conjured—as if his speech could enshrine these things for me—*The Fortunata* brooking wall-high waves that spun it like a casket and shattered its hull, of Saint Elmo's fire shimmering like a silvery nimbus on the sails, and the ship anchoring under cover of darkness at a hidden cove in Cuba. Seasoning camps he recalled, and then his third name—Obadiah, yet still his *kra* remained the same, unspoiled, despite three masters in as many states before he was purchased by Earl Hatfield.

"I know," he said, "who's dead and who *will* be." Now it was midnight. He had not finished his carving of me, had, I realized, hardly cut a niche in the surface of the uncarved block.

"It's not like you said." I walked to the door, looking west, toward Flo's house. "I don't *want* to replace Patrick."

"You tell that to my boy. If you don't find him, he'll find you."

I rode back at half-speed, the horse bounding forward at the touch of my heels. I had seen at Cripplegate none of this ugly struggle for supremacy, since I was, as I say, the privileged ward of Master Polkinghorne. I had not seen, except in George's fear of padderolls and women, this warped and twisted profile of the black (male) spirit, where every other bondsman—everything not one-self—was perceived as an enemy. A threat. There were rumors of a coming war between the states. Sir, we were *already* in the midst of Civil War. Blacks and whites. Blacks and blacks. Women and men—I was in the thick of diversity, awash in the world's rich density. But things were becoming too dense. Everything seemed to create its own cancellation. I wanted this movement to go no further if, as the Coffinmaker said, someone would wind up on a cooling board.

From the stables I ran to the house, pressed my thumb on the latch to the back door, and pushed inside. You could tell by the way Patrick had swept, mopped the floors, and fixed the front rooms—the paintings in Flo's boudoir framed and lined up precisely on the walls, her brushes cleaned, still smelling of turpentine, the lines in the paintings angling the eyes peacefully to the Y where corner and ceiling met, from the high ceiling to the chandelier, like logical implication in Spinoza's *Ethics*—that Reb's son had labored hard that day to outdistance me. He had even done my chores. In the house I heard no sound. Flo had not returned. Or had she? And where was Patrick? Dizziness crawled up from my stomach. I went upstairs to her bedroom, but felt even weaker, for the long hallway to Flo's chamber swam with a smell so strong, so thick, my eyes began to water. It was at first a primal stench, raw and sharp; it hung in the air, like smoke or steam. Her door moved back on its hinges. My voice jumped, "Flo? This is Andrew." Her door banged against the wall. To this day I cannot tell you how many steps I took when I entered, for time played tricks on my mind—I remember seeing the slanting floor, a laky fluid, smudgelike shadows, her stained throw rugs soaking in blood, her bedsheets, then her mattress where Patrick lay naked with his long legs twisted in the red blankets, both dark hands frozen on the shaft of the butcher knife buried deep in his belly.

Trouble, I thought. *This is real trouble.*

And no accident. Flo's butler had pulled the knife, horizontally, in a crosscut from rib to rib. It was exactly my father's method for disemboweling a deer.

To keep from trembling, or fainting—my head was light—I squeezed my hands, then drug deeply for air; I sat down on the bedside. It was now twelve forty-five. Outside Flo's window a tree branch banged on glass. The sound of a carriage, far away, drew closer. There was only the dull certainty, like an ache, that I had done this—I *had* killed Patrick, in a sense, by my presence, and now, as the carriage stopped outside, and Flo's footman fumbled with her packages downstairs, I knew I would have to pay. All hands at Leviathan would agree that I should be hanged. I looked at him. His face even in rest, even in death was condemned to express desire. Standing up, slowly, I went down the long staircase, through the kitchen, and onto a back porch that bellied out, low, into the yard. Yellow moonlight pooled, as in a bowl, between the old gray walls of her garden. A fresh breeze herded leaves toward the stairs. Gripping the railing, weaving from the shock of cool air, I gazed up, up. My vision was porous. And was I through? Had the sick, dull feeling passed? As Ezekiel's student I had ever believed it was man's destiny to achieve freedom from the polarities, to find the Ground, but years after Patrick's death, after I lost Leviathan and Flo Hatfield, this deadening feeling that our particularities limited us, closed us in—created a ceiling low enough to break your neck—remained. Although nearly anything you said about slavery could be denied in the same breath, this much struck me as true: the wretchedness of being colonized was not that slavery created feelings of guilt and indebtedness, though I did feel guilt and debt; nor that it created a long, lurid dream of multiplicity and separateness, which it did indeed create, but the fact that men had epidermalized Being. The Negro—one Negro at Leviathan—was needed as a meaning. So it was; so it was. A mist dispelled. I pressed one hand to my forehead. In my will, my body, I slept. As for Flo. . . .

I had not yet confronted Flo Hatfield. The back door opened with a burst. Before I could turn, I felt small hands slide under my shirt, fingers spreading, palms down, on my chest. Warm breath rushed on the back of my neck. After several moments:

"Andrew?"

"Yes, ma'am?" I turned, sitting on the railing, my back to the yard, balanced like a crow on a clothesline. She looked up; I looked down. "There's something I must tell you."

"Not now."

"It's about Patrick."

"I'm not interested in Patrick."

In the moonlight, with her eyes wet, and brilliant, she was beautiful. And then, in spite of my terror, I touched her face with my fingertips, lightly, and Flo Hatfield held my hand there.

"I want you to kiss me now."

She said again, because I could not respond, "Will you do that?" Flo walked her fingers along my chest, and in a voice soft-breathing, gently singsong, she whispered, "Remember what I told you about Venice? And my education? I'm going to teach you,

Andrew. You have more promise than most men. But everything I do to please you, you must do to please me." On the railing she crushed out her cigarette, then screwed up her eyes. "I haven't embarrassed you, have I? Your ears are red." Then Flo ran her tongue right down to the roots of my throat, moving her head as my fingers climbed her hair, and her mouth spilled water into mine. It was a longish kiss, and when I opened my eyes, I saw through the haze caused by the violence of my desire, saw on a lozenge of grass, between a sundial and an old hawthorne, a figure sewn from darkness, standing a bowshot away, looking like something transplanted from a Russian novel to her yard.

"Just as I thought." Flo pulled away. "You taste milky."

"Did you see him?"

"Did I see who, dear?"

He slipped away like a dream. My pulse was stampeding. My mind: a nest of worms. "You *didn't* see him?"

"It's your imagination, Andrew." The wind lifted her hair. Flo curled her arms round my waist. "There's no one here but us."

She lay her chin on my chest, looking up, and I wondered if, really, there were two of us here, or—for each of us—only one. I asked her, "What do you feel when you touch me?"

"Me." Now her lips were on my fingertips. "I feel my own pulse. My own sensations." She laughed. "I have a pulse everywhere."

"That's all you feel?"

"Yes."

IV

IN THE SERVICE OF THE SENSES (2)

On August 4, 1858, I became Flo Hatfield's lover. That next morning her butler Patrick was buried.

He was, of course, not in the house when my new services at Leviathan began (I will speak of them shortly), because the Coffinmaker came for his son the night of the suicide, saying not a word to me when he tramped upstairs, climbing to the top floor with his hands on his thighs, and nothing to Flo Hatfield, which I thought unfair, for the discovery of Patrick's death nearly paralyzed her. When I told Flo she slapped me. Twice. "I can't handle this, Andrew." Before my eyes she became an old, old woman. Her back wishboned suddenly, tipping her head forward. I helped her inside, her hand light as a child's on my arm. When she saw Reb drag his son outside, the last ember of life in Flo Hatfield winked out; she dropped in a heap to the floor.

For two nights Flo slept in my room, though I had the uncanny feeling that her butler had settled, even there, like an oil stain. He was, if you will, worked into the texture of the house, he stained the things he'd touched like sweat, his fingertips, thoughts, and footprints clung to each object like an odor and left me with the feeling that, though dead, he had soaked, as I sat watching over Flo as she slept, into everything. She looked small and broken on the bed, aging fast-forward like a fairy-tale witch in the final scene. She was now eighty-three. That night of Patrick's death I wrote to Master Polkinghorne, a desperate perambulation that explained all I had experienced since my arrival. The following day Leviathan's veterinarian came by to visit and to ask Flo questions, which I answered—running interference, so she could rest. Flo did not

54

rest. She had nightsweats. Spun dreams so terrible she sat up straight, like a starched collar, and insisted that I keep the lamp burning and sleep with her.

Next morning when I awoke I heard voices moving toward Leviathan's cemetery. My mistress rolled over, her face webbed with wrinkles, mumbling beneath the quilt—she always slept with the covers over her face to keep out the sunlight. "Andrew," she licked her dry lips, "why did you let those things in here?"

"There's no one here." I was up, wedging my knuckles in my eyesockets, looking for the boothooks to pull on my Bluchers. Her dreamwork after Patrick's death often spilled over into morning, nightmares resurfacing in the first thing she said. I said, "Go back to sleep."

"They didn't push me off the roof?"

"You were dreaming."

As she slipped back to sleep, I gently pushed the door shut, took the stairs two at a time, then stepped into a morning too bright for a burial.

The whole day was in bad taste. The air, I thought, had no business being so crisp, the sky so berylline, and Nature so indifferent to Patrick's death when the voice of my education sang the earth as man's home, Being as a vast feminine body, if poetic tradition was trustworthy. (Metaphors are fair.) These rolling hills, these timeless trees and vegetation we genderized—even as we racialized Being, giving them feminine attributes, without asking whether Being, like Anna Polkinghorne and my stepmother, bore an ancient grudge against men. Of course, William Sidney Mount painted her; Emerson sang her; Thoreau fled to her; Paine mystified her. But these were *men*. That morning I thought this vision contained the menacing idea that men, not Man in the abstract, but *men* were unessential, and in the deepest violation of everything we valued in Woman. What was said of Woman was no less true of World. She did not need us for satisfaction, or even reproduction— there were, after all, parthenogenones, all of which cast men as the comical exception in Nature, the luxury, the freak who fell back on thought in the absence of feeling, created history because he could not live Being's timeless cycles. On my way to the hills, I entertained, nervously, pulling at my fingers, the possibility that the sexual war was a small skirmish—a proxy war, with women as the shock troops for a power that waited, mocking the thoroughly male anxiety for progress, ready to (s)mother the fragile male need to build temples to the moon; ready, as in Patrick's case, to remind us, without hope of redemption, that though men were masters— even black men, in the sexual wars—we could not win.

Clearly, I was in foul spirits.

Through white gum trees into woods west of the quarters, the pallbearers traipsed, trailed by mourners carrying their wreaths of white flowers, Patrick's pine box swinging so lightly it seemed filled with straw. They walked on through thick weeds and rough grass that crackled underfoot, alongside humpbacked cairns to the oldest part of the boneyard. Whitherward, I came through the trees, breaking cobwebs as I went, with branches whipping my face, in time to see them lower the bier onto the soft lip of the grave.

Here, the light was poor, but numinous. In a few places cold sunlight shafting through leaves overhead broke into shifting patterns at their feet. Presently, Reb's bald head and sunblistered neck separated from the crowd, the dark fingers of men and women, like fire-licked kindling, dropping away from his shoulders as the Coffinmaker shuffled closer. His voice was faint. A rustle of leaves. Then Reb lifted his head and began to croon in a tongue incomprehensible to me. Another mourner began to sing. Then another. The sound swelled, expanded, ate space, filled the woods like a splash of wind, blended with the air, turned and touched off, one by one, the different voices of the others, then Reb sang louder— or, better, bellowed like a steer. Abruptly, they stopped. My own face was hot and thick, the tears flew back into my nose when I sniffled and burned my throat. It was then, as Reb drove home the first nail to seal his son's casket, as I felt the sound of metal ring on metal in the deepest coils of my ears, that a voice behind me, toadlike, said:

"At least he was spared the mines, eh, Andrew?"

By my guess, I jumped three feet. My heart pounded, for an instant, like the hoofbeats of a horse; I bit down so hard on my tongue that it bled for hours thereafter. The veterinarian, Hiram Groll, had peradventure come secretly, like me, to watch Patrick's funeral from afar. A fat, pursy little man in his late sixties—a failed physician with a rich Old Country burr, and quick, incomplete gestures, he wore, without change, a clawhammer coat, highheel boots with mule-ear straps, and a chimneypot hat. He had two chins. A cyst on the tip of his nose. People said that before arriving at Leviathan, Dr. Groll had worked as an abortionist in Louisiana. As to that, I have no proof, but the Vet had funny ways (like looking at things sideways, as birds do) that made everyone uneasy. He stuck his nose right inside your clothes (almost) when talking to you, like an Arab, as if how you smelled was partly what you were. Damned peculiar. He was not deformed, but gave the impression of deformity, though with a good bath, he might, I thought, resemble Benjamin Franklin (on a bad day). But the Vet never bathed; he had vile habits like wiping his nose with his whole arm, and finished your sentences for you. Worse, he sold bogus funeral policies to slow-witted slaves in Leviathan's quarters, giggled too much for a man of science, and smelled like Flo Hatfield's barn, where he treated her servants and slept.

"I see *so* much of this in my work." He gave a leaky sigh. "When Captain Walters brings bodies back from the Yellowdog Mine, it's me he wants to write a certificate for the cause of death." He sat down against the tree, his heels pulled back, and took off his hat. "Do you know what I tell Captain Walters, Andrew? Do you know what I write on these certificates?" Leaning forward, looking up, he drubbed his thick fingertips together, then giggled, "No life-assurance."

"I do not take your meaning. You mean to say, no life *insurance*?"

"I mean what I said." The Vet made a weak, wheedling smile, but a smile for that: no front teeth. "It's an idea I've been working on for some time, an improvement on the popular Burial Society. Not a year ago I sprang the idea on that boy, your predecessor in the house, Patrick, but he refused to think about his future. He thought he was secure, you see, until you arrived. . . ."

"Then you think I killed him?"

"Dear me, no," said the Vet. "It was the loss of life-assurance. Oh, I've seen it happen before! Some strapping, able-bodied young man strong as a bull decides there's no future for *him*, and keels over. There's no medical explanation, as far as I know, but I *do* know, or sometimes—when bodies pile up like cords of wood in the barn—I think I know the reason." He touched the ground beside me, smoothing down grass for me to sit. "I'm not losing you, am I?"

"A little," I said. "But go on."

"Well," he glanced below as each mourner dropped handfuls of dirt into Patrick's grave. "The cause of death for these black men was, strictly speaking, not physical at all, not a material failure in the usual sense, though their affliction is perhaps the oldest disease in the world. It cannot be empirically measured, or even perceived through instrumentation—we know it through its symptoms, yet despite its mystery, it is invariably the cause of death. I am speaking," he said, fanning himself with his hat, "of the belief in personal identity, the notion that *what* we are is somehow distinct from other things when this entity, this lie, this ancient stupidity has no foundation in scientific fact."

"But, sir!" I said, shocked and, I think, a little angry. "Civilization is *founded* on this belief! There must be absolute presuppositions, bedrock ideas—superstitions, if you like—or everything built upon these ideas collapses."

"Just so," nodded the Vet, though not in agreement. "For the sake of the argument, suppose individuality *is* a fact. What do you feel just now? Foxglove on the wind? The solidity of stone beneath us? The bark at our backs? Now, be frank," he said, spiraling in for the kill, "is it reasonable to say that, since these sensations appear, there must be a separate entity that perceives them? We do not *have* a sensation of solidity; we *are* the sensation, Andrew."

"Then you are calling identity a lie?"

"Vanity."

He gave his crooked smile again. With his fingers and thumb he turned my chin toward the grave. "If not a vanity, then how comes it, Andrew, that the remains of Flo's butler are but a handful of conflicting memories about the man?" Because I thought myself outdone and made no reply, Dr. Groll struggled to his feet—I had to help him stand—then put on his hat. He said, at length, "It's way too early in the morning, I suppose, for ontology. We will continue this conversation later, and perhaps I will tell you about Frederick Mesmer's work on Animal Magnetism."

Filled with these thoughts as the Vet wobbled east and the

others shoveled moist soil over Patrick's coffin, so filled that I could not untangle Groll's mysterious—maybe crackpot—theory, I half-ran, half-walked back to the house. When I walked into Flo Hatfield's kitchen, picking beggarticks off my pantsleg, she had breakfast steaming on the table.

"You must be starving by now." Flo's age had dropped from eighty to fifty. She was wearing a pair of my trousers under her dress. Definitely a bad sign. "I couldn't sleep so I thought I'd fix something."

Breakfast was a big production—grilled fowl, bricks of cheese, tea, eggs and ham. She'd spent the morning cooking, I suspected, to sidestep thinking of Patrick, which meant that if I didn't eat, that awful night would be hugely present again. "Do you want coffee, too?" Flo was talking because she was afraid. "Andrew?" The sight of food, however, and my encounter with the Vet had tired me. I pushed away my plate. Flo looked wounded. So I expected. She began to blubber into her handkerchief. When that was wet, she wept into her hand:

"You blame *me* for what he did, don't you?" She stamped her foot. She put two fingers in her mouth, caught herself, then swung the hand behind her back.

"They think *I* did this to Patrick, don't they?"

"They probably blame us both."

"It was Patrick who left *me*, Andrew!" She sat down in two movements at the table, speaking through hair swinging in her face. "If I could only stand you behind my eyes for one minute. People say a woman is *nothing* without a man! A kind of freak to be pitied! A failure—people tell you—in the grand social scheme of things! The bastards. Maybe you *do* know," sniffed Flo. "Years ago I thought colored men were closer to seeing through this than anybody. Now," said Flo, "I'm not so sure. You've suffered, but you've never been married to someone so stupid he felt threatened if you sat on top, had an opinion, or knew how to tell time. In six years of marriage I didn't come *once*. Did you know that?" Flo sniffed again and pulled at her hair. "I used to ask Earl to explain things in the newspaper to me. I wanted so badly for him to love me and feel intelligent and share things with me and *stay!* He'd foul up the bookkeeping, and the furniture, when he called himself 'fixing things,' and I *let* him, Andrew, because if I said as much as boo about it, or forgot to act helpless, Earl would say, 'Sometimes, Flo, you make me feel like a fool.' " She stroked one hand with the other, like an old spinster sitting before a fireplace. Above her upper lip: the slightest shadow of a moustache. "Even acting helpless doesn't make a difference. You still get old. You get fat. Or too thin. You have female trouble. Your hair falls out and your husband starts fucking everything under the age of twenty-five." Her face fell loose. With a wrench, she looked up. "I *used* to be beautiful. . . ."

I touched her hand. "You still are."

She was a little petted by this. Her face stretched into a smile. "You really think so?"

I gave her a nod.

"Then why am I always *alone?*"

"Begging your pardon, Flo, but maybe you ask for too much."

She gave me a tight look.

"Is wanting tenderness too much?" Flo snatched her hand away. "Or intelligence in a man?" Thoughtful, she munched her lower lip. "Of course, I *also* want sexual satisfaction compliments gifts fidelity a great body cleverness sophistication yet boyish exuberance a full head of hair good teeth and the ability to know my moods." Flo gave me a side glance, cagey. "Is *that* too much?"

"Oh no—if you're going to dream," I offered, "dream big."

"You're the dream, Andrew." She kissed me on both eyes. "You can handle it."

Insofar as possible, I tried to satisfy Flo Hatfield's appetites. This was a job for twelve men. She relieved me of all my duties, except keeping her entertained. And here, let it be said, I devoted myself to becoming a good lover. As with any study, there were a thousand small things to master, skills foolish to a metaphysician, a man trained, as I'd been, in the severe discipline of the *cogito,* but the greatest of these skills was listening. Note well, a lover *listens.* Patiently, I nodded as Flo spoke about her small army of former lovers, her previous acts of sexual terrorism, which she regretted because, "Sometimes," confessed my mistress, "I feel like a Public Utility." My vocabulary, which at Cripplegate had turned on the phrases *But* and *On the contrary* and *Do you mean to say . . .?* was scaled down at Leviathan to *Of course* and *Quite so* and *Any fool can see that.* Philosophers may see this as facile, and that is their privilege, but I merely sought, from my station, to serve.

Sometimes this meant riding into Abbeville with Flo, where we shopped, fingers intertwined, and she made no effort to disguise her affection for me, sometimes it meant playing the most childish games when she felt silly and needed her silliness reaffirmed, at other times she raged and pulled down the books in her boudoir, took a knife to the curtains and irons to the furniture, and broke dishes—on these days she wanted not a playmate, or a lover, but a father—and still other times Flo felt her age—she often feared she had cancer (it was, in fact, indigestion, according to the Vet)—but I played toothless old hubby, both of us sitting beneath quilts on flatbottomed roundabouts, reading the *National Intelligencer* with magnifying glasses, fingering our gums for loose teeth, a hand behind our ear as we asked, "Eh?" The lover of Flo Hatfield's fantasy was polymorphous: husband, ravager, teacher, Galahad, eunuch, swashbuckler, student, priest, and, above all else, *always there.*

It would have been easier to pick cotton.

It made me feel, if I may speak freely, that the Vet had everything backwards. No Self, he said. But insofar as I satisfied Flo Hatfield—and for a year I *did* keep her satisfied—I was, or felt myself to be, several selves, like the Coffinmaker's polyhedral *kra,* which suffered all possible forms. Absorbed sin in all its subtle variations. And sojourned still. "That was sorcery," was what Reb said when I told him about this queer business.

"You don't understand women," was what he said when Flo napped and I returned to his shed. "And you sho don't understand a woman like Flo Hatfield." I feared that Reb blamed me for Patrick's death. He did not. He seemed, in a way, to have known it was coming, was now unyoked from his son, and often said, "I put his casket in the ground a month ago. You the one still carryin' it around, Freshmeat." Something else he often said was this:

"You act like you ain't never been chased by a woman before."

"It shows that much?" I asked.

The Coffinmaker laughed.

"You know, I once worked for a man named Fitzhugh in West Virginia." Scowling down at powder on my face, he pulled the pipe of animal bone from his mouth, wet the tip of his shirt, and, like my stepmother, scrubbed my cheek. "I knew that man better'n he knew hisself. *Had* to. He had the whip. If I couldn't guess what was in his heart before he thought of it, I was hup river without a paddle."

"I don't understand. What's that got to do with Flo Hatfield?" Reb sighed.

"She ain't free," he said. "Some women learn, like slaves, to study men. They learn to think like men. They knows what men want, how they look at women when they think nobody's watchin', they know what men are afraid of, what they *dream* about—just like I knew Fitzhugh. They have to keep one step ahead. If you got no power," said Reb, "you have to think like people who *do* so you kin make y'self over into what they want. She's a slave like you'n me, Freshmeat." Reb's eyebrows speared in toward his nose. "And you best be 'fraid of someone who's 'fraid of you."

"Stop." I organized myself to leave. "All this talk about sex and slavery. . . . It's scaring me. Besides, I'll be going home soon. I'll have my papers. She hasn't paid me yet, but when she does. . . ."

Reb looked around in wonder.

"Boy, can't *no*body be as dumb as you let on! Flo Hatfield ain't studyin' about payin' you! And she ain't gonna let you go." He showered me with laughter. "Without you, she don't know who she *is*. Without her," he showed his teeth in a terrible grin, "you ain't nothin' without somethin'—or somebody—to serve, Freshmeat."

That was, obviously, a cheap shot, but I figured I deserved it. While Flo and I luxuriated in the Big House, the sad pattern of slave life at Leviathan remained unchanged. Ginning. Sorting and moting cotton in January. Winter passed with her bondsmen making brooms, mats, and horse collars. There was the bedding of cotton and ridging of soil in March. In April there was splitting the ridges with plows. Planting seeds. Mending fences. May through August evaporated in endless hoeing. Come September: more picking. Through all this I devoted my year, you'd have to say, to mint tea and clever conversation.

Not that I made love to my mistress the week of Patrick's

OXHERDING TALE

burial, but I did pork Flo Hatfield (her phrase, not mine) two weeks later. This is a delicate matter; I will try to describe that night with discretion. Flo Hatfield belonged, I should say (since these things interest modern historians who report drearily on every affair, every tedious slip in a man's social life), to the class of women called Screamers. Unlike Minty—a girl who was silent when lovemaking—unlike Minty, Flo, a Screamer, could not truly experience her feelings, appreciate her own pleasure, until she whooped, "Oh there!" or "Andrew, don't you dare do that!" which meant, of course, that this was precisely what I *should* do, and then, as our first night of lovemaking dissolved into daybreak—all the servants kept awake by her screams—she clamped shut her eyes in what was more narcosis than sleep.

I was in pretty bad shape myself.

The bedsheets (and Flo) were slick with my sweat. By afternoon I was able to crawl a little, then stand; stand a while, then walk. Have I said that Flo Hatfield needed chemicals to feel? Correction: Opium, which the Vet brought from Abbeville, *lowered* the senses, slowed them down and, in doing so, expanded the skin's sensitivity to the point where the body's edge vanished and blended into other bodies, objects. For men, opium speeded up the heart and slowed sexual response; for women it intensified sex, but made the heart serene. Our portion was four pipes of chandoo in the morning (before breakfast), two in the afternoon (with tea), and three at night (before bed), the effect of each pipe on Flo immediate, on me—well, it is with opium as with Scotch: you build up slowly, rubbing it on your gums, or drinking it, say, after soaking the paper in whiskey, suffering nausea for weeks before the nerves regulated. Slowly, I learned. Gradually, pain gave way to something like clairvoyance—I could see, like Ezekiel who lived on laudanum and perpetually smelled like licorice, the interior of objects. During the day my attention was on the noises that came from outside—the rooms in Flo Hatfield's great house felt hyalescent, but with the rising of night, I began to notice the rooms themselves, the density of the walls, the strange finality of her furniture, and had the feeling there was nothing outside, that only her tiny boudoir, shadow-heavy, close and soundless, was real. By and by, I found a place where there was neither cold nor heat, thought nor memory, time

63

nor motion, house nor field. All this, I remind you, was but prep-
aration—Sensuality 101, Section A—for my real work, as a volup-
tuarian, at Leviathan.

Strange to say, I learned from Flo Hatfield that lovemaking
was magic; was, if properly understood, a Way. There were, I had
heard, many Ways, but if you wished to experience pleasure, you
must—she taught me—give pleasure, and to do this unfailingly the
lover must get the feel of sacrifice and the ideal of service into his
head, which sounded odd when she first said it, sitting naked on
her sofa in the boudoir, her tangled laphair soaking, one hand on
her smooth-muscled belly, for I'd always regarded sexuality as
nothing if not self-gratifying, yet (said Flo) to learn her rhythms
and responses—to play her well, like a finely tuned instrument, I,
Andrew Hawkins, had to transform myself. I speak, sir, of what I
know. Lovemaking at Leviathan, after Flo Hatfield closed her shutters, locked her doors, and spread herself in an *X* on the sofa, was
exactly the inverse of my training—all thought and cognition—at
Cripplegate. She brought me pleasure in places I didn't even know
I had places. Older women, I decided in this daze of feeling, *knew*
things.

Caresses that stripped the skin of movement. Silenced it. She
guided my hands. My hips. Flo Hatfield went through the *Kama
Sutra* page by page, improving, in her own small way, on each
position. She was, as she said, a genius at love. The body (for Flo)
was the touchable part of the spirit; the spirit the untouchable part
of the body. Could thirst and hunger fit into American Transcendentalism? Could desire and the body be accepted, contrary to the
texts I'd studied, as Ways to celebrate man's incarnation?—we used
them so those long fall evenings in Abbeville. For those interested
in ways to improve their sexual performance, I suggest the following:

1. Extinguish the ego.
2. Eat well.
3. Exercise regularly.

To tell in short what happened, we made love like monkeys all
that winter, then spring. In the liquor of an evening late in April,
1859, Flo Hatfield rolled a cigarette and said:

"La, Andrew, you are the best servant I have *ever* had." Lamp-

OXHERDING TALE

light clung to her lashes above eyes bright, incendiary. She made circles around my mouth with her tongue. "You are the most willing to learn, the most promising."

"You are," I sighed, "too kind."

She stood up, picking up hair behind her head in two huge handfuls, and stretched.

"Would you like a sandwich?"

Grudgingly, I agreed. My stomach growled. The aftertaste on my tongue (of Flo) was briny. After five rounds of slow humping all evening I felt numb from the waist down, raw, and needed to replenish my tissues. What talent I'd had for going without food or, for that matter, riding a thought longer than required for after-dinner conversation, was gone. My memory failed me frequently. My palms stayed wet, even when I slept. At least, I told myself, you can still control your heart, Hawkins, and read.

She brought me, as it turned out, a letter addressed to me on a plate, under my sandwich. It was from Hodges.

It was from Anna Polkinghorne.

As I tore open the letter, Flo, lying down beside me, her knees drawn up, oozing her own fluids and mine, began to dry herself on the bedsheet. She ate off my plate. "That was downstairs on the dining room table, lover. What does Jonathan say?"

"It's from his wife." My hands trembled so I could hardly read the letter for my shaking.

Flo sat up. "What does she say?"

"She's sold half the slaves at Cripplegate to speculators."

Flo put down the sandwich. "Why?"

My hand dropped over the bedside; I could not lift my head. "She doesn't say. She tells me to stay here with you."

Flo laid her head sideways on one hand. "Is that so bad?"

The letter was two weeks old. What had gone wrong? What about Minty? And my parents—were they among those sold? Her letter held no clue, no hint of their progress. They were property. Not people. At that instant something slammed dead center against my chest, from the inside; I sat bolt upright in bed.

"What did I do?" Flo made a face. "Andrew, you're acting introspective again. You're no fun when you act introspective."

I told her I was stepping outside to relieve myself, but the fact

65

was that, as soon as I dropped the letter and lay back, my heart clenched like a fist; when I focused consciously on the pain, the constrictions redoubled. If you have ever seen a man's heart fail—his lips pulled back, belching whoops of pain and astonishment, spit flying everywhere, his blind fingers at his throat—you will understand my terror. Straightaway, I decided to see the Vet. I scuffed from the house to the stabling shed, one hand over my heart, fearing that if I brooded about this mystery at home, walked too fast, felt joy or anger too suddenly, belched or hiccoughed more than twice, I would suffer coronary arrest. From Leviathan's stabling shed into a smear of odors—hay and horse manure—coming from Flo Hatfield's barn. Outside, I saw a great war-horse with padded hooves. The pain forked up again: a flurry of birds (crows) in my chest.

The Vet turned round as I entered. There was someone seated beside him in the darkness. "Oh my," said Groll. "Oh my." Recovering, he coughed to clear his throat. "Andrew," he said, "this is Horace Bannon."

It was my first glimpse of the Soulcatcher. To some it may sound peculiar that—but wait; this had best commence a new chapter.

V

A NEW CHAPTER

To some it may sound peculiar that I consulted the Vet for a serious medical problem. In the South before Surrender, men of color were treated, if treated at all, by the local veterinarian. He set slipped discs, served as a dentist, and, when I blundered into Dr. Groll's workshop in the barn, was dressing one of Leviathan's newly dead behind the strawcutter—a runaway hauled back by Horace Bannon—for burial. The boy's hands and feet were tied. Hoping to identify him, I looked into his face. His face? He might have been anyone, given the decay, blisters, the green stains on his groin, gas ballooning his genitalia in a ghastly parody of eros. The Vet saw me wobble. He took my arm.

"He escaped three days ago from the mine," Groll said. "He was returned this evening by. . . ." The Vet looked at the Soulcatcher, then dropped his eyes. "We should step outside."

"Ah was just gettin' mah hat," said Bannon.

The Soulcatcher's voice, I swear, was black. The kind of deep-fried Mississippi Delta twang that magically turned *floor* into *flow*. *Door* into *doe*. Yet, this was the same man, now framed by lofts of hay and straw in Flo's barn, cribs and bins for grain, that I'd seen months earlier in her yard—a manhunter, a great, slack-shouldered monster with a gray Cathedral beard, a racial mongrel, like most Americans, but the genetic mix in the Soulcatcher was graphic: a collage of features that forced me, as he labored toward the door, looking down at me steadily, the corners of his mouth curled up, to stare. Here the deltoid nose of a Wazimba, here a "snotcup" (so my stepmother called them) cut deeply above his lips, which were the sheerest line, a slash; here curly hair coarsely textured like my

67

father's; here heavily lidded eyes, one teal blue, one green beneath a low brow that bulged with veins. Two rifles were strapped on his saddle. And, more startling, his clothes were a cross between house— Rob Roy jeans, a redingote, cartridge belts, and Ivanhoe cap—and fields. I could not shake the feeling that Bannon was in masquerade, a slave who, for reasons too fantastic to guess, hunted slaves.

"You favor somebody," said Bannon. "Would yo father be an oxherd in Hodges? A George Hawkins?"

"Nossir." I stepped back. "My mother is Anna Polkinghorne."

He made a bow. All mockery. "Mah mistake, suh. Ah saw that resemblance, too—in the eyes—but Ah have heard in mah travels that the Polkinghorne's were childless. Well, not quite childless. Ah heard," he paused with one foot in the stirrup, "that Anna Polkinghorne had a son by this scalawag George Hawkins during a night of misunderstandin's. These things interest me, you see, because one drop of black blood makes a Negro, and Negroes are mah trade."

"You have heard from Hodges?"

"A slave uprisin'," he said. "It was squelched the same day. You know how that is: a bondsman loses his temper—the oxherd in this case. He starts swingin'. Others pitch in. They burn their sheds. March on the House. A few are shot. Most sold." Bannon turned his head to Groll. "You called him Andrew, didn't you?"

The Vet shrugged. "Did I?"

"The oxherd Ah mentioned had a boy named Andrew."

"Stillbirth," I said.

Bannon pursed his lips. "Ah see. So you are the legitimate Polkinghorne heir? What might yo name be, son?"

"It might be James."

"Well put," the Soulcatcher slapped his knee—he was definitely enjoying himself. "And it might *not* be James, eh? You's clever, 'James,'" he said. "You'll go far in this world." His horse moved forward; on his saddle, Bannon turned halfway round to face me. His smile flashed again. "But let's hope you'll not go too far."

Having said his say, he left.

"That man makes me nervous," said the Vet. He shook his head. "You can't trust anyone who makes his living repossessing stolen—or runaway—property."

"What about men who sell bogus burial policies?"

The Vet frowned.

"He was," I asked, "one of Flo Hatfield's lovers, wasn't he?"

"Horace Bannon?"

"That boy in the *barn!*" I said. "Do you know his name?"

"He's no one now, Andrew." The Vet watched Bannon's horse canter away, then maneuvered: "On the market, he's worth about ninety-five cents in chemicals—five pounds of minerals, one pound of carbohydrates, one-quarter ounce of vitamins, a few pounds of protein. . . ."

"You haven't answered my question."

The Vet sighed, "His name is—was Moon."

So here was the boy who was replaced by Flo's butler Patrick: pulped, reduced—in Nature's grim perversion of democracy—to liquifying tissue, his head smashed like a melon, chest and belly splintered from gas building like boiler steam in his abdomen, his flesh the color of cooked veal—Patrick would be pleased. I was not pleased. Was this horror the coda of pleasure? There was, it seemed to me, something especially hideous in this end to enlightened hedonism, for the johnson (as we say—pronounced *yawn-sun*) of the lover expanded to Rabelaisian proportions, the testicles bloated bigger than coconuts, as if Death mocked a man's single distinguishing feature by enlarging the genitals, exploded and powdered them green with breadmold: a nest for maggots.

"Andrew?" asked the Vet, softly.

I snapped back, sick, as if from a dream.

"Yessir?"

"Come outside." He covered the body with tarpaulin. "You didn't come here tonight for a chemistry lesson, did you?"

To his credit, the Vet examined me and explained that since my arrival at Leviathan my heart had developed an extra sound: a sort of whisper, or moan on the diastolic downbeat, which meant it never exactly rested now. Would never rest again, he said, "Unless you stop being a Negro." Groll chuckled. "Internal medicine can't help you there." Politely, I laughed, but the last words of my father months before flashed through my mind: "You could pass, if you wanted to." As the Vet thumped my chest, listening, I wondered if life would indeed be easier if I abandoned what appeared to be a no-win struggle for happiness in the Black World. You needed little more proof than I'd received to believe that this world was, had always been, and might ever be a slaughterhouse—a style of being characterized by stasis, denial, humiliation, thinghood, and, as the philosophers said, "relative being." If you didn't believe this—couldn't *see* it—you had only to listen to Leviathan's slaves who, late at night, each swapped tales no man in his right mind would laugh at, but we did—Negro humor was nothing if not a defense against hysteria. Yes, I could turn my back on Cripplegate's bondsmen—circumstance had scattered them like seeds—but how could I leave my only friend on Flo Hatfield's estate: the Coffinmaker?

"There's *nothing* I can do to control my heart?"

"One thing maybe."

The Vet stepped back into the shadows, fumbling through papers near his bunk. "If you had life-assurance, your heart might return to normal." He handed me a sheet of paper. "Does Flo Hatfield pay you a wage—give you something now and then?"

"She owes me," I said, sourly, "a year in back wages."

"Well," said Groll, "if you are willing to pay, and engage in a scientific experiment, I might be able to provide you with a life-affirmative vision."

"What kind of experiment?"

"Mental Healing through Animal Magnetism. As a medical technique, it's new," he said, "still in the hands of fools and faith healers, but its principles are ancient. In Robert Fludd's *Philosophia Moysaica* and Maxwell's treatise *De Mecina Magnetica*, both propose that all creatures have their own heaven—or harmony—within them, which corresponds to the harmony of the universe. Fludd and Maxwell supposed sick persons have wandered, as it were, from the motions of the universe."

"How," I asked, "can a man stop wandering?"

"You need an unshakable faith—fiction or fact, it makes no difference, a life-assurance that will place everything in proportion, including evil." The Vet jabbed the air with one finger. "Especially evil. I've listed several on that paper."

I unfolded the page he'd given me. Depending upon your ability to pay, Leviathan's veterinarian offered a series of values that brought a man peace. These he ranked according to price.

They included: (1) The faith that someday you would be honored by your community for your contributions, $100. (2) That, if not honored, your children would one day regard you as a source of inspiration, $75.00. (3) If neither of the above, you would enjoy the benefits of a good marriage, a little property, and pride in your work, $50.00. (4) If none of these, then you would enjoy *all* the above, plus life-everlasting, in the afterworld, $25.00. (5) If *none* of the above, you would, at least, die mercifully in your sleep, $5.00.

"The last policy is, lately, our most popular," said Groll. "You have only to select a hope. Through the techniques of Friedrich Mesmer, it will seem apodictic."

"That's wicked!" I shouted. "They're all lies!"

The Vet nodded, sadly, in agreement. "What value isn't?"

I took Groll's proposed life-assurances with me and sat on Flo Hatfield's steps, though I still believed these assurances were evil. There had to be, as my tutor hoped, a value greater than the flimsy lies peddled by the Vet—so I reasoned—greater than the dead-end, wheel-spinning life of desire I shared with Flo Hatfield: a male fantasy, I realized, with both Flo and me victims enslaved to an experience—a part of the masculine ego—that neither of us truly wanted. What this new value was, I did not know. And, when she heard me, I had no time to brood on it, for Flo stepped outside.

"Andrew?" She sat down beside me, wearing her trollopee. "Where have you been? I needed you."

"Tell me about Moon," I said.

Flo played with my hair. "He doesn't concern you."

"We have to settle something," I said. "I've been here a year now. . . ."

"It's been a wonderful year. I think you're the one, Andrew."

"The one what?"

Playfully, she gave me a push back against the stairs. "The one I've waited for, silly." And then she said, quickly, as if saying this was admitting defeat:

"I love you."

For a moment I said nothing. That such a woman could love me seemed impossible. She was my superior in so many things, my teacher, the kind of woman men pulled knives and killed over. But Flo Hatfield was in bondage. I said, "We must settle my wages."

"Andrew, I never *pay* for it."

(A man would put it that way. She was the creature of men; she was me.)

"Ma'am," I shifted on the stairs, "I came here to earn enough to buy my freedom. That's all changed now. Everything has changed. I don't know what to do, but if you'll at least pay me in part what I have coming, then. . . ."

"We'll have no more vulgar talk about money," she said. "You're tired." She took both my hands, then led me into her boudoir. "And you don't look well, lover. Let me fix you something."

Except for a single candle, her boudoir was dark. Flo walked barefoot across the room, gliding like a spirit with feet spun from air, and opened a small, painted box on her wigstand. From this she carefully pinched a goodly measure of powder. With a writing quill she lined the powder into six rails, or columns, about five inches long, then handed me the hollow reed she also kept on the wigstand. "Here," she said, "this will relax you."

It was not in my power to refuse.

It did not seem in my power to do anything since I could not return to Hodges. My mistress waited. I breathed in my portion, sneezed (grabbing my heart), and, as I wiped white circles off my nose, Flo opened her cabinet and removed a decanter of wine, which she carried upstairs to her bedroom. There, she closed the door, ran a comb through her hair, closed her eyes, then lifted her arms, her wrists crossed above her head so I could undress her. She had early established this prelude to our lovemaking, this circling round (for me) the object of pleasure, and I must confess that I enjoyed it—she knew I would enjoy it—there being, paradoxically, something of the pursuit of truth in a good lay, an epistemological edge in exposing a woman stitch by stitch to the lamplight, as if knowledge had an affective tone (*Begriffsgefühl*), was somehow *delicious,* and the lover as sincere a seeker after wisdom as any physicist.

Well.

This practice my mistress taught me, but the confluence of opium and wine in my bloodstream, Anna's letter and Groll's cynicism, to say nothing of the dead boy and the Soulcatcher I'd seen made me edgy and impatient. Beside her, I said, "Even if you pay me only half my year's wages, I'll have enough to buy my freedom papers."

"You're *hurting* me, Andrew!" She said, "Be gentle."

I swallowed.

"I hate to talk wages at a time like this. . . ."

"Then *don't* talk wages!" Pushing my hands away, she exhaled heavily. "Andrew, you're spoiling everything. Just get it over with."

As I mounted her, I felt dizzy, a blur of disorientation, and to center myself I tried to reconstruct Minty's face from memory, only to find that I'd forgotten certain features—her skin, nose, and I could not remember her ears. How could I forget the ears of the first woman I'd ever loved? Vertigo washed over me. The chandoo played hob with my sense of touch. Then Flo began to rub against me in a raw, hard way. It was, I thought, like using me as a kind of scratching post. What this action said was: What good are you? You have failed to rouse me. Be still while I satisfy myself. And ever she did this the pain was quick, the insult deep, the self-hatred more complete, and I did not, as she worked toward detumescence, truly exist. Suddenly, I wanted to hurt her. My fist shot up without telling my brain what it had in mind—these things happen—then smashed five times, straight from the shoulder, into Flo Hatfield's nose, which flattened like soft clay—I watched all this in a daze, distant—and the next thing I knew I was standing across the room, wringing my hands.

My knees banged together.

"I didn't *mean* that!"

My mistress held both her hands to her nose. Blood spilled like liquid light through her fingers.

"Are you hurt?"

"Get me something to catch this, Andrew."

I took a step toward her; a step back. I fisted myself on the head. "Something came over me!"

"Will you get me a *cloth*, Andrew?"

I threw Flo her trollopee.

"It's been a *terrible* day!" I said. My hands flew, then froze. "You know I'd never do anything like that if I was in my right mind."

"I'm sure you wouldn't."

"You must hate me."

"I don't feel anything at all for you, Andrew Hawkins."

She was as calm, her voice as cold as when discussing the weather. Thinking this a good sign—better than rage—I came closer to examine the damage, and Flo gave me a glacial look and hissed, "Stay on that side of the room, Andrew. Are all your clothes in the next room?"

"I think so."

"Then," she said, "it might be best for you to gather them up and move to the quarters until you feel better."

"Oh, I feel fine *now*."

Flo Hatfield, pinching the bridge of her nose, left the room. Her leaving had the feel of a death sentence—it was indeed a foretaste of a death sentence. But believing her anger might blow over, I packed my things and moved in with the Coffinmaker.

"You did what?" asked Reb.

I told him again.

"You goin' to the gallows, Freshmeat." The Coffinmaker pulled up his blanket and rolled over, his crinkly hair mashed against his head from sleeping on his side. "And you a fool. I make it a practice never to talk to fools befo' breakfast." Helplessly, I waited beside my heavy portmanteau—it was crammed with gifts she'd given me—still unsteady from the chemicals in my system. I shook his shoulder.

"She loves me—it was a lover's quarrel," I told him. "These things straighten themselves out, don't they?"

"Where you been, boy?" Reb cackled. "On the moon? You didn't hit yo mistress. You hit yo master two seconds befo' she got her cookies. Think about that."

I didn't want to think about it.

He rolled over again, so huge his legs hung over his pallet. Waiting, I watched him curl up, then stretch like a bear in an effort to get comfortable again, trying this side, then that, and, finally, he sat up on one balustrade-thick arm and rubbed his face. Crabby, he fixed me through two bloodshot eyes.

"Just what the hell you want *me* to do?"

"Go to her house," I said. "Tell Flo I'm sorry."

"Be yo lawyer, huhn?"

"Reb," I said, "I'm in trouble."

"You *stay* in trouble, Freshmeat. That's yo nature. You think too damn much. You think too deep. You think yoself into corners. All them high-priced books and expensive ideas—they what gets you in trouble! Even if you'd never seen Flo Hatfield, even if you was white, you'd still be in trouble."

"You really think so?"

"I *know* so."

Grumbling, he swung two shovel-sized feet, without the slightest arch, to the floor, pulled on his shirt (he slept in his trousers), then stepped outside into the weeds, passed water, and made his way, moving so slowly you'd have thought he regulated each breath as he walked, to the Big House.

Note well, I did not truly understand the Coffinmaker, but I trusted and had my theory about him. In his shed, taking long pulls on a reed-covered jug from his table, I found that, unlike Flo's house, or even my former room, Reb's quarters left no residue of its lodger. He appeared busy—the hardest worker at Leviathan—but his shed and many carvings, the wood sculptures that ranged from finely wrought caskets to footstools in Flo Hatfield's boudoir, had the anonymity of Egyptian artifacts. He was not in the shed. Not in his work. Not truly in the thickness of the world-web, as I was—boomeranging from desire to desire—and, waiting, I wondered if Reb hungered for freedom as I did. What did he want? Seldom, if ever, did Reb take the initiative in producing anything. He waited, quiet as a cat. Something acted upon him, a pressure, a shove, a cosmic finger on the spine, and only then did he move. Now and anon, he reminded me of Ezekiel, whose sad fight for spirituality fizzled out in a romance that ruined Transcendentalism forever in South Carolina. Both men, I decided, were subversive, Ezekiel in the sabre-rattling style of Western activists, Reb in a much softer and more devastating Old World way that made Harper's Ferry look foolish. Torching a master's house, Mau-Mauing his property, was fine, for we hated being propertyless—it was exactly a correlate to the emptiness of the ego, and everyone feared *that*, especially Flo Hatfield. Again and again, and yet again, the New World said to blacks and women, "You are nothing." It had the best of arguments to back this up: nightriders. Predictably, we fought this massive assault on the ego, even *inverted* the values of whites (or men)—anything to avoid self-obliteration. And if you embraced this? Absorbed it? Said "Yes" to illness. "Yes" to suffering. "Yes" to liberation. "Yes" to misfortune. What did you become?

The Coffinmaker.

Slavery had made him a saint in 1839. Waiting, I remembered what Reb told me about the deaths of his wife and daughter.

Diseases at Leviathan often became plagues, for the Vet administered potions of castor oil and turpentine for most afflictions, and only those slaves with savings could afford treatment in town. That year Reb's wife Lucy died. His daughter Biddy, he said, showed signs of pellagra—blisters bursting with yellow-green fluid—and he ran fifteen miles to Abbeville. Thereat, Reb begged up and down the boardwalk for coins. He turned his pockets inside-out. He wept. He struck the eleventh man who passed him by, then dropped, as it happened, beside another bondsman, an experienced beggar named Jupiter. "You been doin' it all wrong," said Jupiter. He spit into the street. "I been watchin' you carryin' on about yo girl for half an hour now. Pullin' yo hair. Pesterin' folks 'cause you about to lose somethin'." Jupiter spit again. "Boy, you don't git *nothin'* 'til you *don't* want it." This was such unwanted advice that Reb moved across the street. He would receive no money—that was clear. His daughter would drop into West Hell with Lucy. His only strategy, the one option left, was surrender, accepting—said the Coffinmaker—the shock of nihilation. The knots of his heart were broken. In this poverty of spirit, this resignation, the Coffinmaker felt metal—Mexican coins—and shinplasters splatter onto his lap. These he collected in his straw hat, then carried to a doctor, who rode back to Leviathan, and pronounced the girl dead.

From that day on Reb took nothing on himself. So deep was the experience of sacrifice engraved in him—his forty or fifty years of adjustment to self-denial—that even in his eating he was wont to make sacrifice, saying, "Lawd, you *better* take this food!" So often had food, property, and loved ones been snatched away that now he treated whatever he had as someone else's property, with the care and attention that another's property deserved. Reward he did not expect. Nor pleasure. Desire was painful. Duty was everything—the casket promised tomorrow, a carving for the black-smith's daughter, the floorboards that needed fixing. This was his Way. It was, I thought, a Way of strength and spiritual heroism—doing what must be done, dead to hope—but like Flo Hatfield's path of the senses, it was not *my* Way.

It was now two hours since Reb left.

Trip-hammering again, my heart made the sort of mad, mouse-in-a-cage racing that preceded pulmonary mishap. ("A slight coronary accident," the Vet called it, a phrase that made it equivalent to knocking over your water glass at the dinner table.) What had delayed Reb? He had only to explain to our mistress that I was troubled by Anna's letter—it should have taken no more than a few minutes. I took another pull on the bottle. If she would not have me back, what then? Flight? The Underground Railroad was, I'd heard, a route to freedom. But I had no contacts for escape to Canada. Furthermore, I had seen the Soulcatcher; the man had weapons up the yin-yang, seemed able to sniff out slaves anywhere; had perhaps been a slave himself, even a champion of abolition, a lover of freedom, I speculated, who—like a revolutionary turned reactionary—so cherished the object of his passion that his feelings turned, with equal intensity, to hatred. Thinking of the Soulcatcher made me shiver. Reclining, on Reb's pallet, I busied my thoughts by inspecting his shelf of carvings overhead. Among these was the sculpture—the then uncarved block—he had started of me.

The replica was finished, but only the first side bore my likeness: a face of feathery lines, which felt—beneath my fingers—smooth-grained. Unstained. The second portrayed someone else, the knife marks deeper gouges in wood that gave the portraiture a splintered feel, its expression a worldly blend of ecstasy and pain, sickness and satiation. The third side was stranger still: a Master who had made his fortune long ago; aging, he would be on the Village Board, the Chamber of Commerce—a Whig in political matters, perhaps a church father. The fourth side was blank. The back, I supposed as I drifted off mercifully to sleep, was where one mounted this odd figurine.

Shortly after dawn the Coffinmaker stomped in. Swearing. Dragging his feet toward the pallet. He kicked me awake. Said: "C'mon." His face was pale with the strain of a man who has given too much and must give more. His lips shook. He said, "Decide what you gonna take with you. You won't be needin' all them clothes."

"Did you talk with Flo?" I stood up. My pulse soared. Slowly, I sat again. "Reb?"

"I talked with her."

He went through his boxes, pulling out old shoes repaired with wire, shirts and trousers, which he stuffed into a sack. His face was set now. Polished metal. "You ain't nothin'," he said, "but trouble."

"What did she say?"

"I went walkin'," he said, ignoring me. "Thinkin' 'bout how all my life I been in the wrong place at the wrong time. Washin' in a river when they caught me. Workin' late that evening you come up from Greenwood—I shoulda chased you off as soon as I seen you. If I'd hit you upside the head, things would be the same. And me . . ." he laughed, low in his throat, "I coulda passed my time in peace heah, Freshmeat."

"Reb," I asked, "what did Flo Hatfield say?"

The Coffinmaker folded blunt fingers, like strips of steel, on my left shoulder, and spoke in the slow, guttural voice I believed issued from his belly.

"She say it's our turn in the mines."

VI

THE YELLOW DOG MINE.
KARL MARX AT CRIPPLEGATE.
ALTHEA

North-northwest of Flo Hatfield's estate, the land was blackened by the sites of old shafts and heaps of slate, the air was fouled by carbonic gas and smoke from blasting. Red dust, like plague, settled filmy on the ribcages of workhorses burned in ditches by the road. From five miles off, riding back-to-back in a canvas-covered wagon drawn by four horses, we could see smoke mounting in columns against the sky. The rest of the mine's history we were told by Flo Hatfield's coachman, Sam Plunkett. Dozens of gangs, grimy with dust and from farms as far away as Greenwood, went regularly into the Yellowdog Mine. Trinitrotoluene, dualin, gunpowder, and mica followed on caravans. They poured in—shovelers and wheelers, borers and slave teams—to replace those who perished from consumption. Silicosis. From dust particles in their lungs. Or, above, from camp brawls that broke out over women. A misplaced bottle. An impolitic word. From murder, more often than not.

Josiah Dabner (said Plunkett) was in charge of blasting; Henry Shea handled cuts, embankments, and coal shipments; Captain Noah Walters, a fat, fretful man with a withered hand and dirt in his neckseams, was Chief Engineer. "You come this way just ten years earlier," said Plunkett, talking like a tour guide—afraid no doubt because we were five, the flotsam from Leviathan, the unruly, the lazy, the rejected lovers, and he, Plunkett, a whiskery old man with so little skin on his leathery face he had to shut his eyes to speak or chew, equipped with only an owlhead pistol—Plunkett wondered if he'd ever see his family again. His fears were unfounded. These men, I saw, were shattered—they had the unsee-

79

ing gazes I'd glimpsed on birds my father had shot, just before he finished them, and Reb, even he, had no fight left in him—"you wouldn'ta seen nothin'. Sprawlin' wilderness. Forests fulla deer. Rabbits. Skunks. Maybe a lynx or two." Plunkett forced a laugh. "Wild country so tough the hootowls all sang bass." No one thought this funny. Two miles west (said Plunkett, squirming) the Savannah roared with currents so swift, so treacherous that navigation across was impossible. Not even sturdy lumber rafts withstood its waves. When the mining company's surveying team commenced work two years before, they found no bottomland. No flat shores whatsoever between boiling springs and falls. Twisting through the dark valley between the plantation and the Mine was a path so steep and nookshotten that the surveying team took measurements and calculated levels by suspending themselves from the escarpments by ropes. It would not be an easy place to escape from—I was thinking already of flight. Work (said Plunkett) began January, 1850. Twelve of Flo Hatfield's slaves were the first on the site. Six months later, after some fifteen deaths, the first deep shafts were in.

"There," said Plunkett, looking back again, "that's where y'all goin'."

"You finished?" asked Reb.

"Why, yeah." Plunkett blinked. " 'Course, I don't *approve* of what goes on there! Oh, it's terrible, treating men like animals! Or machines! I'm a Socialist," he blurted, "I'm on your side! You men should pull together. I mean, *we* oughta pull together." Plunkett tugged at his collar for air.

Reb asked, "How come?"

"Because. . . ." Plunkett was silent a spell. "Because all property is theft." He pulled the phrase around him for protection. *"You're stolen property,"* improving a little on it now. "And me, I'm sorta on rental terms, like a cabin." He looked at Reb. "That doesn't work, does it?"

"Not really," said Reb.

"Well," snorted Plunkett, "you get the *idea.* The people on the bottom belongs on top."

"Sam?" said Reb.

"Yeah?"

"Watch the road."

80

On the ridingboard, Reb put his chin on his fist and, like the others, fell silent. We were prisoners. Condemned men with a fool steering the ferryboat, the Underworld but four hours away. "Anybody want a chew?" Plunkett fumbled through his pockets, cackled, "I stole it," and peered back at his passengers. He placed his tobacco on the seat. "You're welcome to it all, if you want any."

Reb broke off a mouthful, handing the rest to me. "You mighty quiet, Hawkins. You ain't gonna be sick are you?"

"Trust me," I whispered. "I've got a plan."

The last thing the Coffinmaker cared to hear was one of my plans; he looked back at Plunkett. The old man tucked his head like a turtle. "I *hate* slavery! Nobody's free, 'specially a workin' man like myself. We're brothers," said Plunkett. "Underneath. Don't let nobody tell you Sam Plunkett ain't for Revolution. . . ."

Plunkett defended himself in vain. Flo Hatfield's work-ruined bondsmen had never heard of Socialism, and Sam Plunkett no more understood this movement than did my tutor Ezekiel before the weekend he entertained Karl Marx at Cripplegate. Reaching back, I remembered Ezekiel planning for weeks in advance—I can see him now, asking Mattie to cook, rereading his underlinings in *The Holy Family,* purchasing Marx's favorite dishes and cigars. On the day of his arrival—a hot June morning in 1850—my tutor nearly collapsed from nervous exhaustion.

Marx arrived at Cripplegate dazed by a dizzying cycle of banishment that bounced his family from Belgium to Cologne and, finally, to a two-bedroom firetrap at 1 Leicester Street in London. These were hard years, those of his London exile. His ratio of false starts to finished copy was twenty to one. He thought of suicide. He wrote poems, his first poems since his days at the *Gymnasium* at Trier, plunged into mathematics for moral consolation against the police, the indifference of bourgeois publishers, and bill collectors, who threw his furniture into the street. The landlord bullied Jenny, his wife, for the preposterous rent of forty-two thalers a month. She was, that May, bleeding at the breast, forced to sell her silver— a family treasure—and, as Marx did algebra at his desk, brought her disappointments to their housekeeper Hélène Demuth. This troubled Marx all the more, though he said nothing—Hélène had been with Jenny for years; he watched the breakdown quietly, took

81

Charles Johnson

long walks on Hampstead Heath, and wrote to his American friends
Jonathan Streitburgher, a printer of an Abolitionist paper in Abbe-
ville, Bob Abrams, an authority on Hawthorne, and Ezekiel Sykes-
Withers. "My children are dying," he wrote. "My work meets silence."

Engels, whom Marx's daughter Eleanor called "The General,"
in regards to his obsession with the history of military operations
("A silly way," wrote Marx, "for a grown man to spend his time, but
I humor him."), was reduced, after the romance of Left Hegelian-
ism, to clerking again in the same Manchester sweatshop where
he'd toiled as a child. His checks were slow. As of late, political
affairs affected Marx physically. When he felt a headcold coming
on, a toothache, he looked immediately for its social cause. A new
tax law had cost Marx a molar. Nearby at a button factory a strike
that failed brought on an attack of asthma. These things were
dialectical. As the political world declined, so did Marx's health. As
for Jenny, she wrote friends in Germany, sparing no detail of their
destitution to bring in charity, another humiliation for Marx, especially since editor Charles Dana at the New York *Daily Tribune*
had written "We'll see" to Marx's offer to work as a European
stringer. "You will readily understand my despair," Marx wrote
Ezekiel in May, "at being destitute after so many books. We are
very, very low. Jenny has been shoplifting our meat; I wouldn't
blame her if she left me. I would give almost anything now to see
America." My tutor mailed him the price of a boat ticket to New
York and back, provided that after seeing Dana he visit Master
Polkinghorne's estate in South Carolina.

His stagecoach was delayed, having thrown a wheel outside
Charlotte. Like any traveler, Marx descended disheveled from his
coach with trenchmouth, his collar wilted and overcoat lopped over
one shoulder, his eyes unfocused as he backsheeshed his driver,
and peered round at Hodges in bewilderment. Stepping forward,
Ezekiel said, "Professor Marx, we're over here," and steered him
toward our rented carriage.

"Streitburgher, too?" asked Marx.

Ezekiel staggered a little.

"I'm afraid I've never met him. The locals aren't very interest-
ing—a little dull," Ezekiel laughed. "There are fewer spots in the
civilized world more bleak than Hodges."

82

"You *don't* know Streitburgher?" He and Ezekiel walked out of step for a second and, for two or three steps, Marx walked sideways.

"No, sir."

Marx pulled one of Ezekiel's letters from his coat and held it up. "Is that you?"

"Yes—yes, you've been corresponding with me."

We walked on for some paces in silence. Our guest stepped into the carriage, settled himself, and asked—it sounded like a challenge—"How long you lived here?"

"Seven years now," said Ezekiel. "Come November."

"As long as that? And you've never met Streitburgher?"

"No."

Our guest was disappointed. That was plain. "Hodges is out of the way. Yes?" he said. "You should maybe stand a mirror at both ends to make it bigger." And he roared. It was Marx's effort to put Ezekiel at ease. Abruptly, I saw my tutor through his eyes: a lonely, unsocial creature unused to visitors, as awkward with people as a recluse. Not a Socialist, as he fancied himself. No, his rejection of society, his radicalism, was not, as he thought, due to some subtle rareness of soul. It was stinginess. Resentment for the richness of things. A smoke screen for his own social shortcomings. Regardless, Marx's spirits remained high. Dana had promised him a series on conditions in Germany. Ezekiel replied, recklessly, that he never read newspapers. "Nor I," lied Marx, politely. His smile flashed. Fell away. If you watched him closely, you noticed a certain discomfiture in his crossing and recrossing his legs, the unease of a visitor at pains to find something in common with his host.

Of this curious visit, Master Polkinghorne knew nothing, and it passed unnoticed in Hodges—as well as world history—because Marx came to South Carolina simply to unwind and see an old friend. At thirty-two, he was half a head shorter than Ezekiel, with crushed-down shoulders, and dark skin (he preferred the nickname Mohr), quick, Jewish gestures, and a tangled beard that would be rabbinical, if he let it go. Mainly, he spoke with his larynx, like most Germans. His hands were cold, thick-fingered, and stabbed the air when he spoke. Soon he would be stout. He was working over notes that summer for *Pre-Capitalist Economic Formations*, a task he dreaded, Marx confessed, since he knew no more about the

East than the errors in Hegel's *Lectures on the Philosophy of History;*
Engels, for his part, was studying Persian, and Marx had found a
bit on India in Mill's *Principles.* Also, he had recently taught himself
Japanese so he could read Kwanzan; spent months at it, too, then
decided Kwanzan—or maybe all Oriental thought—wasn't worth a
footnote, but couldn't figure what to do with all the Japanese. All
the same, his knowledge in June, 1850, was piecemeal on prehis-
tory, shamefully thin on primitive communal societies, and weak
on Africa. What Ezekiel Sykes-Withers didn't know about India
could be written on a postcard, and his guest, though he found the
subject tedious, listened humbly, eager to learn, holding his head
at attention, his knees bumping Ezekiel's in the carriage as we rode
back to Cripplegate.

It should have been a wonderful weekend.

Marx was a charming guest, excited by everything American;
he lavishly complimented Mattie on her cooking, kissed her hand,
which made my stepmother giggle, asked for recipes, and was bored
by nothing said by the bondsmen. But he was short with Ezekiel;
he treated him like the most outstanding brickhead and donzel as
ever broke a biscuit. My tutor had badly mistaken this man. Marx
did not, like Ezekiel, live for ideas, political or otherwise; he was,
in the old sense—the Sanskrit sense—a householder. The Marx of
Ezekiel's fancy, the humorless student radical of the 1830s, was—
you cannot guess—a *citizen* devoted first, and foremost, to his family: a droll, Dickensian husband who, going fat—he would not
exercise—unfastened the buttons on his vest when he ate, called
his wife "Mohme," and loved her dearly, but was not above diddling
Hélène when he cornered her in the pantry. His reverence for
Truth took (for Ezekiel) a strange form. When in their discussion
it became clear to Ezekiel that Marx was right, Marx would at once
shift to another subject—he took no pleasure in the fact that *he* was
right. It rather embarrassed him. To be sure, what he saw of American slavery made him sore. But most often Marx diverted Ezekiel's
conversation from social evil and deep-ploughing philosophy to
the few pockets of well-being made possible by capital. And capital
alone. My tutor was badly disappointed. He thought Marx dull.
And now it came to him that Marx, the materialist, would frown

upon his association with the Transcendental Club, dismiss as alienation—species-being projected into the Absolute—any discussion
of the spirit.

After dinner our guest said nothing about Revolution, prefer-
ring to talk about African customs with me, or fiction—Cervantes
and Balzac, Fielding and Dumas (père)—when not humoring Ezekiel.
Against his better judgment, Ezekiel hauled out his latest articles,
spreading them around grease-coated plates, jugs of whiskey, and
makeshift ashtrays on the table; he talked, waving a slice of bread,
about his recent work (ontology), on the *Theologia Germanica*, which
had a sedative effect on Marx: a twelve-page sleeping pill. Listening, Marx beat one hand on the arm of his chair 224 times. He
began a yawn, which failed and left him sitting like someone in a
dentist's chair. His beard trembled—you would have thought he
was chewing; he was, in fact, grinding his teeth. Finally he re-
marked that Ezekiel's paper had one error. Ezekiel looked from
Marx to me. "Does it?"

"Ja." He gave his tight, in-bitten smile. "You *chose* to be miserable. Why?"

Ezekiel twitched back from the table.

"Can your Mama understand all this noise about the Transcendental Ego?"

"My mother?"

My tutor was divided—he later told me, though I saw it for
myself—between sharing what he had written and fear of severe
criticism: he was a graduate student (again) standing with his dis-
sertation (fifth draft) outside the Great Man's door. "I wrote it,"
Ezekiel said, "for *you*." His voice fluttered. "I had hoped a thoughtful reader, someone who loved truth. . . ."

"Truth?" Marx raised his eyebrows. "Truth is some*one*."

"Well, of course. . . ," Ezekiel scratched through his beard; at
that moment Marx scratched through *his* beard. It was as if a third
person, a puppeteer, had pulled identical strings on two wooden
dolls. "All scholarship is *about* and *for* people, I agree. . . ." His
fingers disappeared into his hair when he swept it back off his
forehead. And then he said one word too many: "But certain lower,
less polished classes of people simply don't. . . ."

The Great Man boomed, "Vhat?" He stood and began to roll up one shirtsleeve. "Young Andrew," said Marx, "please hold my coat and step behind me."

Eyes seeled, Ezekiel said, "Sorry."

For a moment they pulled in different directions. Marx sat, rolling down his sleeve. My tutor's forehead wrinkled with the effort of thought. "I *know* your position on these matters, Professor Marx. I didn't expect you to completely agree. . . ."

"Oh, I *do* agree," said Marx.

"You do?"

"Ja." Marx began unlacing his boots. "Is about the Self's onto-genesis, this paper?" He examined now a hole in his stocking. "You vant to say that the Transcendental Ego is empty—correct?—and exists only through vhat it is *conscious* of, vhich means, as in Hegel, that alienation in the Other is necessary in every act of perception?"

"Yes!" Ezekiel sat up. "Exactly! The point—"

The Great Man touched his arm. "Ezekiel?"

"Yes?"

"Is wrong," said Marx. "A mistake. Oh, your thesis is *großartig*, technically, but you are, by your own argument, *dead.*"

Ezekiel did not move.

"Ja, dead." His fingertips pushed the paper toward Ezekiel. "You argue that to exist is to exist *through* an Other. So far so good. But, as you say, *someone* must therefore be central to your existence, Ezekiel. Vhen two subjects come together, they realize in their re-ciprocal intersubjective life a common vorld. Yes? Compared to this, all other vays of being are fragmentary. Partial. Hollow. No matter how passionately you pursue them. The universal name for this final, ontological achievement, this liberation—Occidental or Oriental—in vhich each subject finds another essential is *love.*" The Great Man stood. He put his hand on Ezekiel's shoulder. "Ja, love. Do you haf a lover?"

The word "love" entangled with Ezekiel's tongue and teeth. He got no farther than the *luh*-sound.

Marx smiled sympathetically. "Then do you live if no Other's gaze intends you as the beloved?"

In his softest voice, Ezekiel, his hands tightly locked in his lap, whispered, "Suppose you've never been loved. What if whenever you try, the Others . . . look away?"

"Then love someone." Marx chuckled and shook his head. "On the stagecoach to Hodges there vas this voman. . . ." He kissed his fingers, then looked, white-eyeballed, at the ceiling. "Vunderful! Hair to her vaist. A voice like a girl. I am grateful to her for being beautiful. For her sake, Ezekiel, I vill finish this book *Pre-Capitalist Economic Formations."* He sighed and gave the air a little sweep with his hand. "Everything I've vritten has been for a voman—is *one* vay to view Socialism, no?"

Now the cabin was silent. I could hear wind wheel outside the windows and slam into the cabin walls like seaswell. I looked from Ezekiel to Marx and found them deadlocked, Ezekiel deeply disappointed, Marx twirling his wineglass, sipping carefully so not to wet his moustache. My tutor poured himself Scotch, slammed his palm down on the cap, and brought out:

"You say it's *reciprocal!* What if the Others don't love back? That girl—she doesn't *know* what you felt! She'll never *read* your goddamn book!"

"Temper," said Marx, *"temper!"* He smoked and thought for a moment. "If they didn't, how vould you feel?"

"It would *kill* me." Ezekiel's voice had no body, no center as he spoke. "I would perceive them as beautiful, and I would obliterate myself to let be their beauty, which only I can do, but on their side they wouldn't know I existed—denying *me* love, they would, strictly speaking, deny me life."

The Great Man pulled out his pocketwatch. Yawning, stripping down to his longjohns, he rubbed his stomach with both hands, then lay on the pallet we'd prepared for him.

Ezekiel said, from the table:

"We haven't finished!" Watching Marx's eyelids lower, he asked, "What would *you* do?"

Marx said, perhaps in a half-sleep, the thing Ezekiel was not prepared to hear:

"Rejoice."

But you have not heard the worst.

Though Marx turned in at ten-thirty, Ezekiel did not sleep,

That next morning he sat leaning into the carriage doorway, saying little as mud flew in a soft, wild rush from the wheels. Marx was ferociously polite. Waving off the stagecoach in Hodges, Ezekiel returned, weakly, to his cabin, took a hammer to the looking glasses in his study, and then fed one by one his papers into the fireplace. The Great Man, Ezekiel decided, had been talking through the back of his neck—his advice sounded like the lyrics of popular songs, which were no better than greeting cards set to music, but the most abstruse philosophy—real philosophy—doorwayed, after a process of infinite complexity, into exactly that stark, simple experience of which philosophers never (or seldom) spoke: *love*. By his own confession, he was prepared for suffering. That was no problem. And he was no less prepared for ruthlessly comparing the actual to the ideal (the actual always lost). But joy? No Revolutionary was prepared for joy. It seemed, when he thought about it, *indecent* to rejoice when, as any fool knew, so much of the world had gone wrong. Was not the spirit enslaved everywhere? The planet raped? The government in the hands of criminals? War prophesied? Where in the particulars of daily life, the flaws and imperfections, was there reason to rejoice?

For two days Ezekiel sat in his study, or lay in bed like a tree stump, his head in his hands. This is the accepted position for those suffering heartbreak. Days ran into days. No matter how he sliced it—so he confided in me—Spirit *was* love, and the triumph of the Spirit exiled in World was in our age, or any age, to embrace things in their *haeceittias*, their thisness, to perceive—mad as this seemed—Matter as holy. And when at last he went through all the home-brewed beer at Cripplegate, he walked bareheaded past unpainted board buildings to a Hodges dancehall, his coat collar up, and sat behind four men playing poker under a newly lit kerosene lamp, drinking until flame forked through his chest. Bootheels stamped. A tinny piano to his left played an unidentifiable tune. Ezekiel laid his head on the table. In this place, in air shaking with flies, and logy heat, Shem Moses, a hired man on the Greenwood farm of Colonel Richard Hart, bowled over beside him. There was something marshy about Shem Moses. He was huge, spider-bellied, smelled like a farmer's shoe, cared for no one, believed in nothing, a swindler and whorechaser. He stood with a slight stoop. His voice was terrible. He had thin, hair-frizzed arms, his nails were nub-gnawed. Also, he had syphilis—this Ezekiel could tell by the way he cursed and wept when passing water behind the dancehall. Ezekiel's first thought was to change tables. Fatigue kept him in his chair. Shem Moses brought a bottle to the table. He ticked off his troubles, as drunken men often do to perfect strangers, and his greatest burden was his daughter, Althea. "Transverse myelitis," Moses slid his yellow eyes at Ezekiel—he sounded the syllables slowly, the way laymen (or church people) pronounce terms from the mysterious realms of doctors and priests. "She's paralyzed from the waist down. It come over her in a week. There weren't no signs." He blew his nose into his hand, squeezed off strands of mucus with his fingers, then wiped his hand on the side of his chair. Through all this, Ezekiel only nodded, lips pursed, suspend-ing judgment, giving a little noncommital headshake as Shem Moses detailed the disease, explaining how the girl had been through an operation that destroyed his savings. And then he produced from his coat a daguerreotype of his daughter, an underexposed print, sfumato, smudged by fingerprints. It was cracked, wine-stained. Moses kept it just out of the lamplight, which forced Ezekiel to crane his neck forward to see.

My tutor squinted. "How old is she?"

"Fifteen."

Moses tucked the portrait back into his shirt pocket. He scratched under one arm, then made a toothpick from wood splin-tered on the tabletop. "She be sixteen in a month, but I don't 'spect she gonna *see* sixteen." He slipped both thumbs into his beltless trousers. "Y'know, it sounds funny to say this but, as God is my secret judge, she might as well be planted right now. I can't do for her—Colonel Hart don't pay me enough to feed a chicken. Won't nobody marry her, being crippled, and. . . ."

"May I see her picture again?"

Moses waited before bringing out the daguerreotype. He put a finger in his mouth to adjust his teeth. "You ain't gonna muss it up or nothing'?"

"No," said Ezekiel.

He wiped both hands on his trousers. Moses handed him the portrait. And what did my tutor think? It is perhaps best to say that he did not think. Althea's image was, by any standard, beautiful—a bit pale maybe, suffering from vitamin starvation, but lovely: a freckled, blackcherry-eyed girl with heaps of golden hair. Yet, she might have been, for all he knew, Zachary Taylor's sister; Moses might have stolen the daguerreotype, or picked it up on the street. All this Ezekiel knew. And this: He could not stomach the idea that the future of such a girl—if the portrait was indeed hers—lay in the hands of a grimy, incendiary-breathed scorpion like Shem Moses, who'd drink anything. Stove fuel. Cleaning fluid. In every particle of the man he read: parasite. One hand pulled out his wallet, the other withdrew his whole month's wages. He said, "I hope this will help."

"You *givin'* me that?" Moses wiped his mouth with the back of his hand. His boulderlike face beamed. Without counting the bills, he stuffed the money into his boot. His clothes gave a thin, dry crack as he leaned forward, dislodging dirt. "I can't pay you back. . . ."

"I don't want it back," said Ezekiel. "And it's for the girl, not you. If you spend it on drink, I'll see that your daughter is placed in someone else's custody."

The hired man bobbed his head, "Thank you."

"No, thank you." He picked up the girl's portrait again. "Can I keep this for a day or two?"

"You ain't with the law, are you?"

"No, I'm a teacher. Why did you ask?"

Moses released air in relief. He began to pick at his nose. "You a real Christian, Mr. Sykes. And we *will* pay you back, Lord willin'." And he had one boot out the door before Ezekiel could reply.

It was, of course, neither Christian nor charitable, from Ezekiel's point of view, to give his July wages to the hired man. It could be, he thought, after Moses left and he again sat alone, staring at the girl's portrait, seen as the most self-righteous and, therefore, suspect thing he'd ever done. There was in every gift the feeling that you had overpowered another, performed a service that—in the gaudiest sense—displayed your superiority, or *used* their suffering to assuage your guilt, or to buy yourself a seat in the sweet by-and-by. But Ezekiel didn't believe in the sweet by-and-by. And he certainly didn't believe in the ego. What he *did* believe, strange as it sounds, was that if he took this business about the Good seriously,

if he faced squarely his weariness with having and getting, he had
to admit that the world seemed to fall into two halves. Not prole-
tariat and bourgeoisie. Not black and white. Not even into wise and
foolish. Granted, there were two halves, but the first, which was by
far the greatest, was known simply by its single utterance, *I need, I
want,* and the second by its quiet reply: *All right.* That made him
reflect upon himself. What sort of self was it? Well, in popular
terms, it was solipsistic; it was emotionally bankrupt; it was empty.
He had a weak heart. Even Cripplegate's bondsmen possessed, it
struck Ezekiel, a greater sense of purpose than he, though they
hated it, waited for the hour they would escape it, the thing Marx
had hinted at, the thing that, once the furor over freedom died
down, made real freedom intelligible:

Something to serve.

In his gift to Moses' daughter—there would be more in the
months that followed—there was a sense of right proportion, a
clean asymmetry: a renunciation of the fruit of his works at Cripplegate, of reward, which created, in Ezekiel's view, no further
action. No evil. No stain. This fat idea (like all ideas) tugged long
at my tutor. He returned each payday and inquired about Althea's
health. Her hobbies. Her friends. Did she have enough to eat? In
what was she interested? Could he help in other ways? The num-
bers in his bankbook spooled backwards. After four such meetings
with Shem Moses, whom he now hated—his oily manner, his whin-
ing and self-pity, the way he leveled everything to the coarsest
common denominator—after five months of tolerating this man,
who always spoke in a stupendous voice, as though each dialogue
was a dispute, Ezekiel knew Althea's history perfectly. On their
fifth meeting, after the girl had received nearly fifty dollars from
Ezekiel, the farmer brought him a letter. And a proposition.

"She's doing way better." A thin smile. "She wanted you to have
this."

Ezekiel slit the small envelope, scented and sealed with candle-
wax, with his thumbnail, filled his mouth with whiskey, which he
sloshed around until it became warm, and, after wiping off Moses'
thumbprints, read:

Mr. Sykes,

You must forgive me for not writing sooner. I owe you

91

letters and letters. I can never repay you for what you have done. I should like to meet you more than anything in this world, but I am afraid you would find me poor company. You are in my prayers. Do believe me when I say that I love you, shall always love you, that you have been like a father to me, and that without your aid I should be lost; I remain, Honored Sir,

Your Servant,
Althea

Now, I must call your attention to Eastern texts that Ezekiel himself made me read, works that said Samsara (the world of appearance) was Nirvana (the world to be attained), which implied, outrageously, that man's highest achievements were won in the realm of Matter. The girl's letter, though brief, made Ezekiel's brow go blank. Was he not obliged to give in greater measure? Was he not, after all, *incomplete* in his efforts to serve? Men saddled with obligations, like Moses—like Master Polkinghorne—would scoff at this, no doubt, seeing how they'd blundered into duty—the quiet, dull triumph of devoting themselves to everyday things, placing children and wife, colleagues and acquaintances in a widening circle that soon enveloped the entire community, before all else. But it kept them honest. It brought out, begrudgingly, the best qualities in the bulk of humanity, whether humanity appreciated it or not.

Ezekiel stuffed the girl's letter in his coat. "What is your proposal?"

"You've read Althea's letter?"

"Yes."

"That part where she says you been like a father?" Moses paused with his glass midway between his mouth and the table. He put one finger in his ear and jiggled it. "You read that?"

"Yes."

The hired man took a deep breath.

"She's for sale. You kin have her. Now, put down that bottle!" His voice jumped. "It's plain *I* can't do for her like you kin, poor as I am. Without a wife. Mr. Sykes, you lifted the bottle again. . . ." Moses waited as Ezekiel put the flask down. "You might's well do for her *directly*. Without me in the way." Quickly, taking another drink, Moses kept his eyes on Ezekiel's hands. "Does four hundred dollars sound fair?"

Ezekiel looked at him in astonishment; he filled his cheeks, then his chest, with air, but held himself still; if he moved he would hang for second-degree murder.

"Four hundred," said Moses, "and you'll never see me again."

"If I do, you're a dead man."

Moses laughed.

"The girl. . . ." He cleared his throat. "When do I see her?"

"After I see the money."

Never in his life had he hated anyone as deeply as Shem Moses. "Next Wednesday week—is that soon enough?"

"I kin wait."

Now began a terrible period in Ezekiel's life. The payment was difficult to come by. What credit he had at Cripplegate was exhausted; he was forced to wire friends in Missouri for the money, explaining that he was engaged, soon to be married. This Ezekiel came to believe. There rose in him, starting at about the fifth button on his vest, a vague feeling of purpose. And order. For the first time in years he had the courage to make plans and prelive the future. A month passed. Two months before the money arrived. While he waited, Ezekiel notified Jonathan of his resignation—he would find other work, work with his hands, perhaps even build his own house outside Hodges—you could do that, couldn't you? Find a center? And ever he fixed his mind on the girl, who was the radix for this revolution in his life, ever his hatred for the hired man increased. By this time, it should be mentioned, my tutor lived only for the promise of this new life. He thought he would be transformed by taking her from Moses; he would enter, he believed, into a life of clarity and law. From his cabin, where crates of books waited for moving, there drifted from the quarters to the Big House the sobbing and broken song of a lonely man desperately in love. This luminary, the object of his new hope—Althea—seemed all the more beautiful for her bondage to Shem Moses, a creature so ashamed of the transaction he failed to show on the day Ezekiel, dressed to the nines, delivered the money to the dance-hall. He sent a slave, a messenger boy named Jeff Peters, who trousered the money for Moses, and gave Ezekiel a map to the Greenwood Farm.

This is what happened now:

He hitched wagons to Greenwood, bought a bouquet of flowers, then hiked six miles to the farm, and this wearied him, for the wind was strong and stirred (red) dust, the path was uneven, the footing poor, with night coming on, and he, painted and powdered as he was, wearing his highhat, his tight, square-toed shoes, and carrying a walking stick, was not dressed for hiking. First he saw a porch sharking onto the yard. A wild pig scrambled down the steps, cutting dirt across the fields. Something clicked in his throat. His stomach turned. He took off his hat and stepped inside to the shock of rooms emptying into rooms. Each step on the old floor was like the crack of a coffin shrinking. The farmhouse had not been inhabited for years. Ezekiel looked in the kitchen, the study, the sitting room; no Althea. Only this toadstool smell floating over black-dark furniture. Broken lanterns. Roots bursting through the floor. Birds nesting on the chimneypiece. Curtains moved behind him and he turned around. Rats. He sobbed—his first sound—dropped the flowers, then his cane, and crumpled at the room's center, his back against a barrel, the shadowy house quiet now, a bony ruin where the only movement was blood pounding in his temples, his heart overheating—searing pain in his chest, and then even the work of this bloody, tired motor went whispering to rest, his spirit changed houses, and he dropped into the solitary darkness like stone.

You will object, and rightly, that I cannot know what Ezekiel Sykes-Withers felt when he died, for this work is first-person, the most limited form. But even this philosophical problem of viewpoint—the autobiographical I—will be answered, I assure you, and I confess, for now, that this account is a tale woven partly from fact, partly from fancy.

I will confess even more:

A quarter mile from the Yellowdog Mine I still had no plan for escape, only a feeling that, if given a moment out of Plunkett's sight, I could wing a way to liberation. The Lord, as my stepmother would say, provided the moment when we cleared the last hill and Captain Walter's shed came into view. "We can walk from here," I told Plunkett.

His head went back. "You can what?"

"You can leave us here," I said. "It's a long ride back."

The coachman bit and moistened his lips. "You're up to something, ain't you?"

"No."

"If you *are*," he screwed up his eyebrows, "it won't work. There's nothing around here but woods." He stopped the horses and, when we'd piled out, said, "They know you're coming."

I assured Plunkett that we would report to Captain Walters—I gave him my word, but the coachman waited as we walked, both relieved to be free of us and suspicious. Reb and I pushed a few paces ahead of the others as Plunkett watched from the wagon. When we reached the shed, the others were several rods behind us. Reb pulled at my arm. I pushed him ahead—timing was important—then, praying he was inside, knocked on the Chief Engineer's door. My knees gave a little; I had gone a day without chandoo. My chest felt like a furnace; my teeth *ached*. Dragging for air, I pushed his door, which opened onto an unvarnished desk littered with surveying maps, a bevy of mining equipment, bottles containing coal and sand samples, and, behind it, the Chief Engineer. Walters lifted his head—he'd been sleeping—and came to his feet: "Yes?" He smoothed down his shirt. "Can I do something for you?"

Stepping back, I let Walters fill the doorway, and said, "I've brought these men from Abbeville."

Looking south, we saw Sam Plunkett wave, then turn round his wagon. Walters threw up his hand.

"You work for Flo Hatfield?"

"The same."

He returned to his desk, sweating, nodding at no one in particular at first, then at me to pull a calf-bottom chair closer to his desk. Reb stood close by me, silent as a wall. Now it took all my effort not to moan; the pain moved, experimentally, in my legs—a light green pain speckled with particles of blue. From his drawer Walters removed a bottle of peach-colored whiskey, which he offered me. It eased the ache of withdrawal by a little.

"It'd be a blessing for a man to break his neck in times like these." Walters laughed, all gloom. "You and your man there must be tired. We'll fix a place for you tonight—"

"We best be leaving now," I said. "Mrs. Hatfield expects us back by morning."

Noah Walters nodded.

"You say hello to Flo for me." He reached into his pocket, dragging keys, dust-sprinkled coins, then a gold watch, which played nicely when he opened it, onto his desk. "She always liked this. You give it to her for me, Mister . . . you musta told me your name, but I forget. My memory," he touched his left temple, "ain't what it used to be."

"It's Harris," I said, "William Harris."

Reb exhaled and rubbed his face.

"He has bronchial trouble," I told Walters. "The dust up here. . . ."

The Chief Engineer gave a headshake.

"She's a fine woman, you know that. I never met nobody quite like her. It ain't every woman can keep a farm going like Flo Hatfield. She used to tell me. . . ." He cracked the knuckles on his right hand slowly. His left. His sad, watery eyes skimmed over me. He said, to draw me out, "She's good in bed, too."

"I know."

His mouth fell open. "You do?"

As it often happens in the world, especially the tiny southern communities of South Carolina, Noah Walters and I had a third person in common: His fifteen year marriage ended, six years before, in Flo Hatfield's bedsheets. He was not free of her yet. Would, I realized as he pumped me for the kind of information only shared by men who have slept in the same places, never be free of her. Did Flo still eat candy for breakfast? Dress her lovers like gigolos?—he still had a suit she'd given him. Did she still blather on and on about her Continental education? The Chief Engineer relaxed and let his hair down and looked at me with the preposterous, intimate, slightly embarrassed love of men who have survived— are trying to survive—the same war. It goes without saying that I had found in Noah Walters a friend; it was almost (I thought, stunned) as if I'd slept with *him* by proxy.

At dusk, Reb said, "Sar, we *got* to go."

"I know, I *know* how she is," said Walters. "I was late once and. . . ." He laughed and put his arm round me as I looked, weakly, to the door. "Can I get you a pair of horses for the ride back? You can bring 'em back when you come through again."

"That," I said, "would be fine."

"And provisions?" Outside, Walters grabbed my shoulders, held me at arm's length, and, like a great, wise uncle, said, "Bill, you be careful now. If you get in trouble, come down here. You can stay overnight. We'll talk about it." His hug lifted me a foot off the ground. "It wasn't until now that I talked about this to *any*body. Maybe," he said, turning back to his shed, "I can get on with my life now. . . ."

The Coffinmaker and I got on, thanks to Noah Walters, with our lives—about forty miles' worth, which was the distance we put between ourselves and the Yellowdog Mine; we rode northeast, skirting Anderson, then stopped to rest the horses. You must remember that I rode sick, with quicksilver down my spine, bowels burning, fastened sometimes to my saddle because, every few miles, I fell off. Reb tethered my wrists to the pommel, pulled my horse at times by its reins through heavily wooded country near Greenville.

"He can't die *now*." He was talking toward Heaven by the time we stopped by a dry riverbed for the night. "You listen to me. . . ." Reb built a fire behind a rock, stretched me out on a blanket, and prayed, "Lord, you brought us out of Abbeville, so You *better* not quit on us now."

"*I* got us out," I said. "It was me—"

"You, *you!*" howled Reb. He hated personal pronouns; the All-museri had no words for *I, you, mine, yours.* They had, consequently, no experience of these things, either, only proper names that were variations on the Absolute. You might say, in Allmuseri, all is *A.* One person was A_1, the next A_2. (These are Western analogues. Don't make too much of them.) "You ain't strong enough to even *ride*, Freshmeat!"

It was so. I was reeling, vomiting and voiding waste, by midnight. His voice and lips were out of sync. Words hung in the air seconds after he spoke. Between the thought *Move your arms* and my body there was no connection, an abyss between will and word, and I sank: the last thing I remember of the Black World was Reb tending the fire, twirling a sliver of kindling; sank: a circle of flame; sank: a brilliant firewheel of inexpressible beauty.

PART TWO

The White World

VII

MIDDLE PASSAGE:
THE ROAD TO SPARTANBURG

It is impossible for me to recollect all that took place our first night, for I was from that point on the poorest of traveling companions; I was unable to ride for long, or too fast, fell dizzily from my horse when we resumed flight, and lost all sense of distance and direction. But worse than all this, I had lost Minty. When I tell you that my urgency for freedom came from my desire to see Minty free, that my well-being depended largely upon hers, you will not believe me. You are going to say that at twenty Andrew Hawkins was infatuated or, like most men, in love with the idea of love, or perhaps propelled by romance. None of that would be true. The view from the quarters changes the character of everything, even love—especially love—and in ways not commonly admitted. This was true of my feelings about Minty, and no less true of the tie between her mother, Addie, and father, Nate, whom my stepmother had reason to call the Toadstool, though for a time he was my father's only friend after the Fall.

My father was not well received when he came back from the Big House. Not at first. As might be expected, his head was lowered a little after the incident with Anna Polkinghorne, his voice was lower, too, softer, more unsure, and for two or three months he stayed clear of scrub balls, church services, and the drunken communion of bondsmen behind the still. He was not unsocial. Then, more than ever, he needed the company of other slaves, but what kept him away, behind the rag curtains over the kitchen window, was the feeling that in one evening he'd lost a lifetime of building a good name for himself, winning his master's confidence, and disproving the grim Negro wisdom that no effort served to alter

101

history and nature. He'd thought himself the exception—thought there could *be* exceptions, other models, if a man just did what he was told. Hadn't he lived closer to Jonathan Polkinghorne than the others? Didn't those years of service count for something? In all this, George decided, he'd been duped. Old women in my mother's Prayer Circle, wearing bonnets of braided horsehair, inclined their gray heads together when my father walked by, as if to say, "Now, there goes a fool," which, I needn't tell you, slowed George's step a little. He'd straighten his back, start to speak, then bite down on his lip and pass on silently into a life that could only be called conditional (if that is the right word). He lay down to sleep, but always conditionally, as if to say, "This is no longer the right or real thing," ate, dressed himself, and did a day's work oxherding, but without once coming out of himself toward Mattie or, after Anna delivered her issue to the quarters like a bad tooth, toward me. One deed, it seemed, could be a destiny. For all but my stepmother, George had done only this one thing—made a total ass of himself, and whenever he appeared outside his cabin the other bondsmen saw, or he thought they saw, not a man who had fallen by virtue of his own free will back among them, but instead living proof of the futility of black pride.

Only Nate McKay, a blacksmith, troubled to visit my father: a friendship of lepers, Mattie called it. George was slow in responding, suspicious of the blacksmith's evening visits, because what was he after? To be near a man shattered by circumstance? Was he the kind of man who drew satisfaction from the suffering of others? There were such men, George knew. They stopped him on the road, making small talk at first, then after a silence they'd ask, "You patch things up with the Polkinghornes yet?" He would lie, of course, say, "We ain't fell out for good." But they needed something else, a different story, a confession that would confirm through his life that all Negroes at Cripplegate, high and low, in the Big House and fields, were united by the deadly upas of color. In the silence that followed their questions he felt water building at the back of his eyes, a catch creeping into his voice, and he would have cried, but that was unmanly. So he lied again: "I'll be back in the House soon," and he stayed clear of festivities in the quarters. In time, my stepmother forgave him; she came to see his confusion that night, but George avoided even her. He had no friends. No one to speak to. Friends could hurt you, as Jonathan had. But Nate McKay wore down George's resistance and won his trust. Some soil is low in lime, high in acid, my stepmother told me. It produces poisonous yet strangely beautiful, brown toadstools and, in the days before Surrender, men like Minty's father.

He was, by any standard, handsome. A long-stalked, high-yellow Negro with "good hair," as bondsmen called it, and a trickle of Cheyenne blood that sharpened his cheeks and gave a feminine lilt to the corners of his eyes: a "pretty man" who, since the day he realized his image was pleasing to others, traded on this, and even my stepmother's eyes twinkled when he came round. He could read. He was proud of his African (Kru) and Indian blood. Children loved to touch his hair, which Nate McKay washed often, twisting it back into a waist-long braid when he worked, which wasn't too often. He was, after all, too blessed to squander himself in hard work or, for that matter, in limiting himself to a single black woman. Although he could have his pick of any woman in Cripple-gate's quarters, he belonged—so he told George—in the company of ladies a little more polished, a saying that made George laugh because he wasn't sure whether Nate was serious or mocking him. He never said outright that black women were beneath him, but he hinted that by selecting one—or several—for his attention he was performing an act of extraordinary sacrifice. He had, some said, twenty-five children sprinkled on farms throughout South Carolina, but this was rumor and my parents only knew that when Addie, his Cripplegate wife, was pregnant or had the Curse, Nate unbraided his hair and brushed it for hours, then slipped away for several days.

The Prayer Circle would meet at Addie's cabin, fifteen women seated in a circle of chairs, an article of Nate's clothing in the center, and their combined thoughts and common prayer—a power like electromagnetism—were aimed at pulling him home. It was then I first saw Minty, and I thought: unfair! She was thin, skinny enough then to fall right through a flute and never strike a single note. And shy. A beautiful girl who, I saw, deserved much better than the man who days later returned home with the smell of strange women in his clothing.

They stayed clear of Nate McKay, his children, until the odor was gone. Addie did not. She wept. She hid his meals in the woods. Many a night, Nate came home asking, "What'd you do with my dinner?" to which Addie replied, "You can't have it!" She'd cooked that day—her children had to eat; but his portion she put where he couldn't find it. His children watched him spend his first hours home smelling it, searching in the outhouse for it, rummaging through Master Polkinghorne's toolshed in a perverse game of hide-and-seek, his stomach growling, and then he'd whale Addie, pound her with both fists, and squeeze her throat until she clawed at his eyes or kneed his testicles. His son Jerome (sixteen), daughters Ann (twelve) and Minty (six) would join in, swinging, trying to unlock his fingers from Addie's hair—the whole family spilled like a creature with ten legs into Nate McKay's yard. It was not a pleasant household, those nights. For hours Addie cried. Jerome cursed and threatened to kill him. Minty and Ann cowered like chickens in one corner of the cabin. Meanwhile, Nate kept looking for his dinner. Often he would find it, cold and fouled by farm animals in the barn. Finger-feeding himself in the darkness, hunched over his plate, he swore each woman's hand was a glove that concealed Satan's claw.

They had this in common, George and Nate: a bewilderment about black women, but there all similarities stopped. Nate treated his wife as a prize Weimaraner would treat the mongrel he'd mated with. He was straightforward with George about his feelings: "I'm a *physical* man, you understand, with powerful drives. It's only natural that when the wife's bleeding I should have somebody on the side." And then he told George about a woman named Delphine, whom he'd been seeing for years; how one winter after not sleeping with her for months he went for a visit when Addie was sick, and found Delphine hemorrhaging in her cabin on a plantation not far away, the softheaded fetus spilling onto the floor in a splash of placenta and blood: a fish, Nate called it, some monster halfway between being a steelhead and his son, and, without saying a word to Delphine, he went outside, threw a torch into her master's window, then placed the matchbox on her porch. Within the week she was sold.

"You did that?" asked George. "Why?"

"I don't need another mouth to feed. Besides," said Nate McKay, "she shoulda known better'n to try an old trick like that to trap me into stayin' with her."

My father quoted the Bible, chapter and verse to him and the blacksmith, shaking his head, cut him off:

"Master Polkinghorne give you that book, didn't he? It's wrong for us, George. Ain't a thing the same between us—we been treated different, so we gotta have different rules. You oughta know that! You did *every*thin' they tol' you, and looka where it got you."

"Was only tryin' to do right," said George.

"Uh huh."

Nate McKay smiled triumphantly.

My father gazed up from under his brow, a little afraid of the blacksmith, but thankful for his company. After a moment, he asked, "Then how do we do hit? Hold our families together when they kin sell us any minute, when it ain't clear what's right or wrong, and one li'l mistake'll destroy everythin' you been workin' fo?" He licked his lips, thoughtful. "Mattie, she don't understand none of this. I feel like a daid man gettin' hup ever' mawnin'— there ain't nothin' to hope for, work toward. How kin you go on, knowin' that?"

Nate McKay nodded, sympathetic.

"You gonna feel daid," he said, "until you back in the Big House and Master Polkinghorne is down heah—permanently."

That made sense to my father. He toyed with the idea, frightening as it was, during the first year of his exile. The problem was that, like so many other ideas a man desperately needed to believe, it came from the mouth of a person everyone at Cripplegate wanted to shoot. It came, to be precise, from the only bondsman who told him his expulsion wasn't fatal, that it was perhaps a period of purification of all things European. This kept George steady. It saved his life, to be frank. Before and after my birth in the Big House, Nate McKay shouldered my father through the worst years of his life, and George comforted him. He fixed Nate a pallet when his wife kicked him out after his wanderings to other women, and shared whatever problems he had with Mattie. The blacksmith laughed easily, and somehow—said Mattie—his humor relaxed George a little. For this reason she tolerated him for as long as five years because he kept George from self-destruction. Also, he brought Minty by to play with me in the yard.

"You like her, don't you?" George would ask me. I was only four then, going on five, but already he was thinking of cementing our families through marriage. My stepmother began to have doubts.

"George, I don't think I want that man in our family."

Nate's my best friend!" said George. "He's the only person said as much as *boo* to me when I come back!"

"He isn't safe," she said.

George stamped his foot. "You just like everybody else! Nobody unnerstands him! Just like you don't unnerstand *me!* We balances each other! Is that hard to see? There's some things a man can't talk about to a woman, or white people! I kin see that now. If it wasn't for him, you wouldn't *have* a husband now."

"And if you weren't so stuck on Nate McKay," said Mattie, "maybe you'd see why he really comes around here."

"Come again?" My father fell silent. He looked at her for what seemed a full minute. "What're you tryin' to say? Has he been . . .?"

"He isn't safe, that's all."

George boomed, "I'll kill him!"

Mattie sighed, "Just leave it *alone*, George." Then she went from the kitchen outside.

Naturally, George had nothing to do after that with the blacksmith. But Minty? She had, I thought, no choice. She was stuck with him, though, as I say, I knew she deserved better. And I had failed her utterly, since she and her family had been sold to Heaven knew where, and Reb and I were in flight.

After such recollections, spun from my sickness, the withdrawal from chandoo and Leviathan, you will understand me when I say that we made but little progress during the night, for often I had to dismount and lie down, leaving the world frequently for fifteen or twenty minutes, and even as I rested I realized how treacherous was the road before us, the reward that would be offered, the bloodhounds, and the feeling that I had betrayed the Race, my father's dream of freedom, and now had the greater problem of reconstructing my life from scratch. By all rights, we should not have gotten this far.

At dawn of the third day we continued north on foot, through briars and thorns, hoping to reach Spartanburg, where we were not known. The sun rose quickly. Within minutes it was daylight and we were again in danger of being discovered. Not far from our hiding place was a small cottage and curb-roofed barn. It being now entirely daylight, we slipped inside the barn, the hayloft providing a comfortable bed after our night under the bridge. It was Wednesday morning, a workday. Fifteen minutes after Reb fell asleep a shirtless man, very thin, stumbled from the cottage to pass water in the weeds, survey his land, then wash himself at an old rust-surfaced pump. He lumbered into the barn, found two pails, then drew fine milk from his cows. From the house his wife held up his shirt and called—a good, fat, beautiful woman, broad as a wine barrel, with red-brown hair and a lovely singing voice, clear and controlled. Behind her: two walleyed children, a boy and a girl. Milk! shouted the boy, and the farmer pulled, below us, harder on his Holstein. Milk! he demanded again, and his face expanded like a blowfish. Biscuits! added the girl. With strawberries! There *are* no strawberries, said the mother. You'll have to eat them plain. No! said the boy, Biscuits and strawberries! Where's Nigger? demanded the girl. As if summoned, a black dog crept from the cottage, sniffed at the barn—we had walked close to the windows— then thought investigating not worth its trouble, and pushed his head against the hand of the girl, who regained her thought: *Biscuits!* Coming, said the mother, weary, herding them inside. Soon the air filled with food smells. Her husband hauled milkpails inside, spilling some in an accident so suggestive of casual abundance and unconscious prosperity, of surplus and generosity, that I cannot now, with pen or tongue, make you feel the wretchedness and envy that descended upon me, the fugitive, as I watched this white family dine. Beyond this, I thought, there was nothing of lasting value. Nothing in books compared. It was this warm, dumb domesticity that destroyed Ezekiel—so sophisticated, so urbane—that we dismissed as *beneath* our sensitivity: the quiet, dull, heroic life of the property holder too busy making biscuits, feeding the pigs out

Charles Johnson

back, to ask the tedious question "Why am I here?" As I was thinking about setting their barn on fire, I first heard, then saw four
men on horseback. The father, who was now busy chopping wood,
addressed the leader as Will McCracken. McCracken asked, "You've
seen no runaway blacks today, have you, John? A big man and a
light-skinned boy?"

"No." The father rested his weight on his axe. "They from
around here?"

"South. They stole two horses."

The wife came to the door, drying her hands on an old dress.
Her husband said, not to his wife, who went inside, then brought
the men a plate of warm biscuits, but to the leader, "Are they worth
looking for?"

"Hundred dollars for the boy, half that for the big man," said
McCracken. "His mistress says she don't care if you bring them
back in a sack, long as you bring them back."

They talked lower now, then the husband kissed his wife, went
inside the cottage, came out with a 44-caliber percussion plains
rifle, and led a horse from the barn. His wife watched this group,
as I did, until they disappeared down the road. When she turned
inside, I woke Reb, and we stayed in the woods until night.

These woods, I should say, were no place for a man "drying
out," cold turkey, from chandoo. We waded through marshy ground
and over ditches, vast and interwoven roots, through thick under-
growth soaked thoroughly by late-afternoon rain. Trees above us
loosed a whirlwind of leaves. The dripping forest echoed with the
clack and chirrup of insects, and now we were out of food. None
of this bothered Reb, but my stomach rumbled. Whenever I bent
forward I felt dizzy. Mushrooms I found at the fringe of the woods,
but I was afraid to eat them. Finally, I demanded that he leave me
behind. "I'm ballast," I said, "deadweight. I'll only slow you down."
The Coffinmaker dismissed this suggestion with a scowl:

"If I'm alone, how far you think I'll git? I never thought I'd be
beholden to somebody 'cause he could pass, but I ain't choosey. If
you kin get us to Canada or Chicago—if that's what the Lord wants—
I sho won't kick none."

"Reb," I said. "You were sleeping. You didn't see those people
back there. No one is going to knock on their door and demand

identification, or feel resentful—not too resentful—if the pleasures of their table increase. Do you see what I'm saying? I can't *fake* that kind of belongingness, that blithe, numbed belief that the world is an extension of my sitting room. Or myself. I'll make mistakes, slips; I'll say or do something wrong, and we'll cook little chicken wings." He left a silence; I looked round to make certain he was still there. "The only reason I don't kill myself is because it doesn't seem worth the effort."

Now Reb was confused.

"You should try Hog's Hoof Tea."

"What?"

"Old medicine," he explained. "Very powerful."

Why I wasted my confession on a man like Reb, a man who slept dreamlessly, I didn't know. This kind of talk made him uncomfortable. In silence, we pushed on for another quarter mile and found ourselves at the tollgate of a public turnpike. At the far end an excited little guard—a boy about fifteen—flapped his arms. Said: "Can't *no* cullud men, Injuns, or Anabaptists come 'cross this heah bridge without a pass or freedom papers." He shook his finger at Reb's face. "Suh, you got papers for this man?"

Since leaving the Mine, this was our most difficult moment. However, I had prepared. During the last quarter mile I had given thought to reinventing my biography by providing myself with comfortable parents, landowners like the couple in the cottage, but wealthy, having made their fortune in American shipping, then lost it, leaving their children penniless; but despite my ill-fortune, I still retained one loyal servant (Reb) and could trade on being the grandson of Edwin Harris, a man who distinguished himself in the Revolutionary War. Harrisburg (any Harrisburg) was named after my Grandpapa. A portly Englishman, generous to a fault, he favored me over my older sister Sarah, my brother James, who was definitely a bad hat, and could trace his (our) tree through fifteen generations. A wonderful biography, you will agree, and I say "reinvent" unflinchingly, for we all rearrange our past to sweeten it a little. Memory, as the metaphysicians say, is imagination.

I gave, in part, this history to the toll guard. And this:

"What money I had, and horses, were taken by two runaway Negroes from Abbeville, near Calhoun Falls."

Charles Johnson

The guard spit in rage. After remarking that all Negroes, in his opinion, were two-faced liars and thieves, lazy and without the wit of a toadstool, to which I agreed, he asked, "And you was travelin' to Spartanburg to see yo sister Sarah?"

"Just so," I said.

I'm hardly being fair to this fellow; he was not a bad sort, considering the day.[1] He not only let us pass, but provided the intelligence that not half an hour before our arrival a buckboard heading for Spartanburg had rumbled through his gate, and that we might overtake this traveler, for he had spoken of making camp nearby for the night. I cannot recall the rest. Vaguely, I remember seeing objects on either side of the road change not in space but serially: trees became fields; an orchard, as I squinted, melted into a log bridge, gave way to intervals of night, and became the glow and crackle of a campfire. Feeling my way, with Reb, through low-hanging limbs, I saw—or perhaps hallucinated—a hazy figure six-feet-four leveling a rifle our way. Whatever the Coffinmaker said—words bubbling under water—assured this traveler that we were not runaways. He lowered his firearm, moved Reb aside, and made a place for me close to his fire. For a time I could not focus distances, or identify our new companion, who threw his cloak over me, and said:

"Yo man says you lost yo horses." His face, inches from mine, angled into view. "Ah know the Negroes who took them, Ah just lost their trail fifteen miles outside Latimer." His laugh had a lot of ironic topspin. "They be in Virginia by now."

Weakly, I said, "Your name, sir?"

Uncorking a jug with his teeth, the traveler took a drink, handed it to me, then moved to his fire, where he began frying eggs for us in a long-handled spider supported on a tripod.

"It's Bannon," said Reb.

Away to the right, the Coffinmaker sat, eating, on a moss-

[1] He is fifteen in my account. In two years this boy—James Travis, Jr.—will be wounded at Fort Sumter, fighting with Major Robert Anderson; his nurse will be a black girl, Zelphy Thomas, and James, finding her with child on August 3, 1861, will choose love over bigotry, moving his new family to southern Illinois, where his great-granddaughter, Ellen, an early NAACP activist, will integrate a lunch counter on April 23, 1935. She will die five years later, on the Northeast Side of Carbondale, surrounded by admirers, white and black.

covered log; I looked his way. His eyes went down. The Soul-catcher, for it was he, brought a wooden bowl from his wagon, then scuffed back to tend his fire. He stoked it, spat a wheylike serum that made the flames flare up, then spent a few seconds firegazing before looking back at me as if we were conspirators. "Ah'm more'n glad to have company." He ladled out hefty portions of reheated meat for me from a battered pot. "You don't mind ridin' to Spartanburg with a bounty hunter, do you?"

It could not, to be frank, have been worse for us. Bannon knew me at first glance from Leviathan. Then why this kindness, this cruel pretending—and poorly—that he had not seen through me? It favored the way George's dog Daisy toyed with her prey before tearing out its throat. Was he preparing a trap? If so, then it was perfectly invisible. Was he simply a tormentor? If so, then he was the best in South Carolina. But I could appreciate the grim comedy of this collision as much as he. "We are thankful for your help," I smiled cautiously. "And I've often wondered what sort of man it takes to gun down women and children like game."

"Ah'll bet you have."

Reb, I saw, had positioned his legs to sprint. I asked "What do you mean?"

"Only," said Bannon, "that gentlemen like yoself, with liberal educations," his smile snapped, "think the work Ah do is criminal, which it is not. But they admit it's necessary. Ah, too, performs a service to Gawd, and Ah performs it well."

I stared.

"That last statement again, if you don't mind."

He paused, like a stage actor waiting for his audience to relax and settle so he could deliver his next line against silence. "Between ourselves, Master Harris, the thought of servin' Gawd through murder usta bother me, like it's botherin' you now, but Ah knows mah nature. It ain't an *easy* thing to accept yo nature, the nature you born with. Am Ah right or wrong?" Again, his conspiratorial smile. His sense of timing was faultless.

"No, it's not easy. But. . . ."

He raised one hand to interrupt me. "When Ah was a boy Ah believed every word of the Gospel, 'specially that First Commandment 'bout not killin'. Mah father was a preacher. Methodist. He'd whale tar outta me if Ah even looked like Ah was thinkin' about women. An awful man, mah daddy. You know what happens when you grow hup in a house like that?" He paused again, bleakly. "If there's a stain on yo mattress in the mawnin', you might's well walk right to the woodshed, drop yo drawers, wait for the old man to wake hup, then hand him the strop. Me, Ah couldn't afford to have no stained mattress. Whenever gism started buildin' in my groin, Ah'd get me a candle, sneak out to the henhouse, and strangle a chicken. During my teens we lost fifty chickens. A whole lot of livestock. Papa wrote it off to poachers. But Ah didn't get beat. No suh. Pretty soon, Ah *enjoyed* killin' more'n pullin' my pud." Horace Bannon gave me seconds on his stew, though I'd hardly touched my plate. "Now, Ah *hated* myself at first—you kin understand that, and Ah prayed to Gawd to make me a peaceful man. Ah prayed the most after Ah moved to bigger things—dogs and horses, then this girl Ah was goin' with named Rebecca, who was pretty horsey her damnself." He blew saliva. Swallowed. Then chuffed on: "But you know one thing? Gawd didn't *want* me to be a peaceful man. You kin always tell yo vocation by the weight it has inside you, Master Harris. If you go 'gainst it, you do yoself harm and defy Gawd. Yessuh. It all come clear to me the night . . . well," he said, looking suddenly at me, "the night Ah poleaxed mah family. I couldn't change. It wasn't mah *business* to change, if everythin' is Gawd's will, but to git better at hit, 'cause one thing Papa usta always say was hit's more Christian to do a half-assed job at the work ordained fo' you than to do another man's work perfectly."

Neither Reb, rocking back and forth on his buttocks, nor I could make answer. There would have been a place made for this man among the Thugees. Noticing the condition of my linen, sweaty and mudstained from our flight, Bannon drug fresh jeans and a white osnaburg shirt a size too large from his wagon for me. As I took off my breeches, I said, "No one could help you?"

"Ah *looked* fo he'p, Ah swear Ah did. Hit was right after my forty-fourth murdah. Ah was twenty. All that killin' was beginnin', you know, to weigh a li'l on mah heart by then." Slowly, the Soul-catcher wiped the corners of his eyes with his scarf. "Whenever Ah shut mah eyes, Ah heard all them voices . . . dead people . . . and a good night's sleep and me got to be strangers. Ah went to this li'l

Methodist church my folks belonged to, and Ah told the pastor
what Ah'd done. His name was Reverend Tyler—Ah remembah—
and he was a good man. He tole me to stay there with him, but Ah
asked him, ain't there *some*thin' Ah kin do to wash away all this evil?
Ah mean, couldn't Ah balance hit with good works or somethin'?
Well, suh, this heah pastor, he tole me that mebbe if Ah went to
every church in the state of South Carolina and made an offerin',
maybe then Ah'd be clean again. . . .

"So Ah did that, Master Harris. There wasn't no church, or
shrine, or temple Ah didn't visit, but the urge to strangle somethin'—or break hit hup—still come ovah me, like a flash of epilepsy.
There was no hope, far as Ah could see, nothin' fo me to do but
git back to Reverend Tyler's li'l church and hide mahself forevah.
Ah made mah way back home, slower this time. Ah slept in the
woods one night, woods like these, and the world of Gawd and
good people ain't never seemed so beautiful to me—the only blem-
ish in all Creation, the only spot that stank, was *me*." He said to Reb,
"And d'you know what happened *then?*"

Reb gulped, "What?"

"Well, Ah heard somethin' funny, like a woman's voice nearby.
Since Ah'd sworn off carryin' weapons, Ah followed hit empty-
handed, clawin' mah way through the bushes and, sho as Ah'm
sittin' heah, there she was—a pretty, li'l cullud gal, and three big,
cornfed cowboys pawin' her. Somethin' in me just went *balooey!* Ah
couldn't stand by and watch no rape, could Ah? But there be *three*
of them and only one of me. Mebbe Ah could take out one of 'em.
Mebbe two. But the third. . . . Then Ah thoughta somethin' worse:
What about mah *soul*? Wasn't hit stained enough? Could hit stand
forty-*five* clear acts of premeditated murdah?

"But by then there weren't no time to think. Forty-four or
forty-five, what did hit mattah? Ah was damned, no doubt 'bout
hit. Ah could nevah save mahself. But at least Ah could save that
li'l girl from them—them animals."

"Then you routed them?" I asked. "All three?"

"Killed one," said Bannon. "Ah smashed his haid with a stone.
Like the cowards they was, them other two took off like they done
seen the Devil."

"Maybe they had," muttered Reb.

Bannon said, "What?"

"Nothing . . ." Reb was holding his breath, and I guessed we both had the same question:

"What about the girl?"

"Oh. . . ." The Soulcatcher looked away. "Ah smothered her with mah saddlebag after they done left. The urge come ovah me again—killin' that first guy got me all worked hup. Believe me, she was better off after what they done to her. . . ."

"And the pastor?" asked Reb.

"Broke his neck after Ah got back." As if in apology, he added, "Just before he died, there was this look of forgiveness in his eyes. He seemed to understand. . . ."

Something in me lifted my left hand to my shoulder to strike Bannon. With my other hand I lowered it, as one might press down a mechanical thing gone haywire, and said, to keep this wild man calm, "We all have our work, I guess."

"Indeedy." He sucked his teeth. "And it wasn't afore long that Ah come to see that the world would always have need for mah specialty. There ain't many men what kin catch, or kill, a Negro the *right* way."

"There is," I ventured, "a right and wrong way to this?"

The Soulcatcher reached for his jug and poured three fingers of warm whiskey into his cup. Leaning back against the log, he rubbed his legs to start blood circulating again. A last rush of chandoo locked in my system, inactive until now, chose that moment to come to life, doubling my vision for an instant, twinning Bannon and the trees behind him. Time dissolved into a deeper silence, the universe breathing outward—a god's exhalation in sleep—then in, pointlessly. It was as though we were the last men in the world, survivers of a holocaust at Hegel's end of history, trying to figure out what went wrong. And then the Soulcatcher laughed:

"You don't just walk hup to a Negro, especially one what's passin', and say, 'Ain't you master so-and-so's boy?' No, it's a more delicate, difficult hunt." Here he stared into his cup. "When you *really* after a man with a price on his head, you forgit for the hunt that you the hunter. You get hup at the cracka dawn and creep ovah to where that Negro is hidin'. It ain't so much in overpowerin' him physically, when you huntin' a Negro, as it is mentally. Yo mind has to soak hup his mind. His heart." Here he shogged down a mouthful of corn and cringed. "The Negro-hunt depends on how you use destiny. You let destiny outrace and nail down the Negro you after. From the get-go, hours afore Ah spot him, there's this thing Ah do, like throwin' mah voice. Ah calls his name. The name his master used. *Andrew,* Ah says, if his name be Andrew; *Andrew.*" I stiffened inwardly, but gave no sign. "Mah feelin's, and my voice, fly out to fasten onto that Negro. He senses me afore he sees me. You *become* a Negro by lettin' yoself see what he sees, feel what he feels, want what he wants. What does he want?" The Soulcatcher winked at Reb, who was brutally silent, chipped from stone. "Respectability. In his bones he wants to be able to walk down the street and be unnoticed—not *ignored,* which means you seen him and looked away, but unnoticed like people who have a right to be somewheres. He wants what them poets hate: mediocrity. A tame, teacup-passin', uneventful life. Not to go against the law but hug it. A comfortable, hardworkin' life among the Many. Don't seem like much to ask, do it?" This he put to Reb; my friend did not answer. But this, too, was an answer. "It wears him down, ya know? Investin' so much to get so little. It starts showin'. You look for the man who's policin' hisself, tryin' his level best to be *average.* That's yo Negro." Here he held his cup in both hands. "You nail his soul so he can't slip away. Even 'fore he knows you been watchin' him, he's already in leg irons. When you really onto him, the only person who knows he's a runaway—almost somebody he kin trust—you tap him gently on his shoulder, and he knows; it's the Call he's waited for his whole life. His capture happens like a wish, somethin' he wants, a destiny that come from inside him, not outside. And me, Ah'm just Gawd's instrument for this, Master Harris, his humble tool, and Ah never finish the kill 'til the prey desires hit."

I said nothing. He did not find me ripe for plucking; he would wait—if his tale could be trusted—until I turned my neck toward the knife. It was a bizarre story, the strangest yet in this odyssey, but it explained (for me) Bannon's Negroid speech, his black idiosyncrasies, tics absorbed from the countless bondsmen he'd assassinated.

"The hunt," said Bannon, suddenly, "is also sweetah when you

115

give the prey a li'l room to run. If Ah ever meet a Negro Ah can't catch, Ah'll quit!"

"Horace," I said, nodding to Reb, "my man and I will travel tonight after all. We've put you out, and I think we can make Spartanburg by daybreak."

"Then Ah'll break camp and take you." Bannon stood quickly, dusting off the seat of his trousers. "Wouldn't do to travel on foot, sick as you look. Besides, Ah know a doctor there—no butchering veterinarian—who kin see to yo bruises." He whipped out a pearl-handled, single-shot derringer, the sort of pistol a brothel keeper might conceal in his boot, from his pocket, played with it, pointed it at me, but remained as polite and unthreatening as a colored preacher talking to the Devil. "Do you know how Ah bagged my fust Negro passin' fo' white?"

I gazed diagonally across the fire at him. The Soulcatcher made another stage wait. Then:

"He lit out from a farm in Wareshoals and reestablished hisself in Due West. Got pretty good at passin', too. They give him this job at a factory. You know what happened?" Bannon grinned; he had four—maybe five—gumline cavities. "His foreman asked him to work on a holiday. This Negro thought on it a spell. He said, 'If'n the Lord's willin', and if Ah sees next sweet potato pickin' time.' Might's well as hung a sign round his neck, sayin' somethin' as bootblack as that." The Soulcatcher, slapping his knee, howled.

My polite laughter rang false, even to me—a timed laugh I'd perfected at Leviathan, which I let linger for a few breaths.

The Soulcatcher only smiled. They lifted me, cloak and all, into the back of the buckboard, and, as Bannon threw dirt on his campfire, Reb pulled the thick tarpaulin over me slowly in order to whisper, "Andrew"—the Coffinmaker only called me Andrew when scared or feeling sappy—"you ain't goin' off with this lunatic, are you?"

"Do we have a choice?"

In the clan-state of the Allmuseri, the griots, Reb told me, advised a man to devote no more than five seconds to untangling any problem. At the end of four, Reb admitted, "No, but you *heard* him! He's crazy—he'll kill you if you slip."

"Then I won't slip."

"That ain't what you said six hours ago."

Reb, poor Reb, I thought; I fumbled round the tarpaulin for his hand, then squeezed his thick, work-ruined fingers. "Maybe rabbits enjoy the hunt, too."

If the Coffinmaker had not been convinced before that I suffered brain damage, now he was sure, and for aught I know, that may be the truth of it, for I found the Soulcatcher's *modus operandi* reassuring; because I knew his techniques, the strategies that poisoned my father, I could stare them down, second-guess Bannon and escape destruction. This struck me as a more certain course, a greater triumph than following the north star. The man did not, on principle, act until a runaway lost hope—this was the origin of all error—and haplessly lay his head on the block; Bannon could not, given his code, the aesthetic laws he lived by, interfere. And, sir, if he was fool enough not to interfere, for whatever reasons, what in this world could I not accomplish?

These were my thoughts—feverish, I admit, the source of my new-found confidence during the twelve hours I rode in the rear of the rocking wagon, beneath a length of tarpaulin that admitted only tiny spicules of milky light like a stretch of stars above me, Reb up front beside Bannon, who cracked a whip over his horses across sumps, loblollies, and thank-you-ma'ams between Belton and Spartanburg. By mid-morning we arrived, powdered with cerise road dust, at the west end of the little town. It wasn't much to write home about. Spartanburg's muddy streets were lined with clapboard structures at the far end. Down that row were houses of public entertainment, two banks, a hotel, brothels, eight saloons, a Big Store, tonsorial parlors, livery stable and saddleshop (combined), a two-story courthouse crested by a cupola, and a small whitewashed church (Anabaptist).

A rather commonplace, pre–Civil War town, but I ask the reader to ride in with me, and see how the case goes.

VIII

ON THE NATURE OF SLAVE NARRATIVES

Before unpacking our suitcases in Spartanburg, it is necessary to speak briefly, and apologetically, about the *form* of this Narrative, which, as you have seen, often "worries," as Mattie Hawkins might say, the formal conventions—as we define them—of the Negro Slave Narrative. To glimpse fully the wheels as they whir beneath the stage, we must first sort and shift awhile in the archival tomb of literary history.

Of the Slave Narratives that come down to us, there are, if I have done my homework, three kinds: (1) the twentieth-century interviews, conducted during the Great Depression by the Federal Writer's Work Project, with black citizens born before 1863; (2) the fraudulent "narratives" of runaway slaves commissioned by the Abolitionist Movement as propaganda for Negro manumission; and, finally, (3) authentic narratives written by bondsmen who decided one afternoon to haul hips for the Mason-Dixon line. These last narratives have, as I will demonstrate, a long pedigree that makes philosophical play with the form less outrageous than you might think.

As a *form*, the third kind of Slave Narrative is related, as distant cousins are related, to the Puritan Narrative, a document written specifically by a member of a religious American community to show—as testimony—that he has accepted Christ. Here the narrative movement is from sin to salvation; it is with only slight variation that this narrative *oomph* becomes, in the work of a Douglass, a progress from slavery to freedom. In point of fact, the movements in the Slave Narrative from slavery (sin) to freedom (salvation) are identical to those of the Puritan Narrative, and *both* these genuinely American forms are the offspring of that hoary confession by the first philosophical black writer: Saint Augustine. In *The Confessions* we notice (and perceive also in the Slave and Puritan Narratives) a nearly Platonic movement from ignorance to wisdom, nonbeing to being. No form, I should note, *loses* its ancestry; rather, these meanings accumulate in layers of tissue as the form evolves.

It is perhaps safe to conjecture that the Slave Narrative proper whistles and hums with this history, to say nothing of the nineteenth-century picaresque novel and story of manners, and all a modern writer need do is dig, dig, dig—call it spadework—until the form surrenders its diverse secrets. However, this hole is very deep, the archaeological work slow, and already you are frowning impatiently, and with good reason, about this essayist interlude. (Only one more intermission follows; I promise.) We will, therefore, rejoin the action in Spartanburg, where Horace Bannon is unloading the human cargo from his wagon.

IX

THE UNDERCLIFFS.
WRITING AND TEACHING.
THE COFFINMAKER'S DECISION

The physician is talking:

"You, my young friend, I mean you, William Harris, *you*, sir, are suffering from a few minor physical complaints, not one of which is fatal, but taken all together, and if not watched closely, their federation will lead to the medical equivalent of the Panic of 1837; you have, for a lad of two and twenty, the constitutional makeup of a matador, a very *old* matador, or perhaps his bull, an adrenal output suited for the Cro-Magnon Era, and, if I had not examined you myself—had I, for example, only seen these readings—I would conclude that my daughter, Peggy, who is much given to pranks, had dropped the neurological chart of an antediluvian shark on my desk. I do not recommend rest; I demand it. I also demand payment for this examination within the week because, after seeing your associates, I doubt that you will have *two*."

The physician—his name is Gerald Undercliff—was, as his attitude shows, a crypto-Schopenhauerean. Not for a minute do I mean to say that Dr. Undercliff had read *The World as Will and Representation*, though he had heard it mentioned at his club, but rather that the good doctor inclined to the opinion of society expressed in the Danzig philosopher's "Parable of the Porcupines": namely, that people, like porcupines, congregated for warmth against winter's chill, but pricked each other severely, and this forced them to disperse into the snow. However, the cold drives them together again, and once more they leap away. At last, after many hopeful turns of huddling and dispersing, they discover that the only tolerable condition for social intercourse is *keeping your distance*. They were, of course, never entirely warm, but neither were they pricked

Undercliff, a tender-eyed old southern gentleman, was blind enough to bump into doors without his bifocal glasses; when annoyed, he removed them, or perched them high on the great granite dome of his forehead, thereby reducing others, including Peggy Undercliff, to a pleasant blur. Retired, except for a few patients he numbered as old friends, with a fertility god's belly, Undercliff, who regarded any man who claimed to be religious as a rascal, divided Americans, regardless of race, into two classes: the Annoying and the Very Annoying (I figured in the second group), and if he had a single good feature, it was his daughter. It was as if the last leather-winged pterodactyl had sired a dove, and it was Peggy Undercliff who let us in after the doctor latched his door.

He did more than latch his door, he drew his curtains when Bannon's buckboard appeared, made his daughter stop playing the piano, and stood, holding his breath, as we rapped the knocker on what was easily the most beautiful house in Spartanburg. A splendid house for the time. A triple-chimneyed Andrew Jackson Downing house with cornices and arched windows, priceless furniture inside (John Henry Porter), paintings (Hudson River School), and curtained bookcases. His laboratory, where we sat, I barechested on a stool, his daughter behind me, was *visually* noisy: a riot of papers, fruitcores everywhere except in his wastebasket, tools I did not understand, and phrenological heads; it so resembled Ezekiel's study, and so differed from the Vet's barn, that I immediately felt comfortable.

Dr. Undercliff never felt comfortable.

"That's all," he said. "You can leave now. Go! Get a second opinion! Many of your troubles will clear up, I believe, with a daily application of soap. You have heard of soap? A remarkable medical breakthrough. I suggest you experience its healing powers twice daily, upon rising and once before bed. And something else. . . ." He pulled the curtains to his bookshelf, frowned at the titles, then brought down a volume, which he handed to me. "You will do well to study this, Mister Harris, beginning with the pages I've marked." Then he galumphed from his lab, saying to his daughter as she plopped onto the chair behind his desk and picked up a pear, "Peggy, I will be in the garden. I leave it to you to determine this gentleman's fee."

It was Benjamin Franklin's *Autobiography* that Undercliff gave me; he'd turned down the pages featuring Franklin's famous Thirteen Virtues, had even, I noticed, filled out the chart to pinpoint his own shortcomings, marking each square with an *X* for a virtue consistently achieved during the week:

TEMPERANCE							
Eat Not to Dullness; Drink Not to Elevation							
	S	M	T	W	T	F	S
Temperance	X			X	X		
Silence							
Order	X X	X	X	X		X	
Resolution		X			X		
Frugality		X	X			X	
Industry		X	X	X			
Sincerity	X	X	X	X	X	X	X
Justice	X	X	X	X	X	X	X
Moderation	X	X			X		
Cleanliness			X			X	
Tranquility	X					X	X
Chastity	X	X	X	X	X	X	X
Humility							

Not much progress on Silence and Humility, it seemed to me, but who was I to judge?

"You shouldn't worry about my father, Mr. Harris," said Peggy. "He enjoys snapping at strangers. He didn't mean half of what he told you, it's just that he dislikes anyone who associates with Horace Bannon."

"No more than I," I said. "But must he be so . . . *cranky*."

"Bitter, not cranky." She smiled; it was as if the window to a prison sprang open suddenly. She began peeling, then biting into an overripe banana. "And it's because he never quite got over what happened to my mother. We moved here from New Orleans when I was three. Mother had her own business, you see, an art gallery; she was very independent, and would not leave until she sold it, and she wouldn't do *that* unless she saw the purchaser. So Father and I went ahead by coach. He found this house, which was built for William Grayson, whose poem *The Hireling and the Slave* Mother much admired, so he knew she would love it here. He arranged everything just so to please her, set up his practice, then wired for Mother to come." She licked her fingers. "Highwaymen raped, then murdered Mother in Georgia. My father lost the power of speech for a week. Nor did he eat. He did, however, telegraph my Aunt Olivia in Boston, who had instructions that, in the event of either of their deaths, they were to be cremated. This was done. Her urn was shipped to Spartanburg." I looked round, feeling that one of the huge vases in the lab, or hallway outside, might be this poor girl's mother. "Oh no," Peggy said, "she's not *here*." Her lips puckered. "She was lost in the mails—Mother is now, as Mr. Melville would say, in the Dead Letter Office somewhere."

"Dreadful!" I began pulling on my shirt. "And your father? How did he take this?"

"He loved it."

"Beg pardon—*loved* it, I heard you say?"

"Oh, he took it badly, but he likes to take things badly. Pleasant experiences make him uncomfortable. They make him suspicious. He's afraid they're a fraud, a trick of some kind. If she had not died, or been lost, he'd have no excuse for being a curmudgeon. Disasters," Peggy added, "confirm his belief that everything is disagreeable—except bullfights, he likes bullfights."

"A doctor and he enjoys violent sports?"

"We all need a day off," said Peggy.

"Then I must pay him." She offered me a pear. I polished it on the front of my shirt, then crunched through the skin; it was on the soft side, having been in the lab for perhaps a day too long. "But I have, as I've told you, only my manservant Reb. He will make for poor collateral."

"You have no job then, Mr. Harris?" asked Peggy.

"Ah, there you have me, madam. As your very own Melville has put it, 'Dollars damn me.' "

"You've read him?"

"I have met him, he is an old family acquaintance."

The pupils of her eyes, very gray with flecks of soft blue, enlarged a bit, as if she had only now come awake to my presence. Deep responded to deep. "I've wanted to talk about *Pierre* with someone for years! Father, you know, doesn't approve of novels. A tissue of ostrobogulous lies, he calls them. With the writer laughing behind each page at the reader's gullibility, and no one else in this dead, dead town *reads*, except for Mrs. Pomeroy, and all she reads is Anne Bradstreet!"

I bowed graciously. "I am, if nothing else, a reader of dry, nerve-deadening books, and delight in circuitous, literary conversations."

Peggy Undercliff gave me what I have often read described in popular fiction as "the eye," though I'll not swear on it, never having seen "the eye" at such close range before—it was, at any rate, a fluttering of her lashes accompanied by a soft indentation in her left cheek, a startlingly plastic pocket of flesh that appeared suddenly, vanished just as suddenly, and made me think: *gee whiz.* "If you are such an avid book reader, Mr. Harris—"

"Bill," I said, "you must call me Bill."

"—a philologist" (Peggy Undercliff trained herself, by the way, to finish five books a week and memorize ten new words a day), "then you could teach. Have you taught? Evelyn Pomeroy, that refocillated old poopnoddy who teaches everyone from fivers to farmers, would like nothing better than a vacation, and I know her pupils need a vacation from *her.*"

"Is this possible? I could repay your father then?"

"And tell me about Herman Melville."

Although I am no expert on women (I didn't have to tell you that), I must say that Peggy Undercliff did not compare to Flo Hatfield; she was (alas) physically as plain as a pike, having nothing distinctive about her hair (bisque) or eyes (like her father she wore bifocals, behind which her eyes ballooned), but she was, inly, ener-getic—an explosion of vitality, rather like a teapot set not to boil over but to bubble and steam, perhaps even beautiful in her vulnerability, candor, and openness. Sitting in her father's chair, with early light (gold) slanting through his east window, dustmotes swirling like mites, and rhododendrons visible just over the edge, Peggy had a casualness, a social ease that I found disarming. She was, if French will help, *déclassée* by choice; she possessed in good measure what is possibly a compassionate, intelligent individual's only defense in America: ironic distance. No wonder she found Spartanburg intolerable. Her speech, the way she reshaped language, which was (as with all women) primarily the way she affected the world, was oftentimes a meld of puns, graveyard humor, her father's habit of posing the rhetorical question or ending her sentences with a stress, and dry wit so devastatingly irreverent, and lightning fast, that no one could match her line for line. Certainly not the town farmers. Showing me her sheet music for Beethoven's Sixth Symphony, after I complimented her playing, which I'd heard briefly from the porch, she asked, "Do you know what he's doing now?"

"Beethoven? He died over thirty years ago!"

"Yes, I know. He's de-composing."

"That's depraved," I said. "Sick, sick, sick!"

Peggy glanced up at me, then down, was silent, for I had struck a nerve, then began writing my bill. "Everyone says that. I *am* sick, I suppose." For half a minute the only sound in the lab was her pen. She folded the paper once, then handed it to me. "You owe my father four dollars and fifty cents."

"As much as that?"

"You're sick, too, William Harris."

"But you misunderstand me. I never meant. . . ."

"I *know* what you meant." She picked another pear from the bowl, pushed her bifocals farther up on her nose with one finger, her father's gesture, and looked toward the door. "I suppose your servant is tired of sitting on the steps. If you have time later this afternoon—I'm sure you have a lot to do now—then I'll introduce you to Mrs. Pomeroy. Are you sure you don't know her, Mr. Harris? She has a hairlip and is quite old—Daddy's already filled out a certificate of death for her; she's quite out of fuel now and running on the fumes, a real zombie, the Salem witch that got away, but perhaps *you* were one of her students years ago. Is that possible?"

At the door I held up my hands. "You win."

Leaning against the architrave to the lab, she said, one cheek
distended by a mouthful of pearmeat:

"I always do."

Evelyn Pomeroy proved to be less a product of E. T. A. Hoff-
mann than Peggy Undercliff promised, and had, I discovered, the
charm of a once beautiful woman—a novelist—quietly going mad.
Now I understood Dr. Undercliff's remarks. At twenty-six, Mrs.
Pomeroy had published one book, a little-read but critically ac-
claimed *roman à clef* ("This must be hailed as one of the great novels
of the nineteenth century," said one giddy reviewer, who no doubt
regretted his enthusiasm later) that cost her a husband (the protag-
onist) and brought one lawsuit (her cousin) that stuck. Her second
book, on which Evelyn Pomeroy had written 12,000 pages, was,
after thirty years, "almost finished, Mr. Harris, I'm fine-tuning it
now." You know what that means. Every day was a crucifixion.
Every year past the publication date of her first book cemented her
silence, confirmed the suspicions of critics—and Evelyn Pomeroy
herself—that the magic had been a mistake that first time. A fluke.
But she did not despair. In the meantime, to make ends meet, she
decided to teach school. This was her twenty-fifth year of teaching.
She slept on a bed behind her blackboard, kept her clothes in a
trunk behind the world map, and took meals at her huge desk.
Although not a novelist myself, I thought these reduced circumstances dreadful, this quiet, lonely fight to regain her former glory
and say *Ha!* to her enemies; but Evelyn Pomeroy carried the burden of failure well. She held no grudges. She had grief *without*
grievances, and this, dear reader, is an achievement beyond art.
Unlike most one-shot, flash-in-the-pan, Johnny-one-note novelists
(she described herself ruthlessly, using the remarks of her worst
detractors), Evelyn still loved and lived for the joy of literature and
music (she'd been Peggy's piano teacher years before), and when
this tiny, frail woman with a neck like a trumpet laughed, her whole
face changed, her chin folded into her throat, her green eyes flashed,
and no one—absolutely no one—in Spartanburg could not secretly
admire her.

However, none of this candies over the fact that Evelyn Pomeroy was crazy. She ironed her paper money. She *oiled* the leaves of plants along the schoolhouse window to make them, as she said, "presentable"; she broomswept the backyard, ankle-high with weeds. During my fifteen-minute interview with her, over milktea and a delicious meatpie, Evelyn Pomeroy carried the conversation.

"Peggy Undercliff recommends you highly, Mr. Harris, and I *do* listen to the dear girl's opinions. She's turned out quite well, though none of us really expected much from her."

"No?" I sipped my tea. "May I ask why?"

"Well, I suppose there's no harm in telling you." Her hands, I noticed, trembled faintly; she kept them under the table, or always held an object—a pen or spoon—to hide the shaking. It was now her napkin. "When Peggy's mother left Gerald to run off with that terrible man, the traveling miracle-cure salesman—"

"One moment. It was my understanding that Mrs. Undercliff's ashes were misrouted in the U.S. mails."

The schoolteacher had heard this. She was, I learned, the historian of Spartanburg, the biographer of its five hundred citizens, though she wrote nothing.

"Peggy prefers that story." Evelyn now played with her fork. "She was *quite* a problem, I can tell you. She was never very popular with the other children, and what pleasure she found was mainly in reading books—romances—and telling her own stories. I did not discourage this. She wrote her first story, about a white girl who is unloved and wakes up one morning as a Negro boy, when she was six, with a big joke-quill twice her size, the kind used for advertising, resting it on her shoulder. No," Evelyn whispered, leaning toward me, "she does not live entirely in the real world."

"Not in the White World, you mean?"

That pulled Evelyn Pomeroy up short. "I suppose not. The Negro *is* a creature of romance, isn't he? How perceptive of you, Mr. Harris." She poured me more tea to the rim. "But let us hope her fascination with them goes no farther than fantasy."

In plain terms, the job was mine for the asking. Evelyn Pomeroy was eager for a month or two to finish her new novel, preferably miles from Spartanburg. She did administer a few tests that afternoon—plumbing my knowledge of philosophy and physics,

127

listening as I read from the Bible, but this examination was nothing after the pansophical education provided me by Master Polkinghorne. Within two days she moved out, Reb and I moved in, and I began the thankless, mind-destroying, spirit-sucking duty of teaching fifteen adults (nights) and twenty-seven children (days) the inner mysteries of the Compound Sentence. Consider: At nine I knew the Platonic Worldview like a part of my body, but I was now correcting comma splices; at fifteen I had memorized the Ten Tropes of Sextus Empiricus, but now I spent each afternoon hunting for transitions in papers that did not justify the killing of a tree. I could not shake the feeling, those first few weeks, that teaching was, when you looked hard enough at it, the perfect racket, a real scam, the last refuge of respectability for idle, fugitive intellectuals and cashiered artists who, skidding on their faces toward middle age (or starvation), wanted both to appear productive and to loaf for a living. Perhaps I am too severe. It was mass education, this cattle-herding to enlightenment, not the special interpenetration of pupil and tutor, artist and apprentice, that brought out the unhappy conclusion that you couldn't teach *anything*. Not anything vital, at least, for the heart was the only genuine schoolhouse, the only gymnasium where the spirit was tried.

Nevertheless, I was pleased to be employed. I was no less pleased that my passage into the White World went unmarked. The ease with which I buried Andrew Hawkins forever and built a new life as William Harris was not peculiar. The Negro, if I may digress to develop my theme of teaching, is, as Reb told me, the finest student of the White World, the one pupil in the classroom who watches himself watching the others, absorbing the habits and body language of his teachers, his fellow students. Now, *some* tics don't transfer to his world. You see this vividly in the black girl, very beautiful in her own terms, who tosses back her head to get the hair out of her eyes. There *is* no hair in her eyes. But she has seen, absorbed this gesture. So, too, had I picked up from the Polkinghornes, from Ezekiel and others the quirks that (now) proved so valuable in presenting a new identity to Evelyn Pomeroy and Dr. Undercliff, who provided me with small doses of laudanum, which cured me of chandoo; his daughter visited my classroom often to confound me with questions about Melville; Reb found work with Spartanburg's mortician, for which he was paid handsomely, by slave standards. And the Soulcatcher?

He was one of my night students, one of the fifteen adults, sharecroppers and shopkeepers in Spartanburg who hoped to get a better handle on the Good Book, maybe even to challenge the Reverend Wendell Blake on narrow matters of exegesis at the Anabaptist Church on Main Street, or wanted simply to keep abreast of their children, or to understand agricultural literature. Reading was a skill rarely seen in the Old South. Some brought the books they wished to work on. Reb hung up their coats as they came in. Bannon, seated in the front row, a bear crammed into a child's seat, with his derringer bulging the soft leather of his boot, finger-read his way, after I insisted, through Aurelius' *Meditations,* a work he found objectionable, but hearing him read aloud, tripping on each syllable like a man stepping down cellar stairs into the dark, sounding out words like a schoolboy, lessened my fear of him by a little. After class one evening, he hung back until the others filed out, then helped me stack primers on the bookshelf.

"Wouldn'ta thought you'd do this well," he admitted. "You should heah what they say 'bout you in town. These people been tryin' to git a teacher to replace Evelyn Pomeroy ever since she started taking off her clothes in class—she done that once to git their attention. Be a shame," he bent to lift a book from the floor, "if you had to go."

"I've no intention of leaving."

Reb threw me a look of panic.

"At least not until I've made a little money and paid my debts. I started this trip with a promise to prove . . . to someone that I was ready for independence. I can do that here." With one hand I touched my chest. "I *am* doing that here."

"I meant," put in Bannon, "that hit'd be a shame to disappoint these people. Hit's happened befo'. They hired a sheriff who turned out to be Lorenzo Phillips, the fellah who run a prostitution ring fo' kids in Chattanooga." At the door he flicked his hatbrim with his fingers, head tilted. "He still in Spartanburg over to Two Hills. Yo man knows the place, he been there." And he left.

I asked Reb, "Where's Two Hills?"

"Mile from here." He pinched out the lamplights with fingertips so calloused he could not feel the flames, then looked across the room at me, invisible in the darkness, a disembodied voice. "It's a cemetery, Andrew."

Toward the end of our first month I received a letter from Evelyn Pomeroy, postmarked in New York, where she had contacted a publisher interested in her second novel. He offered her the opportunity to work as a proofreader in his office until her book was finished. "Contemporary fiction is so *sterile*, William," she wrote, "certainly the things I've been reading are empty. No one seems intellectually equipped to write with truth as their motive. A novel *should* be an experiential *feast*, a three-ring circus of humor, suspense, ideas and images, a whole world of people tied together by *plot*—I will not proofread it if there is no plot. Stylistically, these submissions are competent, most of them," she continued, "but our writers apparently have nothing to say, nothing positive; they are more interested, once they've published, in staying published at any price, showboating in the spotlight, even if they have to cannabalize their first work, or resort to formulae. This is so dispiriting. It's as if these books were written by Committee, or by the Sales Department here at Winters, Anderson, and Hoft. Reading these manuscripts has been an education for me—it is as if Publication were the (Slave) Auction of the mind. Yet, it gives me, personally, new hope," she confided in her last paragraph. "In an age of mediocre artists, as the Japanese say, it is easy to distinguish yourself, and I know my new book, *The Awakening of Eve Yoremop* (my name backwards; I can only write from experience), will go swimmingly into the marketplace."

Naturally, I did not show this letter to the Coffinmaker. Reb counted the days we tarried here. True, we had escaped the brutality of Leviathan, eluded like Brer Rabbit certain death in the Mine, and here in Spartanburg life went ahead—or didn't go ahead—in ways that did not offend reason. But there was, I admit, more freedom for me in this town than for my friend. Furthermore, I had taken an interest in Peggy Undercliff that Reb thought a flirtation with the noose. After work, when he returned home with his tools, after the little schoolhouse emptied, and I sat behind my

desk, grading papers, he would pace the rows of seats, and then—
to occupy his mind—begin ironing our clothes with rocks heated
in the fireplace.

"Freshmeat, you know yo business, but. . . ."

"Never," I say, "address me as Freshmeat, especially when anyone is within earshot. Don't even call me Andrew. It's William.
Master William, at that." Hunched over my book, I swing my eyes
left. "And you're *burning* that shirt!"

"Well, EXCUSE ME, Master William!"

He lifts the hot stone, burns the inner, uncalloused part of his
hand, then whoops, "Will that be *all,* sar, or will you be wantin' yo
milkbath, as usual, before retirin'?"

"No need to get ugly," I say. "You should relax and fix yourself
a cup of tea. And, Reb, while you're up, will you be a good fellow,
and bring me one, too?"

The Coffinmaker smashed, in order:

two desks;
four potted plants (begonias, carnations);
one window;
three glasses;
one trestle table.

He was glaring at me, as if selecting the organs he intended to
remove when I (standing on my desk) said, "I was only kidding!
My God, if it means that much to you, we'll leave at the end of the
week!"

Still breathing raggedly, standing in the middle of bookshelves
busted to flinderjigs, Reb shook his fist at me. "We'd better! This
place is *bad,* Freshmeat, I kin feel it. If you ain't ready in two days,
I'm goin' without you, even if I *do* get caught!"

I thought it best to stay on my desk.

"Fair enough," I said. "We leave Sunday evening."

Plainly, it was *not* a good idea to show Evelyn Pomeroy's letter
to Reb. In all Spartanburg, it seemed the only person with whom I
could discuss my possibly extended employment, now that Evelyn
was working in New York, was Peggy Undercliff. The occasion
presented itself on Sunday afternoon at a dinner she twisted her

father's arm (literally) to arrange. "You sit *here*," Peggy pulled a chair out for me at a table of meadhouse proportions, then the seat next to it, "and, Daddy, you sit *here*."

"You want me to sit *beside* Mr. Harris?"

"So you can talk."

"Eat and *digest* my food beside Mr. Harris?"

"Daddy, I'm going to hit you as soon as I find something."

The doctor lowered himself to the chair, like someone slipping into a hot bath, both hands on the chairarms, dropping his rear slowly to the cushion. "I am *pleased*," he finally looked at me, "that you have discovered soap." His daughter placed a bowl of steaming clam chowder under his nose, which Undercliff watched as if looking for signs of life beneath the surface. "Have you also dusted off Edwin Harris' flintlock?"

I was tying a napkin round my neck. "Whose flintlock?"

"Your grandfather's," he said. "Didn't you tell us your grandfather fought in the Revolutionary War?"

"Oh *him!*" My soupspoon clattered to the floor. "Why should I dust that off, sir?"

"There's a war coming," said Undercliff, "a greater war than anything seen in this country, and all on account of the Negro. I rather thought," he tasted his soup cautiously, "a man with your background—war heroes and whatnot—would leap at the opportunity to prove himself as good as his predecessors."

You are wondering, I imagine, about differences in the White and Black worlds. Well, here is the first: this feeling in both that the past is threatening; in the Black World a threat because there *is* no history worth mentioning, only family scenarios of deprivation and a bitter struggle—and failure—against slavery, which leads to despair, the dread in later generations that they are the first truly historical members of their clan; and in the White World the past is also a threat, but here because, in many cases, the triumphs of predecessors are suffocating, a legend to live up to, or to reject (with a good deal of guilt), the anxiety that these ghosts watch you at all times, tsk-tsking because you have let them down: a feeling that everything significant has been done, the world is finished. An especially painful form of despair, I thought, and I admit to suddenly despising Edwin Harris for placing this burden upon me, although I had spun him from my imagination. No matter; I felt uneasy.

"I am not, like my Grandpapa, a fighting man, Dr. Undercliff."

The doctor said, "I can see that."

"Can't you two talk *nice!*" wailed Peggy. She had seated herself across the table; there was, if I was not mistaken, a watery glint in her eyes. "I asked you to dinner because I wanted you to get *along!* I wanted you to *like* William!"

"But I do like William." Undercliff forced himself to smile—it resembled the effort a paralyzed man puts into his first steps. "If he had not rejected his grandfather's bloody history, I would have shown him to the door. He has graduated in that one instant from the Very Annoying to the Annoying."

Both Peggy Undercliff and I registered shock. Beyond this recategorization no man could aspire. "Thank you," my voice nearly failed me. "Peggy, I am afraid that I am too moved at this moment to do your meal justice."

The doctor placed his napkin on the table.

"William, let us step into the laboratory for a moment. There is a problem I wish to discuss with you. A matter of great importance to me. And to Peggy. Will you excuse us?"

"No," she said, "but you're going off even if I don't."

In Dr. Undercliff's lab, he brought forth cigars. Then bade me sit. He poured us both brandy. "You enjoy my daughter's company, don't you, William?"

"Yes, she has been a true friend."

"Only that?" he asked. "A friend?"

Anger flashed through my chest. "If you're suggesting, sir, that I have taken indecent liberties with your—"

"No, no. . . ." The doctor reddened. "Nothing like that. I am simply saying that you are the only man who has held Peggy's interest for more than a day. I cannot escape her references to what you have said, William, or the way you have improved education at Evelyn Pomeroy's school. . . ."

"Your daughter is too kind."

"Yes, she *is* too kind for a golden-throated tramp who has lied about his past!" Undercliff's features, the tightening of his eyes, were ferocious in the half-lit lab. "I have inquired into your family,

133

William Harris, or whatever your name is. There *was* no Edwin Harris decorated during the war. Not *any* war!" He stabbed his cigar out in the fruitbowl. "You have lied about your background, but the feeling my daughter has for you is not false. I, therefore, am going to make you an offer."

In my chair I was scattered. "I am all ears."

"Well should you be, young man, because if you do *any*thing to disappoint Peggy, if I see her so much as in tears *once,* I will inform the sheriff of my suspicions. I have no idea what you are hiding—wife desertion or theft (you do not have the stomach for serious crimes). It matters not a whit to me. But I will surely dig yet deeper, and see you hang, if the only thing of value to me is hurt by her association with you. That includes, when the time comes, a failure to propose marriage."

"I understand fully, sir."

Undercliff opened his laboratory door. "Pray you do, William."

The dinner became much like the Last Supper for me. Dr. Undercliff's appetite was hearty. He even joked with his daughter. But Peggy sensed the change in me. She asked, "What happened to you two in there?" Her father said, between mouthfuls, "We have finally come to terms." This pleased her greatly. After dessert, I excused myself and dragged home to the schoolhouse. Reb met me outside. With a stick and satchel he had made a traveling bag, which lay inside the door. I could not meet his eyes, passed him without a word, and slumped behind my desk.

"Freshmeat," said Reb. "It's Sunday evening. You can see the North Star, if you look up." He came and stood above me, a black giant whose body contained enough violence to take a wagon apart nail by nail, but who chose gentleness. Most of the time. "Can't go north without you, nigguh."

"You have to. Undercliff peeped my game; I can't go."

He took a breath. He was counting, I could tell, to five. At the end of three seconds, Reb put his hand on the back of my neck and squeezed. He exhaled, "If you get up to Chicago, look for the only colored casketshop in town. That'll be me, Andrew." And then, without looking back, the Coffinmaker stepped outside.

X

THE CALL

Horace Bannon left Spartanburg on Monday morning. Not twelve hours after Reb struck north, the bounty hunter, I was told, turned his war-horse, with enough firepower to exterminate all the timberwolves in South Carolina, in that direction. Two weeks passed. Weeks when I could not prepare lectures properly; I checked each evening at the taverns, the hotels, and the brothels (Bannon's second home) for any news of the Soul-catcher's return. His favorite whore, a great-breasted gorgon named Mamie, who wasn't bad, if you liked deep-sixing in flesh, drowning in a bog of waxy meat, said, "Godamercy, sugah, he don't tell me *nothin'!* He's a strange one. Did you know Horace gets erections at funerals—his emotions get crossed all the time." My heart sank. If he had overtaken Reb, would he return him to Flo Hatfield? Worse, would Bannon—or Leviathan's overseers—come for me? The Soulcatcher, to be sure, would be tight-lipped as a Sioux; he would not lift a finger if they held matches to Reb's face, or fooled with his testicles, or amputated—I remembered the Vet—until he cracked. Bigger men had been whittled down to kindling. For the first time in Spartanburg, for the first time in twenty years, I felt utterly alone. And afraid. If Reb was recaptured, my life as William Harris would not be worth a guinea.

And then Peggy Undercliff proposed.

No, she didn't exactly propose. What Peggy did was plant mines on every path except one, then, looking at me over her shoulder, asked, "Coming?"

We sat in a tavern called the Motley Cow, beneath lanterns lining walls pictured with crude paintings of wagons, wild forests, the L-shaped room softly dark, a little too warm, in late-afternoon light. Peggy was not drinking, legally. House rules forbade women buying liquor. They could sit, however, if accompanied by a man, in a special section adjacent to the bar. This practice put Peggy in bad temper. She boldly slugged whiskey from my glass, she crossed her eyes at Gene Sullivan, the saloonkeeper. How could he object? If you crossed her in this town, Gerald Undercliff might mistake your chart for someone else's and give you the wrong operation. (Phlebotomy, Undercliff said, was his favorite cure for the Very Annoying.) I stared, gloomily, into my glass, swirling the contents in a counter-clockwise motion, my mind on the road to Chicago.

"William!" Peggy's fist made the table jump. "If you don't ask me to marry you this very minute, I'm going to tell *every*one you're 'funny'!"

"Marriage? Fruity," I often called her Fruity, an affectionate sobriquet, given her diet of pears, bananas, and apples, "I'd marry you tomorrow, if my life was in order. Should Mrs. Pomeroy return. . . ."

"She won't be back any sooner than that man of yours who ran away, William, and you *know* it!"

"Fruity," I lowered my voice, "there are things about Reb and I that I haven't told you."

"You *are* funny?"

"Disgustingly heterosexual, a Benedict Arnold in the war between the sexes—"

"William, if you don't get down on your knees right now, I'll throw myself under a train. Wait. We don't have trains here. A stagecoach, then."

On the floor I spread my handkerchief, planted my right knee thereon, pressed my hands together, and proposed. As this was said, the other customers cheered. Sullivan offered drinks on the house.

"Good." She yanked on a pair of butter-colored gloves. "Now you can tell Daddy."

Dr. Undercliff, as was his habit, spent late afternoons in the garden behind his house; we found him removing weeds with a technique—swearing and hacking—that did not bode well for his performance of surgery. Puffing, wearing his ex-wife's flowered bonnet, he gouged around artichokes with an old, rusted scalpel. The doctor was an even color of pink. He was breathing like a locomotive. "Let no one tell you," he huffed, "that gardening, help-ing things grow, is Christian. It's *conceit,* William!" Cautiously, we followed him into the sitting room. Peggy served lemonade and, after a moment, her father said, "Creation doesn't *care!* Is a ruta-baga grateful? Can a carrot lick your hand? Head back, he drained his glass. Then belched. "The only things we cultivate, plants or people, are the things we plan to *eat.*"

Peggy gave him a moment to catch his wind. "William has proposed marriage. He would like your blessing."

"Is this April first, Peggy?" he asked. "If you're serious, you'd better have him analyzed first."

She drew back her arm to peg a candlesnuffer. The doctor threw up his hand. "Blessings, my dear, are as plentiful as green peas. Take all you wish." He poured more lemonade. "I would wish you, as they say, happiness, too, but I fear there *is* no happiness; it is an invention of the poets. *Vitae nomen quidem est vita, opus autem mors.*" Slumped halfway down in his chair, he thought a moment, the glass on his belly. "I wish you what the Greeks called *arete,* 'doing beautifully what needs to be done.' Not much to dance the turkey buzzard about in that, I daresay, but a man sleeps well at night, with *arete,* develops no digestive trouble, or spiritual afflic-tions, and demanding more than this *ataraxia*—another Greek no-tion—is tempting God's patience." Undercliff poured enough lemonade to toast our engagement. "Tomorrow I will talk to Wen-dell Blake. Now, he's a fool, I agree. All ministers are fools. For most people, William, the spinal cord is quite enough; the brain is redundant. But the problem is that even fools have their place in the Grand Design, bumblers hurled down from Central Casting just to hand Brunhilde her shield."

Peggy exhaled, shaking her head. "You're in rare form this afternoon."

"I'm almost happy." He smiled, painfully: a warlock with a full tummy. "Can't you tell?"

My prospective father-in-law was, as he claims, almost happy. At least as happy as a man can be when he frequently said, "When you have had as many patients as I have, William, and performed as many deliveries, it's not unlike seeing a magician's trick one time too many. You *know* the damned rabbit's inside the top hat. The trick," Undercliff told me the night he invited me to his Club, whose members included the mayor, town sheriff, and two land-owners born with half of Spartanburg in their hip pockets—"the trick, young William, was only meant to be seen *once*." To do him justice, Dr. Undercliff was, for all his irritability, a generous man. He promised to contribute as a wedding present the downpayment on a cabin west of town, which, he added, in a stroke of understate-ment, "needs work." "Sir," I reached for his cold, liver-spotted hands, "Heaven be praised. . . ." He said, "Not a word more, William. I would do this for *any*one my daughter married." Perhaps he meant this. Or perhaps he thought, given the obscurity of my origins, that property—the very obligation of property—would keep my nose clean. Be not mistaken. He still didn't trust me. All the papers were in Peggy's name. Then why this gift?

After our engagement was announced, as the wedding ap-proached, and we talked more of the ceremony, I think I saw the reason for Undercliff's generosity, for Peggy's anxiety about mar-riage. I will not dwell on this, only long enough to say that women were dying for young, eligible men in the slaveholding South. Not *any* man would do, of course. Southern custom blinked at, or openly approved in places, the practice of mail-order brides, the men involved being, on the whole, workers flung into New World waste-lands. But what of widows? Or women who refused to stop think-ing in order to get a husband? Or took a profession? Certain it was that Spartanburg offered no eligible men to satisfy a woman of culture, except Reverend Blake, who was fifty-six going on eighty: the last Pelagian. Peggy's prerequisites for a husband, although drawn from the heroes of pathos-ridden novels by Wilkie Collins, whose formula was "Make 'em laugh, make 'em cry, make 'em wait," were not so outlandish as Flo Hatfield's. Yet, again I found myself facing, in my fiancée, the ancient track upon which the spirit endlessly traversed: *loneliness—love,* exacerbated in her case by the fear that all her early advantages, her privileges, her father's power in Spartanburg, narrowed her future to (a) homosexuality, the sympathy and sure touch of another woman, which few men can fake, or (b) the bitter life of singularity (a metaphysical outrage) of the intelligent, talented woman living in something like house arrest, haunting dustwebbed rooms she played in five decades before.

This deep insult Undercliff did not want for his daughter. Nor Lesbianism. There were, according to Evelyn Pomeroy, town historian, a few childhood incidents with Nora Sullivan, the youngest daughter of Spartanburg's saloonkeeper, the natural curiosity of girls who, sequestered from boys, spent their pent-up humors in caresses both frightening and faintly pleasant, the experience beginning innocently enough with talk about boys, what they'd seen through the window of their parent's bedroom (Nora's, not Peggy's, for Gerald Undercliff's greatest virtue—or complaint—was chastity), or in the stables, and then, to demonstrate, a small hand moves toward—never mind. Lord knows, I was not the ideal husband for Peggy Undercliff. My life was a patchwork of lies. My personality whipstitched from a dozen sources. But the doctor was right about one thing: Virtue was doing beautifully what the moment demanded.

To shorten the story of our courtship, the moment demanded—on July 23, 1860—a new, subtle, loss of identity. A moment to explain: The night before our wedding I forgot instructions the instant I heard them; I put my lingerie on backwards. Burned my black, velvet waistcoat chainsmoking myself into a sore throat. Dr. Undercliff, to lower my blood pressure, prescribed a sedative, which made me sleep to within an hour of the ceremony. He came to the schoolhouse, roused and escorted me to the church by three. As I waited, pulling at my tight collar, adjusting my eyes to changing light patterns at the front of the church, my fob-top boots pinching, I heard organ music begin behind me. The dream, if this was a dream (so it seemed), was remarkably thorough—a spectacle staged so often I could not, at first, truly feel that I, as an individual, mattered in the least. We were *fed*, I thought, into a form that flattened out our humanity. My liberal-humanist hackles rose. Better we should create our *own* ceremony! Then my gaze went to the old woman, Beatrice Jackson, who commanded the organ and twisted her head to squint as Peggy's bridesmaids (three girls from the choir) walked down the aisle in flesh-pink, flowing dresses, and I saw it. I saw it clearly. I saw it with the simplicity of a child: every molecule of the old woman, every wrinkle, every cell

139

and ancient desire wrecked or realized in her seventy-eight years, gave the abstract form flesh, glorified this woman—all of us; all through a ceremony that suspended Time. The heart knew nothing of hours. Minutes. It moved on a plane above history, error. The good doctor straightened his glasses. He came forward, bordered by fifty guests, with Peggy against the background of a stained glass window awash with sunlight, the church constructed such that light rippled, ever richer, as it neared the pulpit, like Platonic *nous* emanating from the One. The organist wept. Peggy, holding a spray of roses, wore a white dress with an empire collar. Flowers were embroidered on her bust, her collar, her sleeves. Tears came flying down behind her fishnet veil. *Dearly beloved,* intoned Reverend Blake, *We are gathered here today.* . . . "William," croaked Peggy, "this is *dumb!* It's the gaudiest thing since the carnival came to town. It's silly. And unnecessarily noetic, and"—she hiccoughed; I gave her a hefty whack on her back—"wonderful!" Standing between us, the minister touched Peggy's arm. He hemmed. He hawed. And me? I heard only the run, the gentle ribboning of his words. A longish dream, I thought, pinching myself. Ouch. And, all at once, the guests weren't there. Only the Minister, the Woman, the Man. We stood, I felt, translated, lifted a few feet off the ground, exchanging replies in old, old voices in a different tongue we borrowed from our better selves—the people we were intended to be—in some parallel world, where the absences of this life were presences, the failures here triumphs there, a realm of changeless meaning for which the only portal was surrender.

After the ceremony this nearly mystical feeling of transport faded. We fell back into clock time (the saying of vows had taken only five minutes), fed each other forksful from a four-tiered cake, and received guests at Undercliff's many-roomed house. His parlor spilled over into the hallway, where well-wishers mingled, some wearing the dark blue frock and trousers, the black collars and cuff stripes of the Confederacy; overflowed with enough gifts to open a General Store. The party was difficult for Peggy. Crowds, sixty people in small groups, mirroring each other's postures, made her nauseated. It was not in her nature to enjoy spectacle, much less *be* the spectacle. After an hour of glad-handing and gliding through a blitz of laughter seriocomic chatter and tinkling glasses, her eyes were glazed. Undercliff stood, one hand behind his back, the other rubbing his nose, listening to a guest whose argument for the necessity of Negro slavery drew from the most recent studies in breeding, from the Old Testament, from history, and from the subordination of one creature by another in the natural world. Beneath his voice, in a lower strata of noise, one of the bridesmaids said, to her friend, "*My* problem is that whenever someone gives me a quick feel in a crowded room, I wheel round, naturally, and slug him, then I realize he's Indian, black, or Mexican, and I feel simply dreadful for the rest of the day because I've hurt someone disadvantaged." Sheets of smoke floated over their heads. Sixty voices blurred like a watercolor in the rain. "This country, as I see it, runs on economic *fact*," the guest who'd now trapped Undercliff in the kitchen was saying, "*not* good will. We brought these people here as one essential ingredient in an agrarian society." He kept touching the doctor's sleeve to hold his attention. "Their purpose as a group, and every group has its purpose, its mission, is tied in the Negroes' case to a specific form of production. . . ."

Behind me, as I strained to listen to Beatrice Jackson discuss her recent operation, another guest told a story to kill your appetite. "You've heard the one about the Chinese, Iranian, and Japanese fishermen? In a small boat on the ocean, right? And the boat springs a leak, right? The Chinese had so many coins in his pocket he sank. The Iranian couldn't keep his big mouth shut so he drowned. And the Japanese—get *this*—the Jap didn't know what to do so he copied the others. Ha-aaagh!" Undercliff's antagonist, to be heard, raised his voice an octave, "*If* there's war, and there will be, Doctor, if the Abolitionists get their way, and they will, then the North and the South will move to manufacture and no longer *need* the Negro. May I proceed? Well, we shall always need them poetically, but they will be, as a people, without a national purpose, if you follow me. It will be generations before the Nation discovers what to *do* with them. Can we ship them back, eh? Answer me that. Be careful now." Before Undercliff could answer, his antagonist said, "I ask you, is it reasonable to suppose they are more suited for a life in Africa than they are for full participation in democracy? They are here, but not really here. Do you see the dilemma?" Undercliff, then on his fifth cup of bitters, did not, but for the sake of form, said, "Life is certainly disappointing, isn't it?" His antagonist, a little miffed, said, "Do you see the problem?" to another guest, then looked at Peggy, who'd unlaced her shoes and was carrying them, "Do *you* see the problem?"

"Husband," she gripped my arm weakly with both hands, "if we don't go home I'm going to get sick on everyone."

Out of doors, the air was chilly when we slipped away from the party, the wind playing under Peggy's wedding dress, molding it to her legs. Away from the guests, in her father's wagon, I felt a silence filling the space between us on the riding board. She closed her eyes, leaned back, and my thoughts flew, as they often flew since I left Cripplegate, to my father. What would he have thought of my wedding? Of my new bride? I knew the answer: "Hawk, you gonna sleep *beside* her after what they done to us? You ain't no better'n Nate McKay! Why don't you marry a cullud girl and lift *her* up?" Some nights, I remembered, he prayed, "Oh Lord, kill all the whitefolks and leave all the nigguhs," and Mattie, miffed, slapped him from behind, which made George yelp, "Lord! Don't you know a white man from a nigguh?" He would reject me, claiming I had rejected him, and this was partly true: I rejected (in George) the *need* to be an Untouchable. Despite the fears of Undercliff's guest, the rituals of caste would, regardless of law, live centuries after the plantations died. My father kept the pain alive. He *needed* to rekindle racial horrors, revive old pains, review disappointments like a sick man fingering his sores. Like my tutor, he *chose* misery. Grief was the grillwork—the emotional grid—through which George Hawkins sifted and sorted events, simplified a world so overrich in sense it outstripped him, and all that was necessary to break this spell of hatred, this self-inflicted segregation from the Whole, was to acknowledge, once and for all, that what he allowed to be determinant for his life depended on himself and no one else.

But I loved my father. What would I not have given for him to be at the wedding? Proud of me. To know he approved of Peggy. Was what I'd done so wrong? So contrary to his cracked vision that, if George lived, he would not forgive me?

"Husband?"

Wife's glasses were steamed by tears.

"I've done something?" I asked.

"No . . . no." She shook open my handkerchief to dry her glasses. "I've never been happier."

"If I were a priest and saw you and your father at these moments of hysterical joy, I'd administer Last Rites and lower coins onto your eyelids."

"It's just," Peggy watched me, myopically, over glasses hooked low on her nose, "that I'm not *supposed* to be happy. Does that sound crazy? It's so hard to say this. . . ." She gnawed her underlip. "The wedding was ridiculous and unnecessary and a flagrant betrayal of the Protestant Reformation, and *every*body wants one, I don't care *what* they say! But. . . ." Groping again for words, she found none, and settled on an anecdote: "It resembles a story Evelyn Pomeroy told me once about meeting Harriet Beecher Stowe in Charlotte. About how she read her novel and loved it—and loved her—and thought, 'I *have* to do that.' Evelyn is not, as you know, a crusader. She is, constitutionally, a romatic writer. Not a journalist-muckraker. Nothing she has written will equal the influence of Stowe. When she *saw* that, after writing a hundred pages of a protest novel, she also discovered that she hated Stowe's book. She found faults, first with her novel, then turned on the Novel itself. She dismissed it as dead. She wrote a parody of *Uncle Tom's Cabin*, a clever, sneering lampoon that was, after the first few laughs, *ugly*—ugly and spiteful because it burlesqued something it couldn't be, and all because Evelyn *did* love Harriet Beecher Stowe. She told me she couldn't admit that for years—that she belonged in the audience, cheering. Not on stage. It was tantamount to confessing she was *beneath* the beauty of fiction. Maybe even beneath Stowe. Can you," Peggy asked herself, not me, "still love and believe in something when it's so beautiful it blinds you, and you *know* you can't have it?" Because she had not asked me, I did not answer. "You start feeling that goodness and beauty are for other people. For men, if you're a woman. Whites, if your nonwhite. Even the simple things—especially the simple things—like being wanted for yourself. To keep from feeling like waste, or destroying yourself, you have to destroy them. Deny them *here*." She touched my chest. "And I did that. Does that sound awful?"

"And you still feel that way?" Near the front we stopped, both Fruity and I a little uneasy about climbing the stairs and crossing the front rooms to the bedroom. "That we must deny beauty because, for whatever reason, we fear we cannot have it?"

"No." She lifted, then kissed my hand. "I have it all now."

As you well know, I had never seen a marriage that "worked," as we like to put it. For on my word, I'd seen no evidence that cohabitation didn't end in conflict. At Cripplegate Anna and Jonathan Polkinghorne lived in, at most, "peaceful coexistence," and in the quarters, for George, who once claimed that marriage should be outlawed forever, and for Mattie, for whom men were a necessary evil, matrimony amounted—after the first few months—to a war of nerves. So that I brought no images of prior success into my marriage to Peggy; I felt during the first few weeks off-center, my footing unsure, and without a map of this new territory. As for my wife:

She was not troubled, as I was—as most people are—by the "quality" of marriage (as if marriage were a *thing*, not a relation, and possessed Cartesian properties), and drew no lines except one: the only act forbidden me was infidelity, and to this I agreed, remembering that (for Ezekiel) there was no anguish greater than others turning away, denying you the energy that seemed to beacon from their eyes. Beyond these game rules, she asked for nothing. Peggy did not probe into my past. She did not ask about other women; she even suggested that anything I had experienced earlier with another woman—even in fantasy—should be pursued *con brio* in our bedroom. Needless to say, applying what Flo Hatfield had taught me occupied our nights for a month; and our days, after I dragged home from school, were devoted to restoring the cabin.

It had been built in 1809 by a Finn named Immomen, with leaded windows and wedges in the ends of each log so that they interlocked tighter than bonded cells. The family that preceded us left damages in excess of two hundred dollars. Rats and nests of squirrels I found inside, unverifiable eggs in the chimney. They left broken windows. A bad pump. And gossipy neighbors. "Your neighbor to the left," said our Neighbor-to-the-Right, "is Will Smythe, and he's the queer one out this way; he makes totem poles." "Tom Warren, over to the right," said our Neighbor-to-the-Left, "won't

call the sheriff if you put up a fence a quarter-inch into his property, and he won't say nothing about it, but he'll probably lob a
fifty-nine caliber ball at you, over your heads, until you pull it
back." That first week our neighbors, and two of my students,
helped us patch the roof of handsplit shakes, replace rotting stairs,
and repair the pump. Meanwhile, Peggy devoted her time to knit-
ting dag-wain coverlets for the bed and tables, a fine dodge as Fate
spoiled a fine dialectician to make a poor, hod-carting carpenter:
me. Perhaps a half-dozen small problems inside the house created
for Peggy and me common tasks that eased the clumsiness we felt
when, after dinner, facing the fireplace in a furnitureless room, she
resting against me, her hair smelling faintly of paint, we felt—or at
least I felt—the strange faith involved in being with another, the
audacity behind placing oneself, desires and defects, at another's
doorstep like muddy boots, knowing they must take you in, but
wondering if they should. After all, knowing yourself as well as you
do, would you marry *you*? And since Peggy *had* taken me in, wasn't
that proof of there being something wrong with her? Had I married a loser? Had she? Suspecting these questions were poison—
perhaps not even *real* questions—we did not give them voice; the
house, hammering and scrubbing, kept us focused not on each
other but on a spot between and just ahead of us both. Not, in
other words, on what she wanted, or I. But on what we built in the
interstices. Which was both of us. And neither. But a house can be
repaired for only so long, like a novel, which must be abandoned
before it is overpolished (a few defects in the house, as in novels,
said Evelyn Pomeroy in her letters, were desirable), and we settled
into something like second nature.

"Husband," Peggy would say, sitting in the inglenook, her lap
(and floor around her) littered with applecores, skimming the
Spartanburg *Plain-Dealer*, her bifocals so low on her nose, pressing
down her nostrils, that she must breathe through her mouth; at
the Queen Anne table, gnawing my thumbnail, at my elbow a mug
of cold coffee-soup (it has been in the pot all day over the fire and
has the burnt, Balzacian consistency of syrup), I grade midterm
papers that make me, after the fifteenth essay, uncertain I understand English at all. I work in my shorts (more comfortable that
way), my trousers on the breeches hook in the bedroom. Light

from the fire throws a triangle of gray shadow from Fruity's nose
to the line of her chin. "It says here that the Alabama legislature's
formally resolved to secede if Lincoln is elected. Can they do that?
Secede, I mean. William?"

"Eh?"

"You're biting your nails again, dear. You *always* do that when
you grade Gilbert Finney's papers." She holds the front page over
her head. "Can the country break up like that, if it wants to?"

"Dunno," I say, distantly. Gilbert Finney has spelled *tranquilaty*
at least four ways; I cannot for the life of me remember how it
goes.

"I *wouldn't* chew my fingers if I were you. . . . William?"

"Ah?"

"What happens to *us* if the country breaks down?"

I look up. *Tranquillity?*

"Wife, you're thinking *essences* again. Giving nouns the value
of existence. People endure. Not names. There are no 'Negroes.'
Or 'women.' There are no 'nations.' We tear down one shop sign,
America; we put another, *Atlantis.* And we blunder along as usual.
Patching up the house. Misspelling *trannquility.*" I push back my
chair. "Where the hell's that *Webster's* I brought from school?"

"In the cupboard, behind the canned peaches."

"The cupboard? Wife. . . ."

"You haven't finished the bookcase." She finds a wormhole in
her apple and winces. "It's been on the porch for a *month*, William.
I put all the reference books in the cupboard."

The bookcase: more domestic slippage, like the on-again, off-
again pump, which I'd put aside for a Saturday morning. I stack
jars on the counter, then return to the table with *Webster's*, only to
discover the bad joke of all dictionaries: In order to find a word's
correct spelling (or learn something new), you must know how it is
spelled in the first place. Or have a good hunch. The ignorant
stayed in the cave. The seeker sought, not knowledge, but what he
already knew. Nothing changed.

"William?"

"Oh, for God's sake, *what?*"

She folds her paper, puts it on the kitchen table, under the
fruitbowl, steps over the apples at her feet, and, standing barefoot

behind my chair, affectionately squeezes me round the neck. "Come to bed."

Tranquility?

In all respects truly being-with was so pleasant I almost felt unworthy of it. Marriage was a little choppy in spots, I grant you, but generally, like Donald McKay's fast new clipper, *Flying Cloud,* a sleek, stripped-down beauty which, on waters smooth as isinglass, whipped by older ships freighted with useless cargo; but I must keep to the point, which is this: I had seen so many Ways since leaving Hodges—the student in Ezekiel, the senses in Flo Hatfield, the holy murderer in Bannon (Shiva's hitman), and Reb, who was surely a Never-Returner; but in all these well-worn trails—none better than another—I discovered that my dharma, such as it was, was that of the householder. I wanted, though good fortune made me feel guilty, nothing more than forty years of crawling home from the classroom, my suitcoat lightly dusted with chalk, nerves humming with the peculiar blend of fatigue and exhilaration that follows an inspired lecture, the sort where you scrub your notes (yellowed, obsolete), and sing the Simple Sentence—that, too, was a springboard for speculative thought, the way it warped the world toward Western ontology; having tossed, like birdseed, these linguistic-epistemological gems to baffled farmers, their children ten years later, and their grandchildren, I would drop to the kitchen table, the U-shape handle of my walnut cane hooked on the back of my chair; hands dithering on the tablecloth, I would watch Wife carry food, as slow as Satan's ascent to Paradise, to the table (it takes her half an hour to scuff from the counter), serving something unnameable that twitches, bubbles, and backstrokes in a bowl of tepid water (in forty years Fruity would still be a poor cook), which I praise, "Wonderful! Boiled tuna, you say?" then eat dutifully, lifting my bowl, licking it dry, even if Wife serves meat, for it is more righteous to approve than stand on lofty principles: a quiet life. With the bird flutter of children throughout the house, all as blind as Peggy. But what came to pass, as you've probably guessed, was quite another story.

There were days in November (always November), just at winter's damp hem, with the whole school year leveled toward me like the business end of a shotgun barrel, when teaching was worse than fieldwork. The classroom was a pit. My students, all frightened, had lockjaw. And if they *did* speak, it was to challenge me, corner me, force me to quote from mysterious texts (the ones I deliberately didn't assign for class) to prove my right to be at the front of the room. A monstrous way to pay off my mortgage, it seemed to me, a minor torture from the workshop of the man who invented the Iron Maiden. After one such class I hied home to Fruity badly in need of a hot toddy and a hug.

Usually, Wife was good on hugs. That evening, however, she was not herself. Her head turned when I held her, she let her arms fall at her sides. She had been crying, I could tell: her nose swelled when she wept; it looked rather like a radish, a snowman's proboscis shoved under her bifocals. "What is it?"

She walked, intense and quiet, into the kitchen, and sat, her face vacant, before a small package that rested amiddlemost the table like a bomb. "William, that *awful* man was here!" No bigger than the box cufflinks are sold in, it was torturously knotted with bootlaces. "He said it was a *wedding* present."

Taking a step back from the table, I felt, ever so slightly, the stone foundations of the cabin sink deeper into the soil, through leaf mold through rock to the blind, white tendrils that suck at bier and bone.

"Aren't you going to open it?" Peggy pushed it toward me. "After you do, there's something I want to tell you, so sit down."

Wife waited for me to pick it up, shake it, to say something Voltarian to dispel her disgust. I could not. The package would put me, I knew, in a different, new, and diseased relationship with everything I held dear. At the table, facing it sideways, I extended my hand. The box was moist, soaked perhaps by rain pounding Bannon's saddlebag as he pursued. . . . "William!" Peggy grabbed a knife, "If you won't open it, I will!" She sawed at the string. Upended the box. Shook it. Onto the table clattered a dull ring (orichalc) that twirled on its side, then clinked against the candlestand. A trinket that from time out of mind was the ornament of the Allmuseri *osuo*. Metal worked painfully, like scarification, into the skin during infancy and, like skin, was impleached until cartilage and metal melted back into a common field.

Wife picked up the ring.

148

"Why did he give you this?" She snapped her fingers under my nose. "Hello? You can return to your seat, thank you, now if I could have another volunteer. . . ."

I grabbed her wrist. "Stop playing!"

Peggy rubbed her forearm, a little afraid of me now. "There's something else. . . ."

"*What* else?"

"Never mind!" She tore off her glasses. "You're so *mean!* How can I tell you anything when you look like you just swallowed a bone?"

Without replying—what could I say?—I took Reb's ring, then rode a (now) very tired horse back to town, feeling not so much fear as a throb in my chest, a strange hurting, what I can only call the concrescence of past deeds pushing in upon me: a cathedral ceiling collapsing. Reb had not reached Chicago. His capture was beyond question. How else could Bannon have come by this ring? A terrible thought (I am known for these fits of terrible thought) came to me: The Soulcatcher would have duplicated the Coffin-maker's spirit, reproduced—as his method demanded—the idiosyncrasies of his victim, which meant he would, in a way, *be* Reb. Was that it then? Why Bannon decided this moment propitious to begin the painstakingly slow manhunt with me? But he had called despair the precondition for the death wishes he delivered, and I felt, with Peggy, in my profession, here among friends, anything but despair. No. I had but to face him to call his bluff; but to call his bluff for him to leave us in peace.

At dusk, Spartanburg was deserted. Main Street emptied, as if an epidemic had erased all movement, except for fine red dust forever filtering through the air. The taverns were shut up tight. The evening sun, low in the sky, was cold, casting more light than heat, the shadows gathered thickly on the ground. From where I dismounted, hitching my horse to a rail outside the Motley Cow (closed), I could glance up and down Main Street at the gray, wind-battered buildings, yet what I felt most powerfully was the silence. Except for the panting of my horse, it was quiet enough to hear a cricket clear its throat. Did everyone in town know something I did not? Carriages were abandoned, a mule-drawn wain in front of the General Store had been left unattended.

Yet and still, there was no sound—not the lowing of cattle, nor the brattle of dogs, no dusty pigeons in the court house windows.

Silence.

I climbed the steps to the brothel, knocked softly, sensing some pestilence had swept the town clean. Mamie parted the curtain to the front window. I had come to ask her about Bannon; I asked instead if the town had been evacuated. She kept the door half-closed. I could not see her face. "Don't you know what happens tonight?" Behind her the rooms were dark, no candles lit. "There's a sale at Sullivan's bar."

Not because I wanted to did I walk to the auction, but because I hoped Bannon had brought Reb there. Trading slaves in 1860, shipping Africans, was illegal, but the practice continued in backrooms poorly lighted to conceal the physical deformities, the damages to blackmarket goods, each slave lifted onto a high table, a makeshift Block, with someone (a boy usually) standing watch for the sheriff at the door. But could this happen here? With neighbors and students I trusted completely? It was as if the people I knew, and worked beside by day, underwent a Walpurgis Night transformation at dusk. In Sullivan's tavern stools were stacked on his tables. I stepped around to the rear, the night blacker now than a funeral of bondsmen in a thunderstorm. The storeroom door was open, the interior packed with people from all strata of Spartanburg—the officials, the thieves, the merchants and streetfolk. Gilbert Finney, wearing two top hats, jangled a bell outside, shouted, "Oh yea! Oh yea! Walk right in, gennulmum, for the rarest business opperchunity of a lifetime!" Music drifted from inside. An organ. A Confederate flag flapped above the door. Will Smythe, entering, saw me, and blenched like a man caught outside a burlesque hall, then moved toward a dim spot of light at the end of the huge storeroom; I followed him into a crowd of fifty liquescent shapes milling around a small platform, a hastily constructed bar—and then! I saw the organ used a month before at my wedding! But now it was playing an anapestic rhythm (short, short, long, pause) that was exactly opposite the rhythm of the heart, made it slam violently, skip beats, and left me reeling. It was late; I'd missed the introductions made by the lawyers, the creditors, and the distributors. Cigar smoke thick enough to lean on hung from the ceiling, floating between a hundred brightly colored balloons. The room had the gamy smell of tainted meat, like a flesh market. Which it was. A second boy, an usher in a livery uniform and chimney-pot hat, seated patrons. There was Wendell Blake. Here another of my students. And here Gene Sullivan. Nowhere did I see Reb. And then the room was quiet.

It became quiet and two slaves walked into the soft kerosene lamplight. Twice the auctioneer, a fat man dressed like a circus ringmaster, tapped his gavel. His voice rang out, "*Don't shove! Don't shove!*" I shrank back, certain my shock would give me away, that the crowd would know me for the fraud I was: a counterfeit white man. A spy in the Big House. "Ladies and gentlemen, I'm pleased to open this evening's bidding with some of the best merchandise to be found in South Carolina." In rapid, camera-shutter succession, a woman my stepmother's age was sent through her paces, made to lift her dress and trot around the room after a tossed stick to demonstrate the strength of her legs. Her husband came next. The crowd asked him, "What can you *do?*" "Can you plow?" "Have you ever cared for livestock?" His face glistened with sweat: "What*ever* you want!" One hand muffled a cough that favored the overture to a funeral. "You gonna take me and my wife together, ain't ya? That's *all* I'm askin' fo'. We been tergether fo' thirty years. . . ."

"Forty-eight dollars," said someone up front, "for the man."

How much worse this was than being on the Block! I was, having passed, a witness. The vilest of turncoats to my father's values. To see persecution to others and to be powerless to end it— to be by accident *above* it—was, I saw, the same as consent. My vision slipped. My temples throbbed. All reformed opium eaters feared this sudden vertigo, set off by a sound. A certain song. By the pitch of the auctioneer's voice as he said, "May it please you, ladies and gentlemen, we have one last item on tonight's agenda," and, before he finished, there stepped, slowly, through a stale pall of azure smoke—did I dream—a girl of two and twenty from the adjacent room, a distant Call I could not but answer, the final knot of the heart that is broken—as Bannon said—from inside, bringing difficulties thick and threefold, delivering destiny as your deepest wish.

"This one's Christian name," said the auctioneer, looking down, locating my gaze, locking into it in a crowd of fifty, "is Minty."

XI

THE MANUMISSION OF FIRST-PERSON VIEWPOINT

In this second (unfortunate) intermission there is yet another convention of the Slave Narrative to consider, possibly its only invariant feature: first-person viewpoint. By definition, the Slave Narrative requires a first-person report on the Peculiar Institution from one of its victims, and what we value most highly in this viewpoint are precisely the *limitations* imposed upon the narrator-perceiver, who cannot, for example, know what transpires in another mind, like that of Ezekiel Sykes-Withers, or in a scene that excludes him; what we lack in authority, we gain in immediacy: a premise (or prejudice) of Positivist science. But the Age of Reason overlaps the age of slavery, and it is not, therefore, unseemly to wonder, despite Dr. Marx's dislike of metaphysics, about the transcendental nature of the narrator.

He is, in fact, nobody; is anonymous, as Hume points out in his *Treatise*. Actually, he cannot be said to be *nothing*, for as all Kantians claim, the I—whatever we call the Self—is a product of experience and cannot precede it. The implications are worth noting. The Self, this perceiving Subject who puffs on and on, is, for all purposes, a palimpsest, interwoven with everything—literally everything—that can be thought or felt. We can go further: The Subject of the Slave Narrative, like all Subjects, is forever *outside* itself in others, objects; he is parasitic, if you like, drawing his life from everything he is not, and at precisely the instant he makes possible their appearance. This proposition will doubtlessly infuriate our Positivist friends, who will think it scandalous, but the "Kantian compromise," as it is traditionally called, suggests that to think the Slave Narrative properly is to see nowhere a narrator who falteringly interprets the world, but a narrator who *is* that world: who is less a reporter than an opening through which the world is delivered: first-person (if you wish) universal.

All this the author(s) of the *Uphanishads* and *Bhagavad Gita* probably knew, in their preanalytic fashion—knew, by instinct, that what we loosely call thought, or consciousness, or Mind is, far from being a "blockhouse," instead a restlessness that, refusing to be contained, contains everything.

Having liberated first-person, it is now only fitting that in the following chapters we do as much for Andrew Hawkins.

XII

---❖---

IN THE SERVICE OF THE SERVANT

No one wanted the girl.

After her introduction a few people drifted toward the door, then others followed, lured by Sullivan's offer to open his best keg of beer. The girl, grotesquely outfitted in an antique ball dress (perse), with an accent of velvet flowers at the décolletage, her hair parted down the middle, watched them leave with the resignation, the fatalism of a woman rejected more than once on the road, who expected it, and lowered her cheap parasol—they'd dressed her to favor a girl at the fair—stepping down unsteadily from the table: the token black girl at the beauty contest, forever told, "Maybe next year." Except for a few children, and those signing papers for the earlier purchase, the storeroom cleared, leaving the floor littered as if a trashbin had been upturned, and the auctioneer in the worst of moods, tearing his leaflets from the wall, pulling down balloons, barking at the girl: P. T. Barnum on a slow day, giving the Crocodile Woman her severance pay.

What I could not tell was whether this was indeed Cripplegate's Minty hanging back in the shadows, flinching as the auctioneer shouted, watching him—not unlike a theatrical agent—turn his other talent over to their new owners. And soon even these left, and I stood trying to recognize something of the girl at Cripplegate, in whom the world once chose to concretize its possibilities in the casement of her skin—limiting itself that something beautiful might *be*—in this badly used woman by the table. If you looked, without sentiment, you could see that her dress was too small and crawled up when she moved, flashing work-scorched stretches of skin and a latticework of whipmarks. Her belly pushed forward.

154

From the cholesterol-high, nutritionless diet of the quarters, or a child, I could not tell. She was unlovely, drudgelike, sexless, the farm tool squeezed, with no thought of preservation in the seigneurial South, for every ounce of surplus value, then put on sale for whatever price she could bring. She was, like my stepmother, perhaps doubly denied—in both caste and gender—and driven to Christ (she wore a cross) as the only decent man who would have her.

And, dear God, she *was* Minty. I did not have a hold on my feelings. They slipped from remembered desire, the glandular hungers I'd once felt for her, to a biblical grief (Pauline) for both her damaged beauty and, within me, the inevitable exchange of passion for compassion.

"You want something?" asked the auctioneer, dragging his equipment past me. "The sale's over, son."

"You have not sold that girl," I said.

"Her?" He laughed. "And I probably *won't*." He snapped his head, and she obediently came closer, curtsied clumsily, falling left, then turned around for me to examine her. Someone had, I noticed, buttered over a gunpowder burn on her back. Scar tissue like a bacon-grease mark. Her eyes were too deep, the sockets in a cowskull. My distress was not lost on the auctioneer.

"See what I mean?" he said. "She's sick."

The girl finally spoke: "I can *work!* I *can!*"

"If you believe *that*," said the auctioneer, "there's forty acres of good bottomland in Anderson I'd like to talk with you about." Now he looked tired. "You can turn it off, sweetheart. Tomorrow you go back to Colonel Woofter, and if he still don't want you, then it's too bad, because," he slid his eyes at me, "I been in every village between here and Ware Shoals with her, and you know what, son? No takers." He laughed again, at himself, I thought. "She's bad for business, you know what I mean? You gets a reputation for putting poor stock on the market and. . . ." His shoulders bunched. He walked outside to his wagon, the back of which was loaded with chains—like a pile of coiled snakes copulating—and the girl, for whom every step seemed excruciating, began to cry. In less time than it takes to tell, I was at the wagon, pulling out my purse.

"What will you take for her?"

The auctioneer smiled, then suppressed it, a poker player's slip. "Make me an offer."

"I only have a few dollars, twenty. . . ."

"You need ten times that."

"Two hundred?" My heart swung into my ribs. "You said your-self—not a minute ago!—that no one would have her! Is she so valuable now?"

"My instructions," he said, "are to sell this girl for no less than two hundred dollars. That's what Colonel Woofter paid for her—I ain't saying there ain't been a whole lot of depreciation, but I'll tell you what. . . ." He reached into his coat for a deed of sale. "You teach over at the schoolhouse yonder, don't you?" When I nodded, he said, "So you're good for the money. You kin raise it in a month, can't you?"

He took my name, and took my twenty dollars as "earnest money," then snapped his head again at the girl. "Go on, darlin'. This gentleman just saved you from the auction circuit. No more pancake and greasepaint."

Now that she had been sold, Minty was uncertain; she had not truly looked at me until he eased her off the wagon, and had only one question to ask him:

"What's he gonna use me for?"

"That," said the auctioneer, "is between you, the Holy Ghost, and Master Harris."

I helped her onto my horse, letting her use my hands as a stirrup (the ones on my saddle were too high), then pulled myself up behind her, leading the horse west of town and toward home, but slowly, for it was not clear to me that I could sally into the bedroom and shake Wife from her beauty rest with news that I'd bought a Negro servant, adding, "And will you pay for her, dear?" But if she, or Dr. Undercliff, did not pay, then Minty would be reclaimed. Outside Spartanburg, I spread my cloak over her shoulders. She remained silent, suspicious of me, and we rode twenty or thirty rods more into a field as dark as the ocean floor, where I dismounted, and walked a few yards away from her to think: *If* I could not raise the money, what then? Her only option would be flight. And would I have to go with her? Did I have a choice? Was loss of Wife and home what I had purchased? Behind me, I heard her feet fall softly off the horse, and turned.

"Master Harris—is that your name?'

"Yes."

"I wanna say thank you, and God bless you, sir, for picking me." A prepared speech, this. Said so often, and to so many owners, its meaning dissolved into mere sound. "And I promise I *will* work, if you don't sell me. I been sold *three* times since I left Hodges."

"After Anna Polkinghorne took charge of the estate?" I led her back to the horse. "Was my father sold? And my stepmother? Do you know what happened to Mattie?"

"Your stepmother?"

She made the sort of face Jocasta reportedly gave Oedipus after his interview with the Herdsman. I understood her confusion. (The Old South bred reversals almost as severe as anything in Greek tragedy: the brother and sister, I'd heard, sold to different plantations; fifteen years later, they meet again, fall in love, feeling an inexplicable tug, a partial anamnesis, and produce a brood of Bleeders.) Minty kept me at arm's length. "It ain't right to play with me. . . ."

I moved forward; she moved back.

"Minty, I am Andrew."

You are familiar with the way travelers, trapped at the train depot, listen to people peddling *The Watch Tower?* So Minty listened to me.

"Master Polkinghorne, if you remember, apprenticed me to Flo Hatfield's farm in Abbeville, from which I barely escaped with my cullions (excuse me), after which I, and a coffinmaker—you do not know him—fled north, well, only *this* far north, where I have reestablished myself, taken a new identity, and live nearby with my wife—I have a wife now," Minty's mouth pressed in, "and I've purchased you not to put you to work but, as I promised years before, to buy your freedom. . . ."

There is a place where southern women retire when their nervous systems short-circuit, a pleasant region much like a sanitorium, or a Writer's Colony, and I have often heard it referred to as a *swoon;* I can describe it no further, having never been there:

Charles Johnson

Men pass out, a few faint, others are knocked out, but men do not
swoon, and I thought it improper to trouble Minty about details of
the Ladies' Psychic Powder Room after she checked back in. We
rode slowly. Slowly, I say, for I wanted word of Cripplegate. As it
happened, Minty knew nothing of my parents' whereabouts after
Anna put them up for sale. My father had bolted for the Georgia
border. And Jonathan? It was now he who was bedridden, paralyzed after a particularly vicious crack to the skull from George
(the clivus and anterior edge of the occipital bone were pushed
permanently against the upper anterior surface of the medulla
oblongata), and Anna, the long-suffering spouse who changed his
bedsheets and sponged his backside, grew inversely in vitality (said
Minty) as the old man weakened. More than this Minty did not
know; and she only spoke sketchily of her masters (all men) who
sprang up in her life, one by one, like principals in a gang rape.

"I *am* free then, Andrew?" she asked. "I did hear you say that?"

"No," I sighed. "Not yet. There is the problem of two hundred
dollars. . . ."

"You do not have it?"

"My wife does, or," I averted my eyes, "her father will provide
the money, I'd swear on it. He's the best physician in town."

At mention of Dr. Undercliff, Minty stopped the horse, began
to speak, then failed, her face tumbling into a fresh spate of tears.
"Andrew, I *need* a doctor. People with what I got—pellagra—just
rot away, unless they get treatment. I've had it a *year*. Colonel Woofter didn't care. And no one knows what causes it. It's like something you do to yourself, make a space for it inside, like, a year ago,
when they sold me to Colonel Woofter and I couldn't stand how he
touched me, what he made me do, I stopped caring. I hated being
alive that much. It's like the way you *feel* turns into something solid
and grows and kills you." She pulled her dress to her lap. "Look at
my legs."

As I live and breathe, her bare legs, as I peered over her
shoulder and down, were hideous. *Hideous!* Incredible, the clarity
with which I remember those pustules and bleeding sores like spots
of flame. Above and below her knee, the skin was scaly, reptilian,
peeling like old house paint, seamed with festering fever blisters, a

158

few of which had burst, and secreted down her thighs a green and yellow fluid so clayey, and protoplasmic, it made my stomach clench. Lumpy veins crisscrossed her legs. Old boils had left black places where they'd dried. Despite myself, I felt dizzy. She would die soon. Who could doubt this? I shuddered to think of it. Cells in me, corpuscles in my blood, spoke before I could reason out a reply: "I will see you through this."

This made Minty cry all the more. "I've always done for *myself*, Andrew. You know that. I don't like being trouble."

She was more trouble than she knew. She talked nonstop of the new life she would start, with my help, once she reached a free state, giving little thought to logistics, the long and perilous flight— I speak of running—if I could not buy her freedom. I would not stay. How could I? I had blundered into manumission, milked the Self's polymorphy to elude, like Trickster John in the folktales my father told, springtraps that killed Patrick, crippled my father, destroyed (probably) Reb, and now—as we neared the cabin—would, I feared, take Minty. That failure would be final. It would finish me, for, if nothing else, I had learned that the heart could survive anything by becoming everything. Opening itself to others. And if the others, in whom you lived, died? Slowly, you died. Gradually, it wore you down. In this I saw the hand of Horace Bannon. He waited. He watched. I could let Minty be taken, or move on, forever trudging north, hope like the horizon, Canada a spiritual landscape as unattainable as Ultima Thule, and either way everything was lost but this: the important promise, the essential promise—the act of mercy—that the Soulcatcher offered. In weariness, I would welcome the kill as a wish. Could the trap be tighter?

Minty I told to wait on the porch after we arrived, and what composure I could muster, stepping inside, smoothing back my hair with both hands, disappeared in a sitting room that was no longer the room I remembered—my toe sent a wigstand clattering to the floor—but, in the darkness, a cabin that hurled back no reflection of my presence. Had I really lived here? Minty whispered, "Andrew, did you hurt yourself?" and, in her speaking the name I was called in the quarters, she gave me a nature that broke my mastery over the cabin forever. I stood stock-still: the sweaty fieldhand, a machete between his teeth, who has crawled through his master's window. Minty's scent was still on me. The smell of the quarters. An old, earthy odor of dirt floors. Woods. The cabin smelled different. Its darkness trembled with foreign sounds. An old grandfather clock tocking. A crack as the cabin floor settled. The furnishings no longer felt familiar. I touched things hesitantly like a guest, uncertain if this was the broken chair we propped against the wall and never used: a room of tables that threw out wooden legs to trip me, hanging plants that bent lower to bump my head, tools that rolled suddenly under my boots, bumped me from behind, and felt, I swear, as if they'd been shaped for an alien form—creatures *built* differently than I, with more (or fewer) fingers, no thumbs, or body parts I did not possess. Into this Martian parlor dropped Peggy, also a Martian. "William?" She had wrapped the topsheet from the bed around her. "You *scared* me! It's almost morning." Knuckling her eyes, she stumbled back to bed, and I followed: the first Earthman on the Red Planet, craning my neck in astonishment.

"Did you talk with Horace Bannon?"

Bannon's name snapped the cabin briefly back into focus, but threw me farther from Peggy than Mars. To an image of myself fleeing hell-hounds in the forest. Of the two terrors, I preferred, to tell the truth, being the only Earthman stranded on a strange world.

"No, I went to an auction. There was an auction tonight, in Sullivan's storeroom."

Her legs drew up; she assumed the position (fetal) of sleep to hasten it. "It must have been awful."

"Fruity," I said, standing away from the bed, afraid to sit (why were Martian beds *rectangular*?), "you must ask your father to loan us money. There was a girl there, someone I knew years ago, and she is sick, and I have brought her home...."

Wife sat up in bed. She was instantly awake.

"You brought her *home*, William?"

"Yes—she is outside now. I have a month to make good on the sale."

Wife's hand fumbled on the night table for her bifocals, slipped them on, and this one item—glasses are peculiar like this—made her seem fully dressed. "You have to take her back! You say she is sick? And you still bought her? William. . . ."

"I am *indebted* to her," I tested the bed with my fingertips, then sat, "the way I am indebted to you, and your father, and Reb, and to *my* father, whom I shall probably never see again, though I would give anything for him to know and love you—I *know* that cannot be!—but there are duties I must discharge, if I am ever to be free." I was fast losing her, stabbing at making sense, hoping the sounds would string themselves together on their own natural rhythms, creating order in front of me, for there was little within. "We are born, even slaves, into such richness, and if I cannot some-how repay them, my predecessors and that girl outside, then I am unworthy of any happiness whatsoever, here with you, or anywhere."

"Really?" If Wife understood this explanation, which confused even me, she gave no sign. "Maybe I'd better go outside and see this grand person."

Slipping into her housecoat, she walked from the room. Cow-ard that I was, I could not rise until I heard the Martian Wife and Earthwoman talking in the kitchen, and even then I was too timid to join them. After ten minutes, Wife, very pale, her lips still twisted by what she'd seen, returned and crawled back into bed. "She *is* sick, isn't she?" She blew her nose on a corner of the sheet, and asked point-blank:

"Did you make love to her? Before, I mean."

I needed time to lie. She gave me none.

"William, you can tell me. Was she your lover?"

"Yes."

If I had not lost the chandoo-induced ability to see the interior of objects, I might have glimpsed in Wife what did not show on the surface: the wound I'd inflicted. For a longer time than I thought bearable, Wife was significantly quiet, and if this quiet occurred in fiction, if she were a character in William Wells Brown's *Clotel*, Delaney's *Blake*, or Frank Webb's *Garies and Their Friends* (all books Wife read), it would have been the lull before a cheap emotional outburst, an embarrassing scene: the horror-stricken belle pulls out her tresses like chicken feathers, she throws her husband, the beast, out on his behind. But Peggy Undercliff was no character in a novel. Her freckled hand smoothed a spot on the Martian mattress;

here she told me to sit. Quietly, she said, "I don't know what she means to you, William, but if you care, I care, and I will ask Daddy for the money."

"You *don't* want to know under what circumstances I knew her? Or why she calls me Andrew?"

She shook her head.

"If you decide, later, that you prefer her, and that she can make you happy, I will, of course, throw myself under the nearest train—"

"No trains in Spartanburg," I said. "Remember?"

"—but I will throw myself happily under the train, because I want what you want, even if your pleasure means I experience pain. I had a long time to think about it after you took off." She slipped her glasses down, cleaned them on the pillowcase, and smiled. "We will need help around here, I shall be doing less and, if she can work, she will be a godsend."

I did not understand; I said so.

"Oh, William!" Wife grabbed my shirtcollar like a longshoreman, pulling down my chin. "You're so clever at seeing invisible things—ideas—you can *never* see the obvious until it draws back and dropkicks you: I'm *pregnant,* dummy!" She let my shirt go and pulled her covers over her middle. "And I want you to know I don't like it *one* bit!"

"You'll survive," I said.

Wife gave me a side-glance, then smiled and moved closer to kiss me. "We always do."

This was hardly the turn of events I'd expected; I had prepared myself for oppression by preliving episodes of disappointment, obstacles, and violent death; I felt a shade disappointed that everyone in the White World wasn't out to get me. (The truth, brothers, is that it was pretty vain to think oneself that important: *hubris,* thinking *I,* one fragile thread, made that much difference in the fabric of things.) With no self-induced racial paranoia as an excuse for being irresponsible, I turned—and Wife turned—to the business of Minty's recovery. For someone who suffered so, and still felt stupendous pain, she was cheerful, and this made her optimism in me—her faith in us—all the more difficult. Wife and I prepared an extra bed (not a pallet) for her in the guestroom. The first week after her arrival we insisted she stay in bed until Dr. Undercliff, off to see his patients in Greenville, returned. "I *don't* take charity!" Minty told me. "You know that. If I can't work, then I *will* go back to Colonel Woofter." Wife and I stood to one side, watching her pull out the sofa, pointing triumphantly at lint and whore's wool in the corners. "See! It's filthy in here! Andrew, you never *could* clean." She winked at Wife. "He just wipes in front of things." She sailed into a soap-and-water campaign that shamed our earlier efforts to clean the cabin. Her meals were no less meticulous. Minty, like a mobile library, carried hundreds of recipes from Cripplegate's quarters, dishes I'd not had in years. Patiently, as if she were talking to a child, she explained to Wife, "You never fixed him Salt Fish Cakes? He *loves* Salt Fish Cakes! But you got to go easy on the hot pepper. They give him the hot squirts and running shits."

Soon enough we learned that the best way to handle Minty was to keep out of her way. And what else did she know? Needlework was a sealed book to Wife (our lopsided coverlets testified to that), but Minty, on the other hand, could conjure hoop-dresses from old cleaning rags. She took over Wife's education. And mine. Told me how to landscape my postage-stamp-sized property, how certain chemicals—and in what combination—would coax grass from the bald patches, where to plant cherokee-rose hedges to hide the cabin's bad features. Minty, as you may have guessed, would never implement these ideas. They *would* be done. But. . . .

Bear with me.

When the pellagra, a wasting disease, worsened, spreading to her lungs, Minty never quite caught her breath again, which made her angry at herself, and anger stole what wind she could draw. Midway through her first week with us she began, though she hated this, sleeping ten hours to build enough strength to work three. Wife stayed at Minty's bedside, reading to her, while I taught. We watched her in shifts. Perhaps you don't understand. When Minty complained (which was rare), when she said the new sores on her legs burned, when some nights she experienced roaring headaches that became screaming fits, uncontrollable crying (her head under her pillow so we could not hear), when her hands had, finally, to be tied lest she bite off her fingers, I would come in, anxious and afraid to see her, toss my books on the table, then, entering the guestroom in my stocking feet, press my cheek firmly against hers. Nay, I said nothing. I made no sound. Minty would smile—I smiled right back. She knew what I meant: We were old, cashiered warriors, Minty and me, romantics who knew the risks. But, remarkably, we were not alone. With Peggy, whose fear of sharing love was tested, then transcended, we made it through more bad nights than I care to recall. Take my word on this: I believed, as I believed nothing else, that together we could see her safely to a world where no soul catchers, no driver's pistol-cracking whip, would ever caa her into darkness again.

"Minty," I said to her the second week. "The doctor is back from Greenville. He will be here this evening."

"Help me dress, Andrew."

She turned her head toward me, weaker than I'd seen her in days. Blanket creases were impressed on both sides of her face. All day she had screeched like a madwoman—sometimes she *was* a madwoman, wan and hollow-eyed. Often, she clawed her covers, so sensitive was her skin to the coarse nap. Life in her was low, but a smile played across Minty's lips when I sat beside her.

"Peggy ain't here, is she, Andrew?"

The heat from her hands, in mine, worried me. "She's gone to get her father. They'll be here shortly."

Her eyes shuttered, she squeezed my hands tightly, and my throat grew thick. "She's no slouch. When you told me you was married, I thought, *what*? Can't nobody spoil this silly nigguh as good as me." She had to rest a moment. Wait for wind. "Now, she ain't no rose garden. She can't *see* nothin' unless it bites her nose, but, well, I *approve*." She patted my hand. Then Minty opened her eyes in surprise. She sat up a little and looked at me. "Why you cryin'? What'd I say?"

"Nothing. . . ." I left my head, for a moment, on her side, her hand on my hair. Then I heard Undercliff's carriage. My voice was shaky, strange to me. "They're outside now. You make yourself pretty."

"Sure." She frowned. "Then maybe I'll swim the English Channel."

On the porch, Undercliff, puffing, head down, paused on the stairs, his right foot planted on the porch, his left on the last step but one and, wheezing, had both hands on his right knee.

"William. . . ."

"Don't tell me." I helped him into the sitting room. "I have been redefined from the simply Annoying to the Very Annoying."

"You flatter yourself," said Undercliff. "I am working on a special category for you, the social equivalent to Cerebral Hemorrhage." Standing behind him, Wife helped the doctor remove his coat, then brought the teapot to the kitchen table. Undercliff stood, facing the fireplace, warming himself. He looked back at me over his shoulder. "Peggy has told me about this girl, William. You wish for me to *pay* for her freedom?"

"I will be in your debt forever, Father-in-law."

Undercliff winced, his face wrinkling.

"You are *already* in my debt forever." He walked to the table and poured himself tea. "And do *not* call me that, I've just eaten a fine meal at the Club, and I should like to keep it *down*." Wife gave a groan, which her father ignored. "I am not in the habit of buying pigs in pokes. If she is as wonderful a young woman as you say, the best thing since indoor plumbing, then perhaps—I only say perhaps—I will help you." He finished his tea, set his cup on the hob, and pulled down his vest. "May I see her now?"

The doctor spent the better part of an hour with Minty, the guestroom door locked. Wife and I waited in the yard. Now and again, Minty let fly a muffled scream. I took a step toward the door.

"I know he wouldn't deliberately hurt her, but the way he pulls weeds. . . ."

Wife slipped her arm around me, shifted her weight, and steered me behind the house. "Walk with me," she said. "You'll feel better." And so I did. But, for my part, the examination worried me. Minty had not eaten all day. She smelled *sour*. Sweat. A seaweed odor, as if her cells were breaking down into more basic elements. Wife and I walked in silence, the moon above us high, the air clean, the perennial red dust settling. Feeling her warmth, the mystery that she was to me now—being within being—I walked, saying nothing.

Then Wife stopped, struck by a thought. She could write her Aunt Olivia in Boston. There, Minty could find work. Make her way as a freewoman. She'd grow rich, given all she knew. Wife's decision so pleased me I lifted her into the air, my arms snugly nestled under her small, hard buttocks, then twirled her dizzily until we both dropped, lips locked, in the high dry grass. Everything, friend, was winged. Covered with grass, I turned her back, eager to tell Minty immediately. Yet, with each stride we took nearer the cabin, she brushing dirt from my hair, the screams increased in volume. Undercliff appeared briefly outside on the porch, then hurried back in.

"William," said Wife. "You'd better go ahead."

I broke into a run, thinking, "Not now," ran, fell up the stairs, turning my ankle, then limped into the cabin. Undercliff stood outside the guestroom, blood spattered on his vest, his trousers. My pulse sped up. Blood was at his feet. On the bottom rail of the door, as if Minty had tried to walk and had fallen. I could not control my voice. "How is she?"

Dr. Undercliff started; he had not been conscious of me until I spoke. "William. . . ." He rubbed his eyes. "She has suffered this affliction longer than most. . . ."

"You can't help her?"

He stepped back from the door, making room for me. "There is still time to speak to her, if you have anything to say."

I advanced into the guestroom with one foot always forward, not wanting to face this, afraid, aye, of what I thought I would see: so many profiles of Minty spun before me, like flashcards—a frightened girl condemned to stay forever in the shopwindow, on the Block; a servant whose laughter affected me like straight gin, so gay it was at times, so Galilean in its goodness; and another Minty I did not recognize, reduced to rotting flesh. He face was dark, her mouth hopeless. "Minty?" Seeing her shook a low, queer, animal sound out of me. She was disintegrating. Sugar in water. Form into formlessness. Her left leg had separated from her knee, flowed away like that of a paper doll left in the rain. Frail light from the lantern nearby etched checkered shadows on her blanket. Shadows were deep in the swales of her skin. She had bitten off her middle finger. Undercliff had torn her sheets and bound it.

Her untied hair splashed behind her on the bed. The envelope of her skin expanded, stretched, parted at the seams.

"Minty?" I pressed my lips to her cheek. Warm. "You're going to Boston." The room was spinning. She began to rouse slowly, lifting her head. Fire like spiraling flame shot through my heart, and all of me strained toward her. "You hear me, don't you?" Her eyelids quivered, showing white surfaces gone gray. Milky pupils large as dimes. Her face was distant and strained and incomplete. Cracked lips sucked back against her gums, she focused dimly on my face. "Andrew?"

"Yes! I'm here."

"Tell me," she said, "that you love me."

"I do," I said. "I *do!*"

"Very much?" she asked.

"*Very* much."

Her right hand reached out, tentatively, touching my face. She licked her lips. Something in Minty relaxed.

"You said Boston. . . ."

"Peggy knows someone there."

My chest, I felt, was on fire. "We're leaving tonight." Undercliff, Wife, and, I thought, a third figure, stood in the doorway; I knew that without turning, felt their pressure shift the room's pressure. "As soon as you can travel. . . ." I remembered, at that moment, how Wife spoke of eastern beaches, their colors, which I knew had been planned at the instant of Creation to complement Minty, blues and browns to contrast the warm hues of her skin; and I saw her there, washing herself clean of the petroleum stench of the marketplace. She would have children—I'd never approve of their father, no man was good enough, and I'd nag whomever she chose—children all stamped with her strange beauty; I saw her stand a freewoman, washing her hair, then she stepped lazily back. . . . It was gone. A gush of black vomit bubbled from her mouth onto my hand. The Devil came and sat on Minty, his weight pressing open the valve to her bladder and bowels. I raved, all my eloquence empty, refusing to release her hand. In my chest there commingled feelings of guilt I could not coax into cognition.

Over my shoulder fingers moved to close Minty's eyes, then settled firmly on my shoulder: Undercliff, I thought, yet it felt like my father's hand. Or Reb's. I let it lift me to my feet. The doctor had not moved from the doorway. Nor Peggy. And the voice that belonged to the fingers upon me was made from the offscum of other voices.

"Andrew," said the Soulcatcher, "We got business."

XIII

MOKSHA

Fluid, a crazyquilt of other's features, the Soulcatcher's face, his fingers on my shoulder, beat with the pulsethrob of countless bondsmen in his bloodstream, women and children murdered with pistols knives tramped by his warhorse strangled whipped suffocated lynched beheaded burned to death starved stoned bombed thrown from heights pushed into machinery drowned clubbed impaled killed by flame tortured. Could only *I* see this? These others in Bannon's eyes, exposed in the ironic tilt of his head, flashed to me in the halting, slow way he spoke, were invisible to Peggy and Gerald Undercliff. They saw Bannon, not the tics, the familiar quirks of my friend, nor could they see that only the Soulcatcher knew the secrets of my history and heart. So this was how it worked. Paranoia come to stay. Unpacking its bag, propping its feet on your table: the slayer of souls in a balandranas and kneeboots. The Negro's private flask of hemlock.

"You will excuse us?" he asked Peggy. "This won't take long."

"No!" She put herself between Bannon and me, caught a whiff of him and just as quickly stepped back. "Why do you keep *bothering* us?"

Bannon smiled a million smiles: a cartoonist's composite face of fifty figures—his beard the hair of a black woman; his nose a Wazimba child curled up, knees to chin; his lips an Ibo lying spread-eagled on the deck of a slave clipper, the sea beneath him churned by the storm into foam, breakers roaring.

"Shall Ah leave?" he asked me.

I answered, "No."

If I could have reached Peggy then, if she had not been worlds away, I would have clung to her, but glancing at the Soulcatcher, I realized the futility of resistance. He would eventually speak, now or tomorrow, spilling my checkered history at her feet. Even if she did not care—even if love conquered the illusion of race, this life-long hallucination that *Thou* and *That* differed—I was still bound to him, had produced him from myself, as Peggy was producing a living thing. "This concerns neither of you," I followed Bannon to the door. "He is right—we have business."

Peggy whooped, "Where are you *going?*"

"And at this hour?" Undercliff hooked his arm around her; I stared, deliberately, to drive them deep into my memory, together like that, a portrait I planned to conjure the moment before Bannon. . . . "That woman," said Undercliff, "there are preparations to make. You must go *now?*"

"Yes," I said. "Now."

Stepping outside, into his shadow, I heard the Soulcatcher say, "Been a long chase from Hodges, Andrew." He climbed stiffly onto his canvas-covered wagon. "And Ah got a surprise fo' you." When he did not elaborate, I guessed Bannon meant some new break-through in scientific genocide—he prided himself on being a "scientific killer," as pugilists call themselves "scientific boxers"—and, strange to say, this thought brought to me the sort of comfort known only to suicides. But I was more fortunate. Bannon did the work, the loathsome specifics, for you. When the heart broke under pressure, failed, losing the strength to revive hope, the Soul-catcher stepped in to perform the most merciful of services. He steadied the dark, nerveless hand on the knife. Jerked the trigger, knowing you would quail, go soft, and grab again at the chimera of a world beyond color; and in that one hesitation, you'd blow two-quarters of your head away without finishing the job. Messy. Bannon was not a servant to botch the job. He offered, and for this I thanked God, the clean, quick kill.

He asked as we gained the road, "No second thoughts?"

"No." I could not face him, but I had to know one thing: "You *are* Death?"

He touched his hatbrim, very humble.

"The promised death, yes, sweetah even than the poetry of liberation. The death that defines everythin' befo' hit. Gives it form, as Ah did for yo father. Ah keeps mah tools ready. The blade clean. The powdah dry. No dreamah should suffah' lockjaw from a rusty knife, hit seem to me, at the end. This," he added in a self-distancing tone I did not understand, "has been mah trade fo' as long as Ah kin remembah."

The air was sharp, stimulating to my senses down this last road we traveled together. There were no words between us for a time, and thus no truth or falsity, only the feeling that I had betrayed all the bondsmen I'd ever known: my father, by passing; Patrick, by not risking Flo Hatfield's displeasure; Minty, who'd trusted me; Reb, by failing to leave Spartanburg. . . .

"Where," I asked, "is Reb?"

The Soulcatcher held his reins with one hand. Unbuttoning his shirt with the other, he exposed a barrel chest trellised with tattooes. The designs on his body were elaborately drawn, and almost seemed to move against the flow of his powerful muscles in the moonlight, more figures than I could take in at the moment, and I looked back at the road when he touched the naked skin between the knot of skin stitchings, and said, "Heah, Ah guess—what Ah was able to git."

"Then you have killed him?"

"Did Ah?" He squeezed his lower lip between thumb and forefinger, remembering. Then laughed. "You know how Ah works? In order to *become* a Negro, to slip under his skin, Ah have to open mahself to some mighty peculiar things. Reb was harder to git into than climbin' a peeled saplin', heels upwards. Ah was in pain most of the time 'cause *he* was. Did you know if yo friend passed a butcher shop, and if somebody was sledgehammering a shorthorn, the back of *Reb's* neck bruised?" He chortled and rubbed his own neck. "Did you git the ring?"

I drew in my head and nodded.

"Knew you'd want to have that."

For another few minutes we rode on, and I realized that Bannon had turned his wagon off the road. Now his wheels rumbled over stones into a field. The moon dispensed a diffused light, distorting everything, throwing long shadows (our own) in front of us. My stomach shook. The field, at night, looked infinite, unending. In my entire life I had seen nothing so—not even the hills

171

behind Cripplegate—nothing so stunning; never. . . . The nearness of death did this, I thought. Seated beside me, talking of his hideous techniques, the Soulcatcher's presence drove out every false possibility, stripped perception clean as whalebone, freed it from the private, egoistic interests that normally colored my vision; I could hear—*was*—the sound of a raincrow's song ringing in the tree we approached, the bird's voice disclosing it limitlessly as a swallow, a wren; I saw below the tree bluets unable to know, seeking only to be known, and then the double-trunked tree itself, which dreamed of becoming a man again, climbing the chain—form after form—until it attained the species capable of the highest sacrifices: man. Against my will, I wept. Not because I was to die; I wanted the kill. Nor again because I was returned to slavery; I had never escaped it—it was a way of seeing, my inheritance from George Hawkins: *seeing distinctions.* No, I cried because the woman I had sought in so many before—Flo Hatfield, Minty, Peggy—was, as Ezekiel hinted, Being, and she, bountiful without end, was so extravagantly plentiful the everyday mind closed to this explosion, this efflorescence of sense, sight frosted over, and we—I speak of myself; you will not make my mistake—became unworthy of her, having squandered to a thousand forms of bondage the only station, that of man, from which she might truly be served.

"A guinea," said the Soulcatcher, "fo' yo thoughts."

I could tell him my thoughts, only him.

"Is it . . ." pausing to pull phrases together, "possible that a man may love the Good, pledge his life to it and, in spite of his best efforts, still be the steward of suffering and evil?"

He fastened his reins to the wagon, under the tree. This, I presumed, was where the execution would take place. Climbing down, Bannon moved like the Coffinmaker, as if Time were fiction, all that was and would be held suspended in this single moment, which was forever, using every part of his foot as he walked, like an animal. First the heel falling gently, then the ball of his foot, not slamming down (as I walked), but firmly taking hold of the planet, pushing down as the ground pushed back in perfect balance: a slow, frightening tread, the way, I thought, an *Ubermensch* would walk. Then he answered me: "Ah have kilt many Negroes with this," pulling out his pearl-handled derringer, "whose every good action led to evil."

"Is that fair!" I touched him, then pulled back my hand; it was like grabbing a boa constrictor seconds after it swallowed a family of rats. "Your duty is to destroy, I understand that! There *must* be destroyers. But you sound like a philosopher! A *modern* philosopher—the mechanic who analyzes the propositions of madmen and sages with the same impartiality, refusing to pass judgment!" I shouted again, "Is it *fair* that you destroyed my friend—'only following orders,' you'll plead, and I can appreciate that, the dancing of Shiva from birth to death, the cosmic drama where all creatures are sacrificed, regardless of their personal dreams, to a God moving mysteriously, struggling to spin a well-made story, making some of us walk-ons, or extras—maybe Negroes in the New World were only hired for the crowd scenes—but I ask you, Horace, you, the holy torpedo, the mercenary of Brama, I put it to you, do you *approve?*"

"You still don't see hit," he said. "Ah approves everythin'. Ah approves nothin'."

Under the tree, which was weighted with fruit, the lower plum-heavy branches of the tree doming round us, like a sermon on regeneration, the Soulcatcher, still holding his derringer, asked me to sit. "Mebbe Ah should finish tellin' you 'bout Reb. For me to capture a Negro the *right* way, as Ah told you, Ah have to feel what he feels, want what he wants, 'fore Ah knows him good enough to hep him finish hisself."

"And what," my voice flindered, "did Reb want?"

The Soulcatcher laughed.

"*Nothin'!* That's hit right there—what threw me off, why hit took so long to run him down: yo friend didn't want *nothin'*. How the hell you gonna catch a Negro like that? He can't be caught, he's *already* free. Not legally, but you know what Ah'm sayin'. Well suh, Ah had to think a spell about strategy. Ah's always worked on the principle that the thing what destroys a man, what finally unstrings him, starts off first as an appetite. Yo friend *had* no appetites. There wasn't no way Ah could git a handhold on the nigguh, he was like smoke. So Ah went back to Square One, so to speak: Ah studied him, lookin' fo' a weakness, a flaw somewheres so Ah could squiggle inside and take root, like Ah did with yo daddy—now *he* was an easy kill, oh yeah, Ah did indeed snuff George Hawkins after the Cripplegate uprisin', but he was carryin' fifty-'leven pockets of death in him anyways, li'l pools of corruption that kept him so miserable he *begged* me, when Ah caught up with him in Calhoun Falls, to blow out his lights—"

(There is a Gentlemen's Psychic Powder Room, I discovered, across the hallway from the one used by Minty; upon hearing of my father's death, I excused myself, went into the first booth I found, bolted the door, dropped onto the toilet seat, and cried. When I returned, weaker, to the cafe table, as it were, Bannon was still talking.)

"—yo friend, as Ah was sayin', didn't have no place inside him fo' me to settle. He wasn't *positioned* nowhere." Scratching his head, the Soulcatcher chuckled. "Befo', afterwards, and in between didn't mean nothin' to him. He had no home. No permanent home. He didn't care 'bout merit or evil. What Ah'm sayin'," his fist struck the tree behind us, "is that Ah couldn't entirely become the nigguh because you got to have somethin' dead or static already inside you—an image of yoself—fo' a real slave catcher to latch onto."

"I don't understand," and I really didn't, for my father's death stood, like a screen, in front of all he'd just said. "The ring. . . ."

"Reb *sold* that in Kentucky," said Bannon, "to git shed of anythin' that'd identify him. Hawkins, you owe me thirty dollars, and me'n Mamie gonna need every penny—we gettin' married—since Ah'm outta work. Ah always said Ah'd quit if Ah come across a Negro Ah couldn't catch." He threw his derringer into the weeds. "Only reason Ah couldn't marry Mamie befo, get her outta that cathouse, is 'cause Ah stayed on the road so much."

My long flight from Cripplegate had made me, I fear, a slow and feeble thinker, the sort who needs to hear the argument twice, or see it in a Study Guide, for Bannon was saying—I gathered slowly—that as a bounty hunter he'd been bested by Reb, who was safely now in Chicago. My heart swung up. Then down. What of my father? Did even he deserve this end? I saw, in the weeds, the barrel of Bannon's derringer. He would have placed it, that gun, at the base of George's neck, tucking it under the loose skin where neckbone and shoulders met, locking his arm, then fired, the column of flame throwing George forward, Bannon back, while the pistol burning red on a black Carolina night went flying over his head, trailing smoke as my father fell into West Hell to precisely the reward all black revolutionaries feared: an eternity of waiting tables.

"Did he speak of me?" I asked Bannon. "What I must know is if he died feeling I despised him, or if he," I lowered my voice a little, "died hating me."

And then the Soulcatcher did a strange thing. His shirt had been opened to his navel (it puffed out, a poorly tied umbilicus, I thought), but hid his chest as we talked. Bannon undid the last three buttons, pulled off his shirt entirely, and bid me move closer.

"He's heah," the Soulcatcher said. "Ask him yoself."

This pulled me up short. I waited for the Soulcatcher's explanation, my gaze dropping from his face to his chest and forearms, where the intricately woven brown tattooes presented, in the brilliance of a silver-gray sky at dawn, an impossible flesh tapestry of a thousand individualities no longer static, mere drawings, but if you looked at them long enough, bodies moving like Lilliputians over the surface of his skin. Not tattooes at all, I saw, but forms sardined in his contour, creatures Bannon had killed since childhood: spineless insects, flies he'd dewinged; yet even the tiniest of these thrashing within the body mosaic was, clearly, a society as complex as the higher forms, a concrescence of molecules cells atoms in concert, for nothing in the necropolis he'd filled stood alone, wished to stand alone, had to stand alone, and the commonwealth of the dead shape-shifted on his chest, his full belly, his fat shoulders, traded hand for claw, feet for hooves, legs for wings, their metamorphosis having no purpose beyond the delight the universe took in diversity for its own sake, the proliferation of beauty, and yet all were conserved in this process of doubling, nothing was lost in the masquerade, the cosmic costume ball, where behind every different mask at the party—behind snout beak nose and blossom—the selfsame face was uncovered at midnight, and this was my father, appearing briefly in the dead boy Moon as he gave Flo Hatfield a goodly stroke and, at the instant of convulsive orgasm, opened his mouth as wide as that of the dying steer Bannon slew in his teens,

175

was that steer, then several others, and I lost his figure in this field of energy, where the profound mystery of the One and the Many gave me back my father again and again, his love, in every being from grubworms to giant sumacs, for these too were my father and, in the final face I saw in the Soulcatcher, which shook tears from me—my own face, for he had duplicated portions of me during the early days of the hunt—I was my father's father, and he my child.

The Soulcatcher buttoned his shirt, covering the theater of tattooes. He helped me, a freeman, back to his wagon, then delivered me, dazed, to my wife's doorstep. He and Mamie were not seen in Spartanburg again. On April 23, 1861, Wife bore a girl—six pounds, six ounces—delivered by Dr. Undercliff, who took leave of this life on the eve of Grant's capture of Fort Henry. *The Awakening of Eve Yoremop* (1863) was overshadowed by the American edition of Trollope's *Framley Parsonage,* and was only reviewed, with five other books, in the "Bookbin" column of the Press. According to rumor, Flo Hatfield did not marry again, but took the Vet as her final lover, and in Illinois—in 1865—Reb built his finest coffin, the one in which they laid Abraham Lincoln to rest. After the war, Fruity and I turned to the business of rebuilding, with our daughter Anna (all is conserved; all), the world.

This is my tale.

Selected Grove Press Paperbacks

E732   ALLEN, DONALD & BUTTERICK, GEORGE F., eds. / The Postmoderns: The New American Poetry Revised 1945-1960 / $9.95

B472   ANONYMOUS / Beatrice / $3.95

B445   ANONYMOUS / The Boudoir / $3.95

B334   ANONYMOUS / My Secret Life / $4.95

B415   ARDEN, JOHN / Plays: One (Serjeant Musgrave's Dance, The Workhouse Donkey, Armstrong's Last Goodnight) / $4.95

B422   AYCKBOURN, ALAN / The Norman Conquests: Table Manners; Living Together; Round and Round the Garden / $6.95

E835   BARASH, DAVID, and LIPTON, JUDITH / Stop Nuclear War! A Handbook / $7.95

B425   BARNES, JOHN / Evita — First Lady: A Biography of Eva Peron / $4.95

E781   BECKETT, SAMUEL/ Ill Seen Ill Said / $4.95

E96   BECKETT, SAMUEL / Endgame / $2.95

B78   BECKETT, SAMUEL / Three Novels: Molloy, Malone Dies and The Unnamable / $4.95

E33   BECKETT, SAMUEL / Waiting for Godot / $3.50

B411   BEHAN, BRENDAN / The Complete Plays (The Hostage, The Quare Fellow, Richard's Cork Leg, Three One Act Plays for Radio) / $4.95

E417   BIRCH, CYRIL & KEENE, DONALD, eds. / Anthology of Chinese Literature, Vol. I: From Early Times to the 14th Century / $14 95

E368   BORGES, JORGE LUIS / Ficciones / $6.95

E472   BORGES, JORGE LUIS / A Personal Anthology / $6 95

B312   BRECHT, BERTOLT / The Caucasian Chalk Circle / $2.95

B117   BRECHT, BERTOLT / The Good Woman of Setzuan / $2.95

B120   BRECHT, BERTOLT / Galileo / $2.95

B108   BRECHT, BERTOLT / Mother Courage and Her Children / $2.45

B333   BRECHT, BERTOLT / Threepenny Opera / $2.45

E580   BRETON, ANDRE / Nadja / $5.95

B147   BULGAKOV, MIKHAIL / The Master and Margarita / $4.95

B115   BURROUGHS, WILLIAM S. / Naked Lunch / $3.95

B446   BURROUGHS, WILLIAM S. / The Soft Machine, Nova Express, The Wild Boys / $5.95

E793   COHN, RUBY / New American Dramatists: 1960-1980 / $7.95

E804   COOVER, ROBERT / Spanking the Maid / $4.95

E742   COWARD, NOEL / Three Plays (Private Lives, Hay Fever, Blithe Spirit) / $4.50

B442	CRAFTS, KATHY, & HAUTHER, BRENDA / How To Beat the System: The Student's Guide to Good Grades / $3.95
E869	CROCKETT, JIM, ed. / The Guitar Player Book (Revised and Updated Edition) / $11.95
E190	CUMMINGS, E.E. / 100 Selected Poems / $2.95
E808	DURAS, MARGUERITE / Four Novels: The Square; 10:30 on a Summer Night; The Afternoon of Mr. Andesmas; Moderato Cantabile / $9.95
E380	DURRENMATT, FRIEDRICH / The Physicists / $6.95
B342	FANON, FRANTZ / The Wretched of the Earth / $4.95
E47	FROMM, ERICH / The Forgotten Language / $4.95
B389	GENET, JEAN / Our Lady of the Flowers / $3.95
E760	GERVASI, TOM / Arsenal of Democracy II / $12.95
E792	GETTLEMAN, MARVIN, et. al., eds. / El Salvador: Central America in the New Cold War / $8.95
E830	GIBBS, LOIS MARIE / Love Canal: My Story / $6.95
E704	GINSBERG, ALLEN / Journals: Early Fifties Early Sixties / $6.95
B437	GIRODIAS, MAURICE, ed. / The Olympia Reader / $5.95
E720	GOMBROWICZ, WITOLD / Three Novels: Ferdydurke, Pornografia and Cosmos / $9.95
B448	GOVER, ROBERT / One Hundred Dollar Misunderstanding / $2.95
B376	GREENE, GERALD and CAROLINE / SM: The Last Taboo / $2.95
E769	HARWOOD, RONALD / The Dresser / $5.95
E446	HAVEL, VACLAV / The Memorandum / $5.95
B306	HERNTON, CALVIN / Sex and Racism in America / $2.95
B436	HODEIR, ANDRE / Jazz: Its Evolution and Essence / $3.95
B417	INGE, WILLIAM / Four Plays (Come Back, Little Sheba; Picnic; Bus Stop; The Dark at the Top of the Stairs) / $7.95
E259	IONESCO, EUGENE / Rhinoceros & Other Plays / $4.95
E496	JARRY, ALFRED / The Ubu Plays (Ubu Rex, Ubu Cuckolded, Ubu Enchained) / $9.95
E216	KEENE, DONALD, ed. / Anthology of Japanese Literature: Earliest Era to Mid-19th Century / $12.50
E552	KEROUAC, JACK / Mexico City Blues / $5.95
B394	KEROUAC, JACK / Dr. Sax / $3.95
B454	KEROUAC, JACK / The Subterraneans / $3.50
B479	LAWRENCE, D.H. / Lady Chatterley's Lover / $3.95
B262	LESTER, JULIUS / Black Folktales / $4.95
B351	MALCOLM X (Breitman, ed.) / Malcolm X Speaks / $3.95
E741	MALRAUX, ANDRE / Man's Hope / $12.50

OXHERDING
TALE